"I love you, Daddy."

"I love you, too, darlin'," Matt replied.

He galloped Sarah into her bedroom, tucked her against the feather tick, sat on a stool by her bed and opened Mother Goose. He could see the picture of Cinderella with her blond curls and blue eyes.

Sarah rolled to her side. "I think she looks like Miss Pearl."

So did Matt. "A little."

"A lot." Sarah folded her hands across her chest. Then she did something Matt had never seen her do. She closed her eyes and mouthed words he couldn't hear.

"What are you doing?" he asked.

"I'm praying."

Matt had no such inclination. A long time ago he'd prayed prayers, but not anymore. That boy had turned into a man who had to live with his mistakes. He couldn't change the past, but he could stop others from making the same mistakes. That's why he'd do anything to protect the innocent...anything except put Sarah at risk.

"Daddy?"

"Yes, darlin'?"

"I'm praying for a mama."

Books by Victoria Bylin

Love Inspired Historical

The Bounty Hunter's Bride
The Maverick Preacher
Kansas Courtship
Wyoming Lawman

VICTORIA BYLIN

fell in love with God and her husband at the same time. It started with a ride on a big red motorcycle and a date to see a Star Trek movie. A recent graduate of UC Berkeley, Victoria had been seeking that elusive "something more" when Michael rode into her life. Neither knew it, but they were both reading the Bible.

Five months later they got married and the blessings began. They have two sons and have lived in California and Virginia. Michael's career allowed Victoria to be both a stay-at-home mom and a writer. She's living a dream that started when she read her first book and thought, "I want to tell stories." For that gift, she will be forever grateful.

Feel free to drop Victoria an e-mail at VictoriaBylin@aol.com or visit her Web site at www.victoriabylin.com.

Wyoming Lawman

VICTORIA BYLIN

Steeple
Hill®

Published by Steeple Hill Books™

STEEPLE HILL BOOKS

Steeple
Hill®

Recycling programs
for this product may
not exist in your area.

ISBN-13: 978-0-373-82846-3

WYOMING LAWMAN

www.SteepleHill.com

Printed in U.S.A.

Unless the Lord builds the house, its builders labor in vain. Unless the Lord watches over the city, the watchmen stand guard in vain.
In vain you rise early and stay up late, toiling for food to eat—for he grants sleep to those he loves.

—*Psalms* 127:1–2

To my husband, Michael,
For his patience, support and sense of humor.

Thank you, Bears, for helping with the bad guys.
Only a true good guy would have your wisdom.

Love you!

Chapter One

❧

Cheyenne, Wyoming
October 1875

Pearl Oliver stepped out of the carriage in front of Dryer's Hotel and glanced down the boardwalk in search of her cousin. Instead of spotting Carrie, she saw a little girl with hair as pale as her own. Pulled loose from two braids and wisping around the child's face, it glinted white in the sun. Pearl's mother had told her daughter that a woman's hair was her crowning glory. Pearl knew from experience it could also be a curse.

She turned back to the carriage intending to lift her son from her father's arms. Before he could hand the baby to her, she heard an excited cry.

"Mama!"

Expecting to see another mother, she looked back at the little girl. What she saw stopped her heart. The child, with her pinafore flapping and a rag doll hooked in her elbow, was charging across the street. Behind her, Pearl saw a freight wagon about to make the turn. The girl hadn't looked before stepping off the boardwalk, and the driver wouldn't see her until he rounded the corner.

"Stop!" Pearl cried.

The girl ran faster. "Mama, wait!"

Unaware of the child, the freight driver shouted at the team of six mules to pick up their pace. As the beasts surged forward, Pearl hiked up her skirt and ran down the boardwalk. "Stay there!" she cried. "I'm coming for you."

Instead of stopping, the child ran faster. The mules gained momentum and the wagon swayed. Pearl cried for the driver to stop, but he couldn't hear her over the rattle of the wheels. The child, now halfway across the street, saw only the woman she believed to be her mother.

Praying she wouldn't slip in the mud, Pearl dashed in front of the mules, each one snorting and chuffing with the weight of the load. The driver cursed and hauled back on the reins, but the wagon kept coming.

So did the child.

So did Pearl.

She could smell the mules. Puddles, mirroring the clouds, shook as the animals lumbered forward. With more speed than she rightly possessed, she dashed in front of the beasts, hooked her arm around the child and pulled her back from the wagon. Together they fell in a tangle of skirts and pinafores with Pearl on her belly. Her knees stung from hitting the dirt and she'd muddied her dress.

She didn't give a whit about her knees, but the dress mattered. She planned to wear it to her interview at Miss Marlowe's School for Girls. A woman in her position had to always look her best. One wrong impression and she'd be worse off than she'd been in Denver.

With her heart pounding, she raised her head and looked at the child. She saw eyes as blue as her own and hair that could have grown on her own head. The girl looked to be five years old, but there was nothing childlike about her expression as she clutched her doll to her chest. Like Pearl,

she had the look of someone who'd learned not to hope…
at least not too much.

Her voice squeaked. "Mama?"

"No, sweetie," Pearl said. "I just look like her."

The child's mouth drooped. "You do."

Pearl rocked back to her knees. Reaching down, she
cupped the girl's chin. "Are you hurt?"

"No."

"What's your name?"

"Sarah with an *H*."

Pearl couldn't help but smile. "You must be learning
your letters."

"I am. I go to school."

Pearl wondered if she attended Miss Marlowe's School,
but other questions were more pressing. She pushed to
her feet and offered Sarah her hand. "Who takes care of
you?"

"My daddy."

"Let's find him," Pearl replied.

Sarah looked at the ground. "He's gonna be mad at
me."

Pearl had an angry thought of her own. What kind of
father left a five-year-old alone on a busy street? The more
she thought about the circumstances, the more irritated
she became. Sarah could have been killed or maimed for
life. Pearl's problems paled in comparison, but she'd just
ruined her best dress. Pale blue with white cuffs and silver
buttons, it now had mud stains. She had another dress she
could wear to the interview, but she'd stitched this one
with her friends in Denver. The love behind it gave her
confidence.

As she looked around for Sarah's father, she saw the
start of a crowd on the boardwalk. The driver, a stocky
man with a bird's nest of a beard, came striding down the

street. When he reached her side, he swept off his black derby to reveal a bald head. "Are you okay, ma'am? Your little girl—I didn't see her."

She's not mine. But Pearl saw no point in explaining. "We're fine, sir. I saw what happened. You weren't at fault."

"Even so—"

"You can be on your way."

He looked at Sarah as if she were a baby chick, then directed his gaze back to Pearl. "Pardon me, ma'am. But you should watch her better."

Pearl's throat tightened with a familiar frustration. She'd been in Cheyenne for twenty minutes and already she was being falsely accused. Memories of Denver assailed her…the whispers when her pregnancy started to show, the haughty looks before she'd taken refuge at a boarding house called Swan's Nest. She'd gotten justice in the end, but she longed for a fresh start. When her cousin wrote about a teaching job in Cheyenne, Pearl had jumped at the chance for an interview.

Winning the position wouldn't be easy. As an unwed mother, she had some explaining to do. Not even her cousin knew she had a baby, not because Pearl wanted to keep her son a secret, but because she couldn't capture her thoughts in a letter. The two women didn't know each other well, but their mothers had been sisters. Carrie Hart was Pearl's age, single, a respected teacher and the daughter of one of Cheyenne's founders. If Carrie spurned her, Pearl would be adrift in a hostile city. Even so, she refused to pretend to be a widow. More than anything, she wanted to be respectable. If she lied about her son, how could she respect herself? And if she couldn't respect herself, how could anyone else? She had a simple plan. She'd tell the truth and trust God to make her path straight.

She had also planned to arrive in Cheyenne quietly. To her horror, a crowd had gathered and people were staring. She'd be lucky to avoid the front page of the *Cheyenne Leader*. Her father broke through the throng with her son in his arms. Even before she'd stepped out of the carriage, the baby had been hungry and wet. Any minute he'd start to cry.

"Pearl!" Tobias Oliver hurried to his daughter's side. A retired minister, he'd once been her enemy. Now he lived for the grandson sharing his name. "Are you all right?"

"I'm fine, Papa." She touched her son's head. "Take Toby to the room, okay?"

"But you need help."

She shook her head. "I have to find Sarah's father."

As he looked at the child clutching her doll, his eyes filled with memories, maybe regret. Pearl had once shared Sarah's innocence but not anymore. She'd been raped by a man named Franklin Dean, a banker and a church elder. Her father blamed himself for not protecting her.

"Go on, Papa," she said. "I don't want all this attention."

When Tobias met her gaze, she saw the guilt he lived with every day. He nodded and headed for the hotel.

Squeezing Sarah's hand, Pearl turned to the opposite side of the street where she saw twice as many people as before, almost all of them men. She couldn't stand the thought of shouldering her way through the crowd. Most of the onlookers were gawking.

"Please," she said. "Let us pass."

A businessman removed his hat and bowed. A cowboy tried to step back, but the crowd behind him pressed forward. A third man whistled his appreciation and another howled like a coyote. She turned to go in the other direction, but another crowd had gathered. She heard more catcalls, another whistle.

Sarah buried her face against Pearl's muddy skirt and clutched the folds. The child didn't like being the object of so much attention especially after falling in the dirt. Neither did Pearl. She patted the girl's head and mumbled assurances she didn't feel. Her own breath caught in her throat. She had nowhere to go, nowhere to hide. She was back in Franklin Dean's buggy, fighting him off…. She whirled back to the first side of the street, the place where she expected to find Sarah's father.

"Get back!" she shouted at the mob.

The crowd parted but not because of her. Every head had turned to a man shouting orders as he shoved men out of his way. As he shouldered past the cowboy who'd whistled, Pearl saw a broad-brimmed hat pulled low to hide his eyes, a clean-shaven jaw and a badge on a leather vest. She judged him to be six feet tall, lanky in build but muscular enough to command respect. He also had a pistol on his hip, a sure sign of authority. The city of Cheyenne, fighting both outlaws and vigilantes, had enacted a law prohibiting men from wearing guns inside the city limits. Foolishly Pearl had taken it as a sign of civility. Now she knew otherwise.

When the deputy reached the street, his eyes went straight to Pearl. They flared wide as if he recognized her, but only for an instant. Pearl thought of Sarah calling her "mama" and realized she looked even more like the girl's mother than she'd thought. The man's gaze narrowed to a scowl and she knew this man and his wife had parted with ugly words. Loathing snarled in his pale irises, but Pearl didn't take his knee-jerk reaction personally. She often reacted to new situations the same way…to crowds and stuffy rooms, black carriages and the smell of a certain male cologne.

The deputy's gaze slid to Sarah and he strode forward. When he reached the child's side, he dropped to one knee, muddying his trousers as he touched the back of her head. "Sarah, honey," he said softly. "Look at me, darlin'."

Pearl heard Texas in his voice…and love.

The child peeked from the folds of her skirt. "I'm sorry, Daddy. I was bad."

"Are you hurt?"

She shook her head, but her father wasn't convinced. He ran his hand down the child's back, looked at her muddy knees and inspected her elbows. Apart from the scare, Sarah and her doll were both fine. Pearl watched as he blew out a breath, then wiped the girl's tears with his thumb. When Sarah turned to him, he cupped her chin. "You shouldn't have left the store."

He'd put iron in his voice, but Pearl knew bravado when she heard it. He'd been scared to death.

Sarah hid her face in Pearl's skirt. "I know, Daddy. But I saw a puppy."

The man frowned. "Sarah—"

"Then I saw *her*." She raised her chin and stared at Pearl.

Instinctively Pearl cupped the back of Sarah's head. She'd been close to grown when her own mother died, but she missed her every day, even more since Toby's birth. If she'd ever caught a glimpse of Virginia Oliver in a crowd, she'd have acted just like Sarah.

The deputy pushed to his full height, giving her a closer look at his clean-shaven jaw. Most men in Cheyenne wore facial hair, but the deputy didn't even sport a mustache. He had a straight nose, brown hair streaked with the sun and the greenest eyes she'd ever seen. If her life had been simpler, she'd have smiled at him, even flirted a bit. Instead she pulled her lips into an icy line. Until she secured the job at Miss Marlowe's School, she didn't want to speak with anyone.

He took off his hat, a sign of respect that made her belly quake because she longed to feel worthy of it. The intensity in his eyes had the same effect but for different reasons. He frightened her.

"I can't thank you enough, miss." His drawl rolled like a river, slow and unstoppable. "I was in the store. I had an eye on her, and then…" He sealed his lips. "The next thing I knew, someone said a child was down in the street."

Pearl knew how he felt. Toby had suffered a bout of croup once, and she'd been worried to death. Her heart swelled with compassion, but she blocked it. "As you can see, your daughter's fine. If you'll excuse me—"

"But I owe you."

"No, you don't." She tried to step back, but Sarah tightened her grip.

The man skimmed her dress the way he'd inspected his daughter for injuries. "Your dress is ruined. I'll buy you a new one."

"No!" She could only imagine what kind of talk that would cause.

Instead of backing off, the lawman thrust out his hand. "Forgive my lack of manners. I'm Matt Wiley, Deputy Sheriff."

If she accepted the handshake, she'd have to give her name. She'd be trapped in a conversation she couldn't have until she spoke with Carrie and the school board. The less she said to this man, the safer she'd be. She indicated her muddy glove. "I don't want to dirty your hand. I have to go now." Before he could argue, she pivoted and headed for the hotel.

"Wait!"

The cry came from Sarah. Every instinct told Pearl to hug the child goodbye, but she couldn't risk a conversation with the girl's father. Walking faster, she skirted a puddle and stepped on to the boardwalk. Thinking of Toby, her father and the new life she wanted for them all, she hurried to the hotel.

No way would Matt let Miss No Name walk away from him. He owed her for the dress and he always paid his debts. He scooped Sarah into his arms and settled her on his right hip. His left one sported a Colt Peacemaker in a cross-draw holster he'd worn for ten years. It had been a gift from Howard Cain, the confederate captain who'd welcomed a weary soldier into the ranks of the Texas Rangers. Matt had stopped being a Ranger, but he still liked the chase.

"Hold up," he called as he followed the woman.

Miss No Name ignored him.

Fine, he thought, she didn't want to talk to him. He didn't want to speak with her, either. She looked enough like his wife—his former wife, he reminded himself—to be her sister, except Bettina had abandoned her daughter and Miss No Name had ruined her dress to save her. At the very least, he intended to pay for the gown. She could have it laundered or buy a new one, whichever she preferred.

First, though, he had to catch her. He tightened his grip on Sarah. "Hold on, darlin'. We're playing horsey."

She giggled and nestled against his neck. "Go fast, Daddy!"

Matt broke into a jog that brought him within three feet of Miss No Name. Just to hear Sarah's laugh, a treasure he'd almost lost, he made a neighing sound. As she squealed with delight, the woman turned her head and gaped at him. He hadn't seen a colder stare since Bettina left. Either she didn't like horses or she didn't like men. Matt didn't care. He didn't like blondes, so they were even except for the dress.

He reached her side in three steps. "Sorry to startle you."

"What do you want?" she said coldly.

"Like I said, I owe you for the dress, either a new one or a good cleaning."

"That's not necessary."

"I say it is."

Matt didn't like owing favors. In this town, a man's debts came back to haunt him. He'd learned that lesson his first week on the job when he'd let Jasper Kling give him a deal on a pair of boots. Never again. The merchant had expected special treatment for a measly six-bits off the already-inflated price.

Her eyes darted over his shoulder and down the street. Earlier he'd attributed her unease to the crowd of rowdy men. Now he wondered if trouble had followed her to Cheyenne. Matt didn't give a hoot about a person's past. Everyone in Cheyenne had a story, including him. But he cared very much about the here and now. He'd have to keep an eye on this woman.

Still tense, she looked back at his face. "If you must, you can pay for the laundering."

"Fine."

He set Sarah on the boardwalk, dug in his pocket and extracted a handful of coins. Before he could sort through the silver, Sarah grabbed the woman's skirt and looked up. "Would you braid my hair?"

His daughter had caused enough trouble for one day. Matt gritted his teeth. "Sarah, don't pester—"

"Pleeese," she whined to the woman. "My daddy can't do it."

That was a fact. He could splice rope, shoot straight and smell trouble a mile away, but he couldn't braid his little girl's hair. The white strands slipped through his fingers just as Bettina had done a year ago. For Sarah's sake, he wished he'd held on tighter. Instead of chasing Indians and outlaws with Captain Cain, and then dealing with the corruption of the Texas State Police, he should have stayed home and raised cattle. Maybe his wife wouldn't have cheated on him, and they'd still be a family.

He didn't miss Bettina at all, but Sarah did. His daughter needed a mother, someone who could make proper braids and teach her about life. A better man would have married to meet that need, but Matt couldn't stand the thought of repeating the mistakes he'd made with Bettina. Neither did he think a sham of a marriage would benefit his daughter. They were doing just fine, and he intended to keep things as they were…except his daughter was clinging to this woman's skirt and she looked so hungry for female attention that it made his chest hurt.

Pushing back old regrets, he touched Sarah's shoulder. At the same instant, Miss No Name dropped to a crouch and clasped Sarah's arms. Face to face, they looked like mother and daughter, mirror images separated only by time. Matt thought of Sarah's book of fairy tales and wondered if a child's dreams really could come true.

The woman spoke in a voice just for Sarah. "I wish I could do it, but we don't have a brush."

Sarah's lower lip trembled.

Matt didn't want to owe this woman another favor, but he'd swallow fire for his little girl. He also had a comb in his pocket, a tortoiseshell trinket shipped to Cheyenne from Boston. He'd learned to neaten up before doing business with busybodies like Jasper Kling. He took out the comb and held it in front of the woman's nose. "Here."

Looking both pleased and mistrustful, she plucked it from his fingers, straightened and clasped Sarah's hand. "Let's go in the hotel," she said to his daughter. "We can sit in the corner of the lobby."

Where people won't see us.

She didn't say the words, but Matt heard them. He glanced down the street, saw nothing suspicious and stepped in front of the females to open the heavy door to the hotel. As the woman guided Sarah inside, she skirted the desk and went to a group of chairs behind a pedestal holding a vase of dried flowers. Matt couldn't stop his eyes from admiring the sway of her dress. The front of it was a mess, but the back looked brand-new. He didn't know beans about fashion, but the bow at the small of her back made him think of tying knots...and untying them. Being a gentleman, he blocked the thought by silently whistling "Dixie," especially the part about looking away.

Miss No Name sat on a brocade chair, set the comb in her lap and removed her gloves. "Now," she said to Sarah. "Stand right in front of me."

Looking solemn, Sarah squared her shoulders.

Matt stayed by the pedestal, watching as the woman freed the disheveled braids from their ribbons and went to work with the comb. He couldn't stop himself from watching her hands. Maybe he'd learn something about braiding hair...at least that's the lie he told himself. In truth, he found Miss No Name attractive in a way he'd sworn to forget. He'd never marry again. Not even for his daughter's sake.

With a deft stroke, the woman parted Sarah's hair down the middle, wrapped one half around her hand and pulled it tight. Matt made a mental note of her firm touch. He worried so much about hurting Sarah that he didn't pull hard at all.

Miss No Name looked up and frowned. No one liked being watched, but she had an air of worry that went beyond natural reserve. She looked scared and angry. As a deputy, he had an obligation to find out why. As a man, he had instincts that went beyond duty. Unless he'd lost his ability to read people, this woman had a weight on her shoulders, one she couldn't put down.

To put her at ease, he sat in the chair across from her and set his hat on the table. He indicated the growing braid. "You're good at that."

"I've had a lot of practice."

Sarah tilted her face upward. "Do you have a little girl?"

"No," the woman replied. "But I know about braids."

As calm as she sounded, she'd blushed at the mention of having a child. Matt searched her hand for a wedding band, the cheap kind a woman bought for herself to hide an indiscretion. He saw nothing on her slender fingers, not even a hint of white where she might have worn a ring. The more he watched her with Sarah, the more curious he became. He wanted to ask her name, but he didn't want to make her uncomfortable. Sarah, though, had no such qualms. She was chattering about her doll, hair ribbons, last night's fairy tale and what they'd had for breakfast. Whatever crossed her mind came out of her mouth, including the question Matt had wanted to ask.

"What's your name?" the child asked.

The woman took a breath. "I'm a teacher. You can call me Miss Pearl."

She sounded natural, but Matt figured she'd omitted her last name for a reason. Whatever secret she had, it concerned a lack of a husband. He draped a boot over one knee. "Is that your given name or your last?"

She paused to stare at him. "It's how I wish to be addressed."

He raised an eyebrow. "Even by strangers?"

She shrugged as if she didn't care, but her cheeks turned even pinker. Looking back at Sarah's hair, she braided the last inch, wrapped the end with a ribbon and jerked it tight. Matt counted it as both a lesson in hair braiding and a glimpse of Miss Pearl's character. She could be tough or tender. He liked that in a woman.

Fool!

He'd never marry again, not after the misery he'd known with Bettina. In Matt's experience, there was no middle ground between companionship and craziness. Looking at Miss Pearl, he felt sure of it. When she smiled at Sarah, he felt soft inside. When she looked at him with her troubled eyes, he tensed with the instinct to protect her.

The woman handed the comb to Sarah. "You're all set."

"Thank you, Miss Pearl."

As the females hugged, Matt stood. He still owed her for the dress, so he reached in his pocket and held out the silver coins. "For the laundering."

"Use it for Sarah." She touched his daughter's silken head. "Buy her something pretty."

In that instant, Matt forgot all about paying debts and surrendered to his curiosity. Who gave Pearl pretty things? Who made her smile when times got hard? He didn't know, but a thought stuck in his mind and wouldn't budge. He'd express his gratitude for saving Sarah's life, but not with a visit to the laundry. Instead of paying for the dress, he'd buy Pearl something pretty.

Chapter Two

Pearl unlocked the door to the suite, shut it behind her and leaned against the wood. She'd never forget the way Matt Wiley had looked at her when he'd thanked her for saving Sarah. She'd felt honorable, whole. If she were honest, she'd felt something even more powerful. She refused to give voice to secret hopes, but she blushed with an undeniable truth. Matt Wiley made her feel pretty again.

"Pearl?"

"I'm here, Papa."

Tobias came out of the back bedroom with Toby in his arms. At the sound of her voice, the hungry baby let out a wail, kicked and tried to get to his mama. Pearl reached for him. "He needs to nurse."

Tobias handed her the squirming infant. "I gave him water, but he's not happy. Is everything all right with the little girl?"

"Just fine." She jiggled Toby to calm him. "Her father's a deputy. He found us."

"Good."

"She misses her mother," Pearl added. "Apparently I look like her."

With Toby in her arms, she thought of Sarah's hopeful

eyes. Under different circumstances, she'd have given Matt Wiley her full name. She'd have offered to braid Sarah's hair again. If he'd asked her to supper, she'd have said yes and worn her prettiest dress. Toby kicked again, reminding her such dreams were foolish. What man would want her now? She was damaged goods and had a baby to prove it.

"I better feed him," she said to her father.

Tobias motioned to the second bedroom. "Your trunk's in there."

"Thank you, Papa."

"We have plenty of time," he added. "Carrie left a message at the desk. She's expecting us at six o'clock for supper."

Pearl had mixed feelings about meeting her cousin. Four months ago, when the trouble in Denver had reached a peak, Tobias had written to Carrie and asked for information about Cheyenne. She'd written back and invited them to visit her. They'd accepted, and Carrie had generously made arrangements for Pearl to interview at Miss Marlowe's School for Girls.

Tonight Pearl would tell Carrie about Toby and the circumstances of his conception. She'd either keep her cousin's respect or she'd lose it. If she lost it, she wouldn't have a chance of being hired as a teacher and would have to find another way to earn a living. Tobias had a small pension from his years as a minister at Colfax Avenue Church, but it wasn't enough to support all three of them. Neither did Pearl want him looking for work. Twice in the last month he'd had bouts of chest pain.

Sighing, she glanced at the clock on the mantel. If she moved quickly, she'd have time to feed Toby, wash the train grit from her face and take a nap. Determined to be at her best, she closed the bedroom door and did all three.

An hour later, a rap on the door to the suite pulled her out of a troubled slumber. In her dreams she'd seen the wagon bearing down on Sarah. The picture had shifted and she'd been braiding the child's hair. It had turned to shining gold, and Matt Wiley had been watching her hands.

The knock sounded again.

Had Carrie come to meet them? Pearl bolted upright and inspected herself in the mirror. She'd put on her oldest day dress and her hair looked a fright. The knocking turned hammer-like. Not Carrie, she decided as she turned from the mirror.

In the sitting room she saw her father, pale and stiff, coming out of the other bedroom. He motioned her aside, but she couldn't bear the sight of him trying to hurry. Ignoring his gesture, she opened the door and saw a delivery boy holding a small package wrapped in brown paper.

"Are you Miss Pearl?"

"Yes, I am."

"This is for you." He held out the package and Pearl took it. Perhaps Carrie had sent a welcome gift, though the gesture seemed too formal for cousins.

As the boy waited expectantly for a coin for his trouble, Pearl looked at her father. Tobias reached in his pocket, extracted a few pennies and handed them to the boy. As he shut the door, Pearl fingered the package in an attempt to guess its contents. It felt soft, like fabric of some kind. Perhaps a pretty handkerchief. That seemed like the kind of gift Carrie might send. Pearl lifted the card bearing her name and turned it over. Instead of her cousin's prim cursive, she saw bold strokes in a man's hand. As she read the message, her cheeks flushed pink.

"Who's it from?" Tobias asked.

"Deputy Wiley."

Her father hummed a question. "What does it say?"

"'To Miss Pearl with our deepest gratitude. You are

a woman of uncommon courage.'" She looked up at her father. "It's signed 'From Deputy Matt and Sarah.'"

His gray eyes misted. "I like this man."

"Papa, don't—"

"Don't what?" He scowled at her. "Don't hope for happiness for *my* little girl? Don't believe God for a second chance?"

Pearl wanted the same things, but she couldn't go down the same road, not one lined with mysterious gifts and the curious shine in Matt Wiley's green eyes. She set the card on the table, then looked at the package. The brown paper spoke of ordinary things, but someone had tied it shut with a lace ribbon instead of twine. Pearl didn't know how to cope with a man's interest, not anymore.

Her father nudged the package with his index finger. "Open it."

She felt as if it held snakes, but she tugged on the ribbon. The bow came loose and the paper unfolded in her hand. Instead of snakes, she found hair ribbons in a dozen shades of blue. The colors matched the sky in all seasons, all times of day. Some of them matched the dress she'd ruined saving Sarah. Others were the pale blue of her eyes.

Pearl would have known what to do with a snake. She'd have cut off its head with a shovel and flung it away. The hair ribbons struck her as both treacherous and lovely... but mostly lovely. Startled by the thought, she caught her breath.

Her father touched her shoulder. "What's wrong?"

"I think you know."

Tobias indicated the divan. "Sit with me, Pearl."

"I should check Toby."

He gave her a look she knew well. For ten years he'd pastored the biggest church in Denver. He'd learned when to bend and when to fight. Right now, he looked ready for a fight. Pearl gave up and sat next to him. "There's nothing to say."

"Yes, there is."

Looking older than his fifty-eight years, he lifted a cobalt ribbon from the pile of silk and lace. "Look at it, Pearl. What do you see?"

She saw a pretty snake. It declared a man's interest and tempted her with hope. To hide her feelings, she shrugged. "I see a ribbon."

Her father held the silk within her grasp. "Touch it."

"No."

"Why not?"

Because hope would sink its fangs into her flesh. Her mind would spin tales of princes and husbands, and she'd see Matt Wiley in her dreams. What woman wouldn't be charmed by the deputy? He loved his daughter and did honorable work. His brown hair framed a lean face and his eyes were the color of new grass. They had a subtle sharpness, a sign of a fine mind, but they also looked steady and true.

Her father turned his wrist, causing the ribbon to shimmer and twist. Her fingers itched to touch it. Knowing Tobias wouldn't budge until she surrendered, she lifted the ribbon from his hand. As the silk slid across her palm, she thought of braiding Sarah's hair and telling the deputy to buy his daughter something pretty. Had he bought ribbons for Sarah, too? She hoped so.

Tobias gripped her hand. "We came to Cheyenne for a fresh start. If a man's interested in you—"

"Papa!"

"I'm serious, Pearl." He pushed to his feet, crossed to a mirror etched with leaves and faced her. "If your mother were alive, she'd know what to say. I'm not much good at woman talk, but I know one thing for certain." He paused, daring her to ask and forcing her to listen.

"What's that?" she finally said.

"A man sends a gift to a woman for just one reason."

"He *had* one." She nudged the card with her finger. "He's saying thank-you."

Her father harrumphed.

Pearl wanted to fire back a retort, but she couldn't look her father in the eye. Deep down, she wanted to believe him. How would it feel to be properly courted? Blinking, she flashed back to Denver. Two days ago she'd caught the bouquet at her best friend's wedding. She'd imagined—just for an instant—wearing a fancy dress and saying "I do" to a faceless man. That man wasn't faceless now. He had green eyes.

Pearl placed the cobalt ribbon on top of the others. "I'm a daydreaming fool."

"No, you're not," her father insisted.

Could he be right? Did she have a chance at love? Looking at the ribbons, she thought of all the things the gift could mean. Hair ribbons could be casual or personal, practical or romantic. She thought of the card and how he'd signed it. "Deputy Matt" echoed "Miss Pearl," a sign that he'd understood her need for discretion and accepted it. She thought of the purpose in his eyes as he'd said goodbye. Were the ribbons more than a thank-you? Was he asking the first sweet question between a man and woman?

What if…

She didn't know, but she wanted to find out. Never mind the fear chilling her feet. Never mind the threat of humiliation. Matt Wiley had called her a woman of uncommon courage. Like her father said, she'd come to Cheyenne to start a new life for her son. Most important of all, she had faith in the God of second chances. She touched the card with her fingertip, then looked up at her father. "I suppose I *should* send a thank-you note."

"That would be very fitting."

"It's just…" She shrugged.

"Just what?" her father said gently.

"It's hard to start over."

He lowered his chin as if she were Sarah's age. "That's true, but we worship a God who loves his children. I can't explain what happened to you, Pearl. It was hurtful and ugly and I'll never forgive myself—"

"Don't say that." She didn't blame her father for the violence she'd suffered. She blamed Franklin Dean for being evil.

He held up one hand. "Let me finish."

She obeyed but only out of habit.

"God has a plan for your life," he said. "It's good, but you need the courage to walk that path. You can do it, Pearl. You're brave and smart and as beautiful as your mother. Any man in Cheyenne would be blessed to have you for a wife."

She wanted to believe him, but her father saw her through rose-colored lenses. When he kissed her good-night, he still called her "princess." Even so, she smiled at him. "Thank you, Papa."

"Now go write that note."

Her stomach twisted. "I don't know—"

"I do." Tobias aimed his thumb at the secretary in the corner. "Get busy. We'll ask the clerk to deliver it when we leave to see Carrie."

"If you're sure…"

"I'm positive." He gave her a look he'd often used in the pulpit. "It's about time you showed a little faith—both in God and in people."

Pearl had no assurance Matt Wiley wouldn't laugh at

her note, but she had walked with the Lord as long as she could remember. "All right. I'll do it."

"Good." Tobias glanced at the wall clock. "I'm going to finish that nap."

As he left the sitting room, Pearl went to the secretary, opened the drawer and removed stationery, an inkwell and an elegant pen. She positioned the paper on the blotter, filled the well and wrote the note. Both formal and friendly, the wording struck her as just right and she blew the ink dry. On a whim, she added a P.S., then sealed the note and checked on Toby. Satisfied he'd stay asleep, she took the note to the front desk before she could change her mind about asking a "what if" of her own.

The instant Matt set foot in the sheriff's office, his friend and partner, Dan Cobb, held up two envelopes and grinned. "Here you go, Romeo."

Scowling, Matt snagged the letters. They were both written on ivory stationery and sealed with white wax. One displayed his name in a script he recognized as belonging to Sarah's teacher. Miss Carrie Hart taught the youngest girls at Miss Marlowe's School, and she frequently sent home glowing notes about his daughter. They often chatted when he met Sarah after school, and they'd become casual friends.

The other letter displayed pretty writing that said, "To Deputy Matt and Sarah." Pearl must have gotten the hair ribbons.

Fighting a smile, he dropped down on his chair and started to open the letter from Pearl. As the seal popped, Dan's chair squeaked. Matt looked up, caught his friend staring and scowled. "What are *you* looking at?"

Dan grinned. "Looks to me like a couple of pretty ladies have their eyes on you."

Matt had no interest in ladies, pretty or otherwise. He held up the first envelope. "This one's from Carrie Hart. She's Sarah's teacher."

"I know Carrie." Dan sounded wistful. "I see her at church."

Matt saw a chance to take a friendly jab. "Judging by that hangdog look, you're sweet on her."

"What if I am?"

Matt huffed. "Beware, my friend. Marriage isn't what it's cracked up to be."

"That's your opinion."

"It's the voice of experience." He'd never forget quarreling with Bettina, how she'd cried when he'd left to go with the Rangers. He'd felt guilty for leaving and even worse the times he'd stayed.

Dan wagged his finger at the second envelope. "Who sent that one?"

"None of your business."

"Sure it is," Dan replied. "We're partners."

Matt considered the deputy his best friend, but he didn't want an audience when he read the notes. He gave Dan a pointed stare. "Don't you have some outlaws to catch?"

"No, but I hear you had a run-in with Jasper."

"Unfortunately, yes."

The quarrel especially rankled because he hadn't been on duty when Jasper summoned him. Matt wore his badge and gun all the time, but he'd taken the morning off to be with Sarah. Last night she'd fussed about his long hours, so he'd promised to spend the morning with her. To his chagrin, she'd wanted to play dolls. Matt wasn't much on dolls, so he'd suggested a tea party with real cake at Madame Fontaine's bakery. Halfway to the shop, Jasper had waylaid him and Sarah had run off.

Matt told Dan everything except the part about Sarah's

braids. Neither did he mention his trip to the dress shop. After choosing the ribbons—all the blue ones he could see—he'd arranged for a delivery to Pearl, then left Sarah eating cookies with Madame Fontaine while he patched up things with Jasper. It hadn't gone well.

"Jasper's a nuisance," Dan complained. "What did he want this time?"

"Same thing as before."

"The Peters kid?"

"You guessed it." Matt propped his boots on the desk. He didn't usually sit that way, but something about Jasper inspired bad manners. "Teddy Peters swiped some candy off the counter. My gut tells me Jasper put it out to tempt him. The kid bolted, and now Jasper wants him tossed in jail."

Dan shook his head. "Seems like a talk with his folks would be enough."

"That's what I did. Teddy's mother made him pay, and he's doing extra chores."

"Sounds reasonable."

"Jasper didn't think so." Matt could hardly believe what he was about to say. "He threatened to have my badge."

"He *what?*"

"He thinks I'm too soft for the job."

"That fool!"

"Don't waste your breath." Matt swung his boots off the desk. "Jasper's a thorn, but I've dealt with worse."

Dan stayed silent a moment too long. "Don't underestimate him, Wiley. The man's got a dark side."

Matt's brow furrowed. "What are you talking about?"

"Secrets," Dan answered. "Jasper's got one, and I'm willing to bet he'd do anything to keep it."

Matt knew about secrets. He had one of his own. "Tell me."

"You know the hog ranch north of town?"

Dan wasn't talking about farm animals. *Hog ranch* was slang for the lowest form of prostitution. Women in that regrettable line of work had often taken a downhill slide from fancy brothels to run-down saloons. As they lost their looks and their health, they slid further and ended up at wretched establishments located on the outskirts of town. Such places were called hog ranches, and they attracted men and women who couldn't sink much lower. As a Ranger, Matt had walked into such places in search of wanted men. "Are you saying Jasper—"

"Yep."

Not a week passed that Jasper didn't send a high-and-mighty letter to the newspaper about prostitution. Being caught at a hog ranch would shame him more than anything. Matt had to hold back a snort. "The man's a flaming hypocrite. How'd you hear about it?"

"Ben Hawks told me before he left."

A fellow deputy, Ben had left town shortly after Matt arrived. An aunt in St. Louis had died and left him a small fortune. Matt hadn't questioned the timing, but he did now. Had Jasper bought the man's silence?

Dan steepled his fingers. "After Ben left, Jasper started up with those letters. Just before that, the other trouble started."

Matt's brow furrowed. "You mean Jed Jones."

"And the fire at the livery."

A month ago Matt had found Jones, a suspected horse thief, hanging from a tree in Grass Valley. A few days later the livery had been torched. Some folks thought the owner had bought stolen horses. Last week the Silver Slipper

Dance Hall had been the target. Riders wearing masks and black derbies had shot out the windows while chanting "Go! Go! Go!"

Matt recognized the work of vigilantes, but who were they? And why were they striking now? Both questions had possible answers. Horse thieves had raided Troy Martin's place three times since August. Another rancher, Howard Moreland, had lost a prize stallion. The men were friends and active in the Golden Order. Matt didn't care for the civic organization at all. The group tended to make unreasonable demands like the one Jasper had made about Teddy. Chester Gates, a banker, served as president. Jasper belonged to the G.O., too. He'd been a founding member.

The news about Jasper's secret made Matt wonder about the trouble at the Silver Slipper. What better way for the shopkeeper to hide his visit to the hog ranch than by attacking another place of prostitution? Chester Gates also had a beef related to the dance hall. The owner, Scottie Fife, had outbid him for some prime land. Whoever owned the property would make a fortune if the railroad expanded its headquarters.

Matt had taken "Go! Go! Go!" to be a command, but perhaps it had been a calling card. Everyone in Cheyenne knew G.O. stood for "Golden Order." If these men had gone bad—a strong possibility, Matt had seen corruption in Texas—they had to be stopped before innocent people suffered.

Matt knew the cost of such violence and not as a victim. As long as he lived, he'd be ashamed of what he'd done in Virginia. Until that night, he'd been a man who prayed. Not anymore. He looked at Dan. "We need to keep an eye on the Golden Order."

"I agree." The deputy gave a sad shake of his head. "Jed

Jones was a liar and a thief, but he didn't deserve a necktie party."

A lynching... Matt's blood turned to ice. With every nerve in his body, he wished someone had stopped him and his men the night they'd tossed a rope over the branch of a tree. He couldn't change what had happened to Amos McGuckin, but he could stop it from happening again. "We'll stop these men. The only question is *how*."

"Any ideas?"

"Not yet, but I'll figure it out."

Dan went to fetch his hat. "We won't catch anyone sitting in the office. I'm going to take a walk."

"Watch your step," Matt replied.

As Dan passed Matt's desk, he noticed the letters and put his hand over his heart. "Romeo...Romeo..."

"Shut up," Matt joked.

Dan put on his hat. "You ought to take one of those ladies to see *Romeo and Juliet* at the Manhattan."

The new theater offered fine plays and bad acting. The performance of *Romeo and Juliet* was said to be particularly awful. "Forget it," Matt answered.

Chuckling, Dan walked out of the office, leaving Matt alone with the notes. He knew what the one from Carrie would say. Yesterday she'd invited him to bring Sarah to have supper with some cousins of hers, a minister and his daughter arriving from Denver. He figured the daughter was a little girl who liked to play with dolls. The note would be a reminder to come at six o'clock. The thought of an evening with a minister set Matt's teeth on edge, but he could tolerate anything for a couple of hours. Except church, he reminded himself. He hadn't set foot in a house of God for ten years, and he didn't plan to change his habits.

He ignored Carrie's letter and lifted the one from Pearl.

He liked how she'd called him Deputy Matt, echoing the way he'd signed the card with the ribbons. Pleased, he peeled off the wax and read.

Dear Deputy Matt and Sarah,

Thank you for the beautiful ribbons. I've never seen lovelier shades of blue and will enjoy them very much. You've made a newcomer to Cheyenne feel welcome indeed.

Regards, Miss Pearl

Below the curly writing, she'd added a P.S. in block printing. It read, "Sarah, if you'd like me to braid your hair again, I'd be happy to do it."

His daughter couldn't read the words, but she'd know the letters.

Matt read the letter again, grinning like a fool because he'd charmed Miss Pearl out of her shell. Why he cared, he didn't know. Not only did she have blond hair, he'd been straight with Dan when he said marriage wasn't for him.

He opened the note from Carrie and saw exactly what he expected. Her cousins had arrived and were coming for supper. Good, he thought. Sarah needed a friend.

Matt glanced at the clock. He had a couple of hours before he had to be at Carrie's house, so he opened the office ledger and recorded his conversation with Jasper. If vigilantes were at work in Cheyenne, they had to be stopped. And if Jasper and Gates were behind it, they had to be brought to justice. Matt wished someone had stopped *him* that night. He wished for a lot of things he couldn't have…a mother for Sarah, a good night's sleep. Maybe someday he'd be able to forget. Until then, he had a job to do.

Chapter Three

As the hired carriage neared her cousin's house, Pearl considered the neighborhood. Cheyenne still had the ragged feel of a frontier town, but railroad executives and entrepreneurs had brought their families with the hope of bringing a touch of civility. Carrie's father had been among the Union Pacific leaders. An engineer by trade, Carlton Hart had built a fine house for his wife and daughter. Tragically, he'd died two years ago in a blasting accident. A few months later, his wife had succumbed to influenza.

Rather than go back east, Carrie had taken a position at Miss Marlowe's School for Girls. Pearl hoped to carve out a similar place for herself, but she had no illusions about her chances. Toby, swaddled in blue and snug in her arms, called her character into question. Some people would gossip about her out-of-wedlock child. Others would shun her. She knew from her experience in Denver that only a few would be kind. Without Carrie's support, Pearl didn't have a chance of being hired as a teacher.

As the carriage rolled to a halt, her father touched her arm. "You can still change your mind about explaining to Carrie. I'll talk to her first."

"No, Papa."

She hadn't come to Cheyenne to be a coward. If she couldn't face her cousin, how could she manage an interview with the trustees of Mrs. Marlowe's School? Meeting Carrie would be good practice. That's why she'd worn her second-best dress, a blue-gray silk with a lace jabot. For added courage, she'd tied three of Deputy Matt's ribbons into a fancy bow and pinned them to her hat. Not only did they complement her dress, they also matched Toby's baby blanket.

Tobias climbed out of the carriage, paid the driver and offered his hand. "Are you ready, princess?"

She wished he'd stop using the nickname. It made her feel small when she needed to be adult. She'd have spoken up, but her father looked as nervous as she felt. Being careful not to jostle Toby, she took her father's hand and climbed out of the carriage. The door to the house opened and she saw a young woman with a heart-shaped face and brown hair arranged in a neat chignon.

"Pearl! Uncle Tobias!" Beaming with pleasure, Carrie hurried down the path. "I'm so glad you're—" She stopped in midstep, staring at the bundle in Pearl's arms. "You have a baby."

"I do."

Her brows knit in confusion. "I didn't know you were married."

"I'm not." Pearl took a breath. "I wanted to tell you in person. A letter just didn't…I couldn't…" She bit her lip to keep from rambling.

As Carrie stared in shock, Pearl fought to stay calm. First reactions, even bad ones, meant nothing. She had them all the time, especially to men who reminded her of Franklin Dean. A person's second response was what mattered.

Carrie's gaze dipped to the baby, lingered, then went back to Pearl. She didn't speak, but her eyes held questions.

Pearl didn't want to explain herself in the street. She wanted the privacy of four walls, the dignity she'd been denied by the man who'd taken her virtue. Thinking of the ribbons on her hat, a declaration of her courage, she squared her shoulders. "I'll explain everything, but could we go inside?"

Carrie touched her arm. "It'll be all right, cousin."

Pearl's throat tightened.

"Whatever happened, we're family."

"You don't even know—"

"I know *you*," Carrie insisted. "We've been writing for months now. Besides, our mothers were sisters."

Tears pushed into Pearl's eyes. No matter what happened, she had a friend.

"Don't cry," Carrie said. "You'll get all puffy."

As if being puffy were the worst of her problems… Pearl laughed out loud. She tried to speak but hiccuped instead. As she covered her mouth, Carrie pulled her into a hug. The gesture shot Pearl back to Swan's Nest where Adie Clarke, now Adie Blue, had opened her home and her heart. Mary, another boarder, had taught Pearl to be bold. Bessie and Caroline had delivered her baby and proved that a faithful woman could survive any heartache.

Courage, from her friends and from the ribbons, gave her the strength to spell out the facts for Carrie. "I was attacked by a man I trusted. I refuse to call him Toby's father."

Carrie hugged her as hard as she could. "You poor dear!"

Eager to get past the ugliness, Pearl blurted the facts. She'd gone for a buggy ride with Franklin Dean, the man she'd expected to marry. A wolf in sheep's clothing, he forced himself on her and left her with child. He'd demanded marriage, but Pearl had refused. Instead she'd taken refuge at Swan's Nest, a boarding house for women in trouble.

By the time she finished the story, Carrie had guided her up the steps and into the foyer. Her father had followed at a distance, giving them time to talk. As he approached, Pearl gave him a watery smile. "We're going to be all right."

"More than all right," Carrie insisted.

Relief brightened Tobias's silvery eyes, but the creases edging his mouth had deepened. "We're grateful to you, Carrie."

The brunette waved off the praise. "We'll talk about the school over supper. I've invited a friend. I hope that's all right."

"Of course." Pearl loved the women at Swan's Nest. She hoped to make good friends in Cheyenne.

Her cousin's eyes sparkled. "His name is Matt Wiley."

Pearl gasped.

"Don't worry." Carrie reached for her hand. "I know you're in a delicate situation, but Matt's not one to judge. He might even help us. His little girl goes to Miss Marlowe's."

Tobias touched Pearl's back. "We've met Deputy Wiley."

"You have?" Carrie's brows arched.

As Tobias told the story about the freight wagon, Pearl's cheeks burned with embarrassment, not with humility at his praise, but because of the note she'd sent. The ribbons had been a thank-you, nothing more. Even worse, she'd flirted with a man her cousin seemed to like. Deputy Matt— Deputy Wiley, she reminded herself—would be here any minute. The ribbons had to come off her hat *now*.

She turned to Carrie. "I need to check Toby. Is there a place—"

Three knocks rattled the door.

"That's Matt." Forgetting Pearl, Carrie flung the door wide. Light fanned across her full cheeks, revealing faint freckles and the smitten glow of a woman in love. Pearl wondered if she'd ever feel a similar pleasure in a man's presence. Envy at Carrie's innocence ripped through her, but she shoved it away.

With a blush on her cheeks, Carrie stepped back to make room for the deputy and his daughter. "Come in," she said. "I want you to meet my cousins."

In a feeble attempt to hide her hat, Pearl moved closer to the coat rack. Maybe Matt Wiley wouldn't notice the ribbons. Maybe the clerk had been slow to deliver the note and she could get it back.

Sarah came through the door first. Carrie crouched to hug her, but the little girl stopped short. Unruffled, Carrie touched the doll in Sarah's arms. "You brought Annie. She looks pretty today."

Sarah scowled. "She's *mine*."

"Of course, she is," Carrie said gently.

Pearl ached for them both. Her cousin plainly cared for the man and his daughter. Sarah, though, probably saw her as a rival. Pearl knew how she felt. When a child lost a mother, life became fragile. When Carrie straightened, Sarah spotted Pearl, cried out with delight and ran to hug her knees. Pearl shot Carrie a look of apology. When her cousin forced a smile, Pearl knew they'd be as close as sisters. They thought alike. They loved alike.

Pearl smoothed Sarah's hair. Smiling, she made her voice bright. "Did you know Miss Carrie's my cousin?"

"What's that?" Sarah asked.

"It means we're family, and I like her very much. She likes you, too."

Pearl glanced at Carrie for approval. Her cousin mouthed "Thank you," then crouched next to Sarah. "I like Annie, but I know she's yours."

Sarah stayed by Pearl, but she held up the doll for Carrie to see. "Her dress got dirty, but I changed it."

"You did a good job, darlin'."

That Texas drawl could only belong to one man. Knowing she'd be looking into Matt Wiley's green eyes, Pearl dragged her gaze upward. Just as she feared, he was staring at the bow she'd made from the ribbons. She forced a nonchalant smile. "Good evening, Deputy."

He took off his hat with a gallant sweep of his arm. His hair, a bit shaggy, touched the collar of a green shirt topped with a dark vest. "Good evening. It's a pleasure…again."

The scent of bay rum tickled her nose. So did the lingering smell of lye soap. Did he have a housekeeper, or did he send his clothes to the laundry? The thought twisted in her mind until it formed a hard knot of truth. She had no business wondering about Matt Wiley's laundry.

He stepped deeper into the entry hall and reached back to close the door. As he turned, the vest pulled across his broad chest. With six people in the small space, including Toby in her arms, she had nowhere to hide. Deputy Wiley's gaze landed on her son, lingering while he grappled with his thoughts on her marital status. Gurgling, Toby scooted up her chest like an inchworm. She loved it when he moved against her, and she smiled in spite of the awkward moment. As she shifted the baby's weight, the deputy watched her son with a father's knowing smile. She wondered if he'd held Sarah the same way.

Carrie straightened. "You've met, but I should finish introductions. Matt, this is my cousin Pearl and her father, Reverend Tobias Oliver."

Tobias held out his hand. "Good evening, Deputy."

As the men shook hands, Pearl tried to signal Carrie for a place to remove her hat. Her cousin didn't notice. She had eyes only for Sarah and was already leading the little girl into the parlor.

When Matt broke his grip, Tobias offered his arm to Pearl. "Shall we join Carrie?"

Before she could reply, Deputy Wiley spoke in a low tone to her father. "If you don't mind, sir. I'd like a word with your daughter."

Tobias wrinkled his brow. "I don't think—"

Pearl interrupted. "It's all right, Papa." She wanted a word with him, too. If he'd received her note, she needed to make her position clear. She'd been completely unaware of his interest in Carrie and her cousin's claim on him. She'd still braid Sarah's hair, but she'd invite Carrie to join them.

As Tobias stepped into the parlor, Deputy Wiley glanced again at her hat. "I see you got the ribbons."

"Yes. They're lovely."

Using a quiet tone, one meant for Pearl alone, he said, "I got your note."

He'd spoken as if they had a secret, a thought that shamed her because of Carrie. She had to make her loyalty clear. "My *thank-you* note," she said.

"Exactly." He looked relieved. "Since I sent the ribbons to *thank* you, and you sent the note to *thank* me, I'd say we understand each other."

Pearl sagged with relief. "Yes. Of course. We certainly do. Thank you…again."

Why was she babbling? And why were his eyes twinkling with pleasure? She didn't know, but she sensed goodness in this man. If it weren't for Carrie, she wouldn't have regretted the note at all. She'd have mustered her courage and gone after Deputy Matt Wiley with her best smile. But that could never be. Not only did Carrie have a claim on him, Pearl was damaged goods and she knew it.

* * *

Pearl's discomfort hit Matt with surprising force. He didn't know why he felt compelled to protect her dignity, but he knew the impulse went beyond gratitude. He liked her. Unless he'd lost his instincts concerning women, she'd needed courage to add the P.S. to the thank-you note. Like a lot of the folks in Cheyenne, she'd probably come to Wyoming for a fresh start. Looking at the baby, he thought he knew why but wanted to be sure.

The blue blanket clued him to the child's gender. "Is that your son?"

"Yes."

"He's a cute little fellow. What's his name?"

"Toby." She raised her chin, daring him to ask the obvious question.

He spoke gently. "And your husband?"

"I don't have one."

So the preacher's daughter had skipped "I do" and gone straight to "I will." Matt didn't hold it against her. His own slate had enough marks to cover a barn.

With a baby in her arms and no husband, she had a good reason to be reserved. People would judge her to be lacking in moral character. The ribbons on her hat told him she had even more courage than he'd guessed. He felt bad about discouraging a friendship, but it had to be done. That's why he'd asked for a private word. She deserved to know he'd been flattered by her interest, but she wouldn't be braiding Sarah's hair.

The baby in her arms made a funny squeak. The sound reminded him of Sarah as an infant and he grinned. "He's lively, isn't he?"

"Very."

With her blue eyes and tilted chin, she reminded him of the picture of Cinderella in Sarah's book of fairy tales.

He blinked and imagined a white coach and glass slippers, a prince chasing after her and mice turning into dashing white horses. His mind went down a long, strange road before he pulled himself back to the entry hall.

Pearl jiggled the baby. "We should join the others."

As he motioned for her to lead the way, Carrie came back from the parlor. She smiled at Matt, then focused on Pearl. "There's a guest room behind the stairwell. You can tend the baby there."

As Pearl went down the hall, Matt watched the ripple of her silver-blue dress, thought again of Cinderella and scowled. He had no business thinking about glass slippers and Pearl in the same breath. He'd been a lousy husband to Bettina, and he'd doubtlessly make the same mistakes if he ever lost his mind and remarried. As much as Sarah wanted a mother, she'd have to make do with Mrs. Holcombe, the widow who lived across the street from them. Mrs. Holcombe loved Sarah and treated her like a granddaughter.

"Matt?"

He turned back to Carrie and saw a sweet smile. He truly appreciated the interest she'd taken in Sarah. The preacher's daughter hadn't been a little girl like he'd expected, but Sarah would enjoy a fancy dinner with feminine touches. He could see why Dan liked Carrie. She had a good heart and generous nature. And his friend had no reservations about marriage.

Pleased for Dan, he felt good as Carrie led him into the parlor. She sat on the divan, so he took the armchair next to Reverend Oliver. Sarah sat at his feet with her doll in her lap, talking to Annie as if she were a real girl. Her loneliness punched Matt in the gut. So did Pearl's arrival in the parlor. Instead of the hat and ribbons, he saw a braid wrapped so tight he wondered if her scalp hurt.

Holding Toby, she scanned the room for a place to sit.

Carrie patted the divan. "Sit with me. I want to hold the baby."

Pearl sat and handed over her son. Cuddling him, Carrie looked at Matt and smiled. He liked babies, so he smiled back. He wanted Pearl to know he didn't hold her indiscretion against her, so he studied Toby a long time, then said, "He looks like you."

When she beamed a mother's smile, Matt recalled the joy of being a family. For a short time, life with Bettina had been good. Pearl made him long for things he couldn't have, things he didn't want because he'd be a bad husband. At the same time, he enjoyed pulling her out of her shell. Wise or not, he wanted to know more about her. As the four of them chatted about the train ride from Denver, Matt gauged her expression. When she looked relaxed, he ventured a question.

"What brings you to Cheyenne?" He'd addressed the question to both Pearl and her father, but his gaze stayed on Pearl.

When she stiffened, Carrie answered for her. "Pearl's going to teach at Miss Marlowe's School."

"That sounds rewarding."

"I hope so." She knotted her hands in her lap. "I don't have the job *yet*. I'll be interviewed first."

"You'll do fine." Carrie patted Toby's back. "The interview with the school board is next Tuesday. That'll give us time to meet with Miss Marlowe. She's going to love you."

"You'll do great," Matt added.

He tugged on Sarah's braid, a reminder to Pearl that she'd risked her life for a child. At the same moment, Toby fussed. The cry brought another truth to light. A single woman with an out-of-wedlock baby would have some explaining to do. He didn't know if the people of Cheyenne would look past her indiscretion. Matt wanted to help her and he had the means. If he wrote a letter describing how she'd saved Sarah, surely the board would see her true character and forgive her past mistakes.

When Pearl cooed to soothe him, the baby wiggled and reached for her. Carrie scooted toward Pearl and handed him back. "I think he wants his mama."

Pearl propped Toby against her shoulder. In spite of the difficulty the baby posed, her smile turned radiant. Matt's belly clenched again. Pearl loved her son far more than Bettina had loved Sarah.

Carrie stood. "If you'll excuse me, I'll check with the cook about supper."

"Can I help?" Pearl asked

"No, but Sarah can." Carrie smiled at his daughter, still glued to his leg. "Would you and Annie like to see what's for dessert?"

Sarah needed all the female attention she could get, so he patted her back. "Go on, sweetheart."

"Don't tell your daddy." Carrie feigned a whisper. "But I baked cookies. I don't think tasting just one will spoil your supper."

Ah, temptation! The war waged on Sarah's face until the cookie won. She pushed to her feet. "I like cookies."

With Annie in tow, she crossed the parlor. Carrie guided her out the door, leaving Matt to consider how different this day could have been. If Sarah had been hit by the freight wagon, he'd have been burying her instead of waiting for a good meal. He'd thanked Pearl with the ribbons, but he still owed her a favor. The interview at Miss Marlowe's School gave him an opportunity and he decided to take it.

"I don't know how much it will help," he said. "But I'd be glad to write a letter to the trustees about what happened today. We haven't been acquainted long, but what you did proves you'll be a good teacher."

She bristled. "Thank you, Deputy. But no."

"Why not?"

"My situation is…complicated."

He'd figured that out already. "So?"

Tobias cleared his throat. "Why would you offer? You barely know my daughter."

"I know her better than you think." Matt spoke to the reverend but kept his eyes on Pearl. "Not many people would do what she did today. I owe her." He'd told the truth, but there was more to his reasoning. Guilt for what he'd done in the war never left him. Every time he helped someone, his conscience eased a bit. By helping Pearl, he'd sleep tonight instead of tossing like he usually did.

She looked at him with hope and hesitation. "I appreciate the offer. It's just that…" She shook her head.

"You want your privacy," he finished for her.

"Yes."

"I understand about private matters." He flashed a grin he hoped would be roguish. "If you don't ask questions, neither will I."

If Pearl knew he didn't hold her son against her, maybe she'd accept his help. If she accepted his help, he could feel good about paying her back. He didn't know who had fathered her baby, or why the man hadn't married her, but he knew how it felt to live with a bad decision. Hoping to persuade her, he gentled his voice. "I'm not the most influential man in Cheyenne. The letter might not change any minds, but it won't hurt, either."

Pearl looked at her father.

He gave a crisp nod. "Say yes, princess."

Matt smiled at the nickname. He didn't like ministers, but he was impressed by Reverend Oliver. The man clearly loved his daughter in spite of her mistake. Pearl, though, looked mildly irked at the childish moniker.

She turned to Matt. "Thank you, Deputy. I accept."

"My pleasure."

She smiled, then blushed and looked away as if she'd committed a crime. Matt had no idea what she was thinking, but he liked knowing he could make her grin…and blush. The thought gave him pause. He had no business flirting with Pearl Oliver, except he liked her and she'd worn his ribbons. Not only did she make him want to whistle "Dixie," he admired her integrity. Matt didn't know what to make of his wayward thoughts, but he couldn't deny a simple truth. He liked Pearl Oliver far more than was wise.

Chapter Four

"Carrie!" Pearl cried. "It's lovely."

The women were in the parlor ready to leave for the meeting with Miss Marlowe. In the middle of the room sat a baby carriage. Pearl had never seen such a fine buggy. Narrow spokes graced the large metal wheels, and powder blue satin lined the wicker basket. Earlier, when Carrie announced she had a gift for Toby, Pearl hadn't known what to expect.

"Do you like it?" Carrie asked.

"I *love* it." Pearl pulled her cousin into a hug. "You've been so kind. I can't thank you enough for what you've done."

Not only had Carrie arranged a private meeting with Miss Marlowe, but she'd also invited Pearl and her father to move out of the hotel and live with her. Pearl now had the pleasure of Carrie's company and the benefit of a housekeeper and nanny. Martha Dinwiddie, a widow, came daily to cook and clean. When she'd set eyes on Toby, she'd vowed to spoil him like a grandson. With Martha's help, Pearl and Carrie had aired out the rooms on the second floor. While beating rugs and laundering bed linens, they'd become as close as sisters.

Carrie touched the wooden handle of the carriage. "I know you planned to leave Toby with Martha, but I think we should take him."

Pearl's nerves prickled. "Are you sure?"

"Miss Marlowe loves babies."

"But this is an interview."

"Not exactly," Carrie replied. "We're going to her house, not the school. Toby can sleep in the carriage. If he gets fussy, I'll hold him."

Pearl had mixed feelings about going out in public with her son. She wanted the world to know she had a beautiful baby boy, but his lack of a father raised questions she didn't want to answer. Today, though, she had to answer them for Miss Marlowe. Having Carrie at her side made the decision easier. She refused to be ashamed of her child. "We'll do it."

Her cousin beamed a smile. "Get Toby. I'll meet you outside."

Pearl hurried up the stairs. By the time she returned with the baby, Carrie had the carriage pointed down the street. Pearl set her son on the cushion and tucked a blanket around him. She'd nursed him earlier and hoped he'd be content. Keeping him fed and happy while she taught was a big concern, but she had a plan. Carrie's house was a short walk from the school. She could hurry home during lunch. In a pinch, he'd be satisfied with goat's milk she'd keep in the ice box.

Carrie looped her arm around Pearl's elbow. "Are you ready?"

"I have to be."

Steeling herself for curious neighbors, Pearl pushed the carriage down the street. As they bumped along, Toby opened his little mouth and found a new sound. He sounded like a tiny locomotive. Laughing, Pearl touched his cheek.

Carrie turned wistful. "He's wonderful, Pearl. I can't wait to have a baby of my own."

Toby had come at a cost, but Pearl loved him without shame. "It's the best feeling in the world."

"I want a *huge* family," Carrie declared.

A long time ago, Pearl had felt the same way. "Three boys and three girls?"

"Maybe." She sighed. "First I need a husband, and Matt Wiley doesn't know I'm alive."

Pearl had to agree with her cousin's assessment. While preparing the bedrooms, they'd spoken at length about Matt. Carrie had met him in September, the first day of school when he'd brought Sarah. They often chatted, but he hadn't done more than express appreciation for her interest in his daughter. Thanks to watching Adie and Josh at Swan's Nest, Pearl knew what love looked like. Matt had been friendly to Carrie, but he didn't look smitten.

At least not when he looked at Carrie. To Pearl's chagrin, she'd seen a spark in his eyes when he'd noticed the ribbons, and again at dinner when she'd passed the potatoes. Not that his mild interest in her mattered. As far as Pearl was concerned, Matt belonged to Carrie.

A gust of wind tugged at their skirts. Carrie tightened the shawl around her shoulders. "I wish I knew what to do. Matt said more at supper than he's ever said before."

"Really?"

"You impressed him. I'm glad he's writing a letter."

Pearl had told her cousin about Matt's offer after he left. Carrie had sung his praises, and the women had talked about the evening for hours. True to his word, Matt hadn't asked a single nosy question. Instead they'd all shared stories about children and growing up. Sarah had glowed with the attention, and Pearl had been happy to show off Toby. They'd all agreed he was exceptionally bright and destined to be president of the United States. Sarah had announced she wanted to be a teacher at Miss Marlowe's School.

Pearl hadn't been that relaxed in a year. "Matt definitely enjoyed the meal."

"I guess that's a start."

"I hope so." She meant it. More than anything, Pearl wanted Carrie to be happy.

Her cousin twisted the ends of the shawl. "It's just that Matt doesn't *see* me. I'm nothing but Sarah's teacher."

"Maybe he's been hurt," Pearl said. "Do you know what happened to Sarah's mother?"

Carrie's mouth formed a grim line. "They're divorced. She left him. She left Sarah, too."

"I can't imagine—"

"Neither can I." Carrie leaned into the wind. "He told me so I wouldn't say something awkward to Sarah."

Pearl couldn't imagine a woman abandoning her child, though for a short time during her pregnancy, she'd considered giving up Toby for adoption. In those dark days, she'd feared Franklin Dean and she'd had no way to support herself. Her friends at Swan's Nest had come to her rescue and she'd be forever grateful.

Carrie broke into her thoughts. "Matt's wife broke his heart when she left. You can see it in his eyes."

Pearl understood too well. She'd seen that look when they'd first met. "How long ago was it?"

"A year or so." As they turned toward the school, Carrie squinted against the sun. "I know Matt likes me. He's just scared. He needs to know I'd never hurt him."

"Of course, you wouldn't."

Carrie bit her lip, then released it. "He needs convincing, that's all."

Pearl didn't doubt her cousin's sincerity, only her reasoning. Matt hadn't shown even a spark of interest. "I don't know."

"I do," Carrie insisted. "Matt needs a push."

Pearl loved her cousin, but she had strong feelings about *pushing* anyone. Even before the attack, she'd been pressured by Franklin Dean and she'd resented it. She considered sharing her doubts with Carrie, but what did she know about men and courtship? Her perspective was skewed and always would be. Carrie's instincts had to be better than her own. "What do you have in mind?" she asked.

"I don't know. Any ideas?"

"Not a one."

Carrie's eyes twinkled. "How about a supper party? I could invite a few people over."

Pearl couldn't bear the thought. Carrie would invite single men. They'd tease and flirt with her.

"It's perfect!" Carrie declared. "You're new in town. The party will be in your honor."

"No, Carrie. I'm not ready for something like that."

"Please?" She made a winsome face.

How could Pearl say no? She owed Carrie for the food on her table, the roof over her head. She wanted to say yes, but she croaked with panic. "I'll think about it."

"It'll be great," Carrie insisted. "It's just what Matt needs. And you, too!"

Right now, Pearl needed to collect her thoughts. They'd reached the school. Behind the main building she saw a cottage. She tightened her grip on the handle of the carriage. "Is that Miss Marlowe's house?"

"It is," Carrie answered. "Isn't it charming?"

Pearl loved the little house. Ivy climbed the porch railing, and the gabled roof boasted a turret. As they walked up the path with the baby carriage, Miss Marlowe herself came out the door. Pearl saw a woman in her forties with chestnut hair and ivory skin. Petite and wearing a pea-green dress, she looked more like a leprechaun than the founder of a prestigious girls' academy. Pearl relaxed, but only until the carriage hit a rut and Toby started to fuss.

"Oh dear," she murmured. If he didn't settle, she'd have to pick him up. Meeting Miss Marlowe with her son tucked in the carriage would have been challenging. Meeting her with a crying infant in her arms made Pearl shake.

Miss Marlowe greeted them with a wave. "Hello, ladies!"

"Be brave." Carrie touched her hand. "She's going to love you."

"And if she doesn't?"

Carrie shot her a look of confidence. "I'll still love you, and so will Toby. Don't be afraid. We're in this together."

Pearl squeezed her hand. "Thank you, cousin."

Carrie waved a greeting to Miss Marlowe. "This is my cousin, Pearl Oliver. We have someone very special for you to meet."

Thinking of the hair ribbons—a gift to a woman of uncommon courage—Pearl lifted her squawking baby out of the carriage. Mercifully he found his fist and started to suck. As Carrie moved the carriage into a shady spot, Pearl climbed the stairs alone and faced Miss Marlowe.

"This is my son," she said quietly. "I'll tell the story now, but I won't repeat it. A year ago I was attacked by a man I trusted. I was—"

"Oh, child."

Miss Marlowe's pale eyes asked questions—*the* question—and Pearl answered with a nod. The woman touched her cheek, then lowered her hand, leaving a warm spot that felt empty. Pearl's heart turned to stone. Sympathy didn't mean Miss Marlowe would approve of her desire to teach.

Carrie joined them on the porch. "We wanted you to know Pearl's circumstances before the board meeting."

"Of course." Miss Marlowe indicated the door. "Come inside, girls. We'll talk over tea and scones. I made them myself."

Carrie gave Pearl an encouraging smile. "Miss Marlowe is known for her scones."

The older woman indicated a cane rocker. "Have a seat, dear. New mothers need their rest. Carrie and I will bring the cups."

"Thank you," Pearl managed.

She sat and put the rocker into motion. The rhythm delighted Toby and he kicked for the fun of it. Arching back, he gave her his first-ever smile. Happy tears pushed into Pearl's eyes. She longed to share the moment with a husband, but her friends would have to do. She'd tell Carrie on the way home, and tonight she'd write to everyone at Swan's Nest.

Miss Marlowe arrived with the tea service and placed it on a low table. Carrie added a plate of scones and a pot of raspberry jam. After serving the refreshments, Miss Marlowe sat tall on a chair that resembled a throne. She studied Pearl for several seconds. "Let me be frank, dear."

"Of course."

"I've reviewed your application and am satisfied with your qualifications. Carrie has provided a wonderful reference for you. As for your son, I have no doubt you've been victimized. In fact, I greatly admire your forthright handling of the situation. A lesser woman would lie to save face. You chose an honorable path. Not the easy one, mind you. But the right one."

Pearl's belly started to unknot. "I did, and I have no

regrets." Toby burrowed his head against her neck. She loved the tickle of his hair.

Carrie cradled the teacup in both hands. "We understand Pearl's situation will raise eyebrows."

Miss Marlowe's eyes twinkled. "I'm quite accustomed to raising eyebrows."

Carrie grinned. "I think you enjoy it."

"I do," the woman declared. "So let's do some politicking. There are five board members including myself. We need three votes. I should be able to twist my nephew's arm, but the third vote will be a problem."

Pearl's heart soared and crashed in the same breath. She'd earned Miss Marlowe's support, but she had a fight ahead of her. As Carrie and Miss Marlowe debated the options, Pearl heard references to Chester Gates and Lady Eugenia. Both women thought Lady Eugenia could be persuaded, but that Mr. Gates would be difficult. Carrie named the fifth board member. "What about Jasper Kling?"

Miss Marlowe grimaced. "The man annoys me."

"Who is he?" Pearl asked.

Carrie set down her cup. "He owns a shop on Dryer Street. I'm not ready to write him off."

Miss Marlowe wrinkled her brows. "I must admit, I don't know Jasper well. Why do you think he'll bend in our direction?"

"He went to church with my parents."

"I see." Miss Marlowe sipped her tea. "You're hoping he'll respect Pearl's refusal to lie."

"Yes."

"He might." She set down the cup. "Jasper's quite determined to build moral character among our girls. Just last week he championed the purchase of McGuffey Readers for the entire school."

Pearl had fond memories of the textbook. The primer

was full of Bible stories, moral tales and lessons for life. If Jasper Kling believed in the principles of truth and honesty, he just might support her. "There's always hope," she said to Miss Marlowe. "I'll have to persuade him at the interview."

Toby kicked and the women chuckled. Pearl saw envy in Carrie's eyes and something deeper in Miss Marlowe's. Maybe regret. The older woman offered the scones. "I'll speak to the trustees myself. You won't have to tell your story, but you might have to answer questions."

"Of course."

After Pearl took a scone, Miss Marlowe set down the plate. "You have two letters of reference. One from Carrie and one from Reverend Joshua Blue. Do you know anyone in Cheyenne?"

Before Pearl could answer, Carrie told the story of Sarah's rescue from the freight wagon and Matt's offer to write a letter.

"Excellent," Miss Marlowe replied. "A letter from a parent will carry weight. He's new to Cheyenne, but he's respected.

Carrie looked at Pearl. "It's going to work out, cousin. You'll see."

Pearl hoped so, but she felt like Sarah alone in the middle of the street staring at a team of mules. Needing to be brave, she thought of the ribbons. Matt belonged to Carrie, but Pearl valued his friendship. Hopefully, his letter would tip the scales in her favor.

Matt didn't like cooking supper, but he did it for Sarah. He liked washing dishes even less, but it had to be done. As he dumped the scrub basin out the back door, he thought of his little girl tucked in bed, wrapped in the pink quilt she'd clutched all the way from Texas. The blanket no longer reached her toes, but the fabric still held the softness of a mother's touch.

As he shook the basin dry, he thought of his last chore for the evening. This morning he'd bought stationery and a bottle of ink. All day he'd composed the letter for Pearl in his head, but nothing sounded right. With her interview just two days away, he had to deliver the letter tomorrow. He didn't regret his offer. He just wished he knew what to say.

He looked at the sunset and thought of her cheeks, flushed pink as she weighed his offer to write the letter. He stared up at the sky, a medium blue that melted into dusk. He thought of the ribbons and felt good that he'd brightened her day. Inspired, he went back into the house, stowed the basin under the counter and fetched the stationery and ink from the shelf where he'd put them out of Sarah's reach. He sat at the table, smoothed a sheet of paper, uncorked the bottle and lifted the pen. In bold strokes he wrote the date, then added, "To Whom It May Concern."

He wrinkled his brow.

He scratched his neck.

He'd have been more comfortable throwing a drunk in jail, but he'd made a promise and he'd keep it. He inked the pen and wrote, "It's my pleasure to provide a letter of reference for Miss Pearl Oliver."

So far, so good. He dipped the pen again, wiped the excess and described how she'd run in front of the wagon to save Sarah. As the nib scratched against the paper, he relived the rattle of the wagon. He imagined his little girl lying in the mud and Pearl protecting her with her own body.

He owed this woman far more than a letter. Not only had she saved Sarah, she'd restored a sliver of his faith in human beings, even in women with blond hair. Bettina had thrown Sarah to the wolves. Pearl would have died to save her. The thought spurred his hand and he told the story with ease. By the time he finished, he couldn't imagine anyone not hiring her. In closing, he described her as loyal, honest, dedicated and kind. After the way she'd handled the awkwardness of the ribbons, he believed every word.

He blew the ink dry, then closed his eyes. As he rubbed the kink in his neck, his mind drifted to Jed Jones hanging from a cottonwood tree. Matt had seen men hanged, but he'd never cut one down after three days. He'd lost his breakfast and done his job, but he'd paid a price. The nightmares from Virginia had come back with a new intensity. He hadn't slept well since then, and he doubted the dreams would settle until he figured out who was behind the recent violence.

His mind wandered until he felt a tug on his sleeve. As he looked down, Sarah leaned her head against his arm. The warmth of her temple passed through the cotton and went straight to his heart. Earlier he'd laced her hair into a single braid. Long and smooth, it gleamed in the lamplight. Thanks to Pearl, he'd gotten the hang of fixing hair. The trick was to pull with a firm hand. Before he'd seen how she did it, he'd worried too much about hurting Sarah's head.

Dressed in a store-bought nightie, she looked up at him with her big blue eyes. "Daddy, I can't sleep anymore."

He draped his arm around her shoulders. With her tiny bones, she reminded him of a baby chick. "You will if you try."

"I want to hear *Cinderella* again."

The week they'd arrived in Cheyenne, he'd bought a storybook with colored pictures for Sarah's birthday. He'd found it at the fanciest shop in town, and a clerk had told him the story behind it. A Frenchman named Charles Perrault had collected fairy tales in a book called *Tales of*

Mother Goose. Someone else had translated the stories into English, and someone else had drawn pictures that sent Sarah into raptures of delight. She didn't like the gruesome parts, but she enjoyed the rest. Matt had read *Cinderella* so many times that he had passages memorized.

"We already had a story," he said. "It's bedtime."

"Pleeeease."

Whining couldn't be tolerated. It reminded him of Bettina. "No, Sarah. It's time to sleep."

She tried to climb on his lap. Matt picked her up by her underarms and plopped her down on his knee. Rather than march her to bed, he'd play one last game of Horsey, then tuck her in with a kiss on the nose. She liked that.

As he scooted the chair back, Sarah saw the stationery. "What's that?"

"A letter."

"Who's it to?"

"It's for Miss Pearl." He wanted Sarah to show respect, so he'd used the "Miss." "We're helping her get a job as a teacher."

"*My* teacher?" She wiggled with excitement.

"Maybe."

Twisting in his lap, she put her hands on his shoulders. The lashes fringing her eyes fluttered upward. "Maybe she could be my mama, too."

The question didn't surprise him. Sarah had been talking about mamas since the day she'd seen Pearl. At supper she'd asked him why she didn't have one anymore. Matt had given the only answer he could manage. *Something happened, sweetheart. She had to leave.*

What else could he say? *I let your mother down and she ran off. She found another man...a better man.*

A five-year-old couldn't fathom such things, but someday Sarah would want to hear the truth. What could he say?

That he'd been a rotten husband? The thought turned his stomach. Sarah needed a mother, but there was no reason to think he'd become a better man. Never mind Pearl's pretty hair and easy manner. Matt had no business noticing her.

"Come on," he said to Sarah, lifting her as he stood. "You talked me into one more story."

She wrapped her arms around his neck. "I love you, Daddy."

"I love you, too, darlin'."

He galloped her into the bedroom, tucked her against the feather tick, sat on the stool by her bed and opened *Mother Goose*. If he angled the book toward the door, enough light came from the hall that he could make out the words. He could also see the picture of Cinderella with her blond curls and blue eyes.

Sarah rolled on her side. "I think she looks like Miss Pearl."

So did Matt. "A little."

"A lot." Sarah folded her hands across her chest. Then she did something Matt had never seen her do. She closed her eyes and mouthed words he couldn't hear.

"What are you doing?" he asked.

"I'm praying."

Matt had no such inclination, not anymore. A long time ago he'd prayed the prayers and he'd felt relieved of his misdeeds, but not anymore. That boy had turned into a man who had to live with his mistakes. All that remained of his faith were the pangs of guilt that had driven him to work harder than any lawman in Texas. The effort had cost him Bettina, who hadn't liked playing second fiddle to his badge.

Matt couldn't change the past, but he could stop others from making the same mistakes. That's why he'd do anything to protect the innocent…anything except put Sarah at risk.

"Daddy?"

He stumbled back to Sarah's land of fairy tales. "Yes, darlin'?"

"I'm praying for a mama."

Matt didn't expect God to answer Sarah's prayer, but neither could he burst the bubble of a child's faith. He brushed a strand of hair from her cheek. "Go ahead and pray, sweetheart. There's no harm in it."

"Mrs. Holcombe says it's good to pray. She says God listens."

"Uh-huh."

"She reads me Bible stories."

"That's nice."

"I like fairy tales better," Sarah said with authority.

So did Matt, though he didn't believe in either one. "Close your eyes now."

As she breathed out a sigh, he started to read about the poor girl enslaved by a wicked stepmother. By the time he reached the second page, Sarah's eyes had drifted shut and her breathing had settled into the rhythm of sleep. He closed the book without making a sound, then went to the kitchen where he reread the letter for Pearl. Satisfied, he folded it into thirds and sealed it.

As he put the stopper in the ink, he wished he could bottle his feelings as easily. His insides were churning and not only because of Pearl. Tonight he'd dream about Jed Jones and bullets flying at the Silver Slipper. Neither could he forget Jasper Kling and his strong reaction to the Peters kid. No one got away with anything in front of Jasper, not even a crude joke. Matt knew all about men who lived two lives. They did things in the dark they'd never do during the day.

Jasper had that tendency. So did the other members of the Golden Order. Matt knew how easily a good organization could go bad. Politics had turned the Texas Rangers into the Texas State Police, and not everyone had been honorable. Rather than become part of it, he'd come north with Sarah. They'd done well together, and he hadn't had nightmares until Jed Jones's lynching. Since that day, he hadn't slept more than a few hours at a time. He doubted he'd sleep tonight, but catnaps were better than nothing. Hoping the dreams wouldn't come, he blew out the lamp and went to bed.

Chapter Five

Matt woke up tired but not because of the usual nightmares. Instead of dreaming about Jed Jones or that night in Virginia, he'd been visited by Cinderella. Blue ribbons had graced her hair, and Sarah had called her "mama." He didn't know which dreams he found more disturbing. He knew how to deal with shame and darkness. Cinderella's smile filled him with false hope. As much as Sarah needed a mama, Matt had no desire for a wife.

Yawning, he threw his legs over the side of the bed, rubbed his jaw and decided not to shave. After splashing water on his face and chest, he got dressed and went to the kitchen to fix Sarah a bowl of mush. As he lit the stove, a cantankerous thing he wanted to shoot dead, he thought of mornings back in Texas, the good days before he'd gotten short-tempered with Bettina. He had his doubts about marriage, but he'd have welcomed bacon and eggs in place of the fare more suited to life on the trail. When he'd ridden with the Rangers, he'd lived on jerky and had been fine. Sarah had taken to calling their morning meal "gruel." Today he had to agree with her. It looked awful.

As he filled a chipped bowl, she walked into the kitchen. She'd dressed herself for school, but her hair was a tangle.

She chattered mindlessly while she ate, then she fetched her hairbrush and Matt did the best job ever of fixing her braid. Just as Pearl had done, he pulled the hair tight and tied it off fast.

With Sarah helping, he washed the dishes and put an apple, cheese and good bread from Mrs. Holcombe in her lunch bucket. Sarah picked it up and headed for the door. Matt put Pearl's letter in his pocket and together they walked to Miss Marlowe's School. Knowing she had the interview tomorrow, he wanted to hand it to Miss Marlowe himself.

Still tense from his dreams, Matt enjoyed Sarah's chatter as they walked. When they arrived at the school, he saw Carrie waiting for her students and waved at her.

Smiling broadly, she waved back. Matt considered asking her to deliver the letter, but he wanted to do it himself. As he handed over Sarah, he spoke quietly to Carrie. "Is Miss Marlowe around?"

"Not yet." Carrie beamed at him. "She'll be in around noon. Can I help you with something?"

"No, that's all right."

"Are you sure?" Her eyes clouded with worry. "If it's about Sarah—"

"It's not." He wanted to keep the letter to Pearl as private as possible. "I'll catch her later."

Carrie's expression dimmed. "Sure."

Matt glanced around for Sarah. She'd joined a group of girls and looked happy today. The move to Cheyenne could have been far worse than it had been. He owed Carrie a great deal for making the move easier. He looked at her now and saw a good woman.

"Thank you, Carrie," he said in a quiet tone. "You've made things easier for Sarah and I'm grateful."

Her eyes sparkled, an indication of how much she loved

children. "Thank you, Matt. She's a wonderful little girl. If there's anything more I can do, I'd be glad to help. I could take her to buy clothes or teach her to sew. I'd love to…" She kept rambling, but Matt stopped listening. He'd never understand why women talked so much.

When Carrie paused to catch her breath, he excused himself with a tip of his hat and headed for the sheriff's office. He pushed through the door and saw Dan looking cantankerous. Matt didn't bother to sit. His gut told him there had been trouble and he'd be making calls this morning. "What happened?"

The deputy made a show of rolling his eyes, then he clapped his hand over his heart in a display worthy of the actor playing Romeo. "It was terrible, Mr. Deputy. Just *terrrrible!*"

Matt grimaced. "This has to involve Jasper."

"Yep."

"The Peters kid again?"

"Nope."

Matt propped his hips on his desk. "Spit it out."

"You're not going to believe it."

"Try me."

"One of Scottie's girls did some shopping in Jasper's store yesterday. Only she didn't buy anything. She just looked." Dan threw up his hands in mock horror. "She *touched* a hairbrush. Jasper says he can't sell it because it's tainted."

"That's silly."

"It gets sillier." Dan rocked forward in his chair. "I know this girl. Her name's Katy. She cleans the saloon because it's the only work she can get. Her husband died, and she wants to go back to Indiana. She's saving for train fare."

A ticket to Indiana wasn't cheap, but Matt knew the stationmaster. Maybe he could get the girl a bargain. He went to the potbelly stove in the corner and poured himself coffee from an enamel pot. "What does Jasper want?"

"For us to arrest her."

"On what charge?"

"He didn't say, and I didn't ask." Dan shook his head. "I figured you'd have better luck with him."

"Thanks," Matt said drily.

His friend flashed a grin. "That's what you get for being new around here."

"It's been two months."

"I've got seniority. That means *I* don't have to deal with Jasper and *you* do."

Matt swallowed the dregs of the coffee, then put down the cup. "As my mama used to say, there's no time like the present."

As he headed for the door, Dan called after him. "Good luck. You'll need it."

With the sun in his eyes, Matt walked the four blocks to Jasper's store. Merchants opened their doors and bid him good morning. Wagons rattled by and drivers nodded in greeting. In the time he'd been in Cheyenne, he'd made a point of getting to know people. They talked to him. They trusted him. To stop the rash of violence, he'd need those eyes and ears on every corner.

As he approached Jasper's shop, Matt passed the display window where he saw wares from back east. Jasper changed the merchandise often, and today Matt saw women's hats, lace gloves and hankies. No wonder Katy had stopped to browse. Matt went inside and sauntered down the aisle, taking in the assortment of whatnot. The clutter irritated him, but Sarah would have been enchanted by the pretty things.

"Good morning, Deputy."

Matt turned to the counter where he saw Jasper. What

the shopkeeper lacked in height, he made up for in fancy clothing. Today he was wearing a green-and-yellow plaid vest, a starched shirt and a fancy tie. A mustache hid his upper lip, and wire spectacles sat on his pointy nose. With his hair slicked behind his too-small ears, he reminded Matt of a rat. "Good morning, Jasper."

"It's about time you got here."

"You're my first call of the day." Matt spoke amiably, but the sniping annoyed him. The clock had just struck nine. Jasper's store had been open for three minutes. Annoyed or not, Matt resolved to be polite. "I hear you've got a complaint."

"I do."

"Tell me about it."

"One of Fife's girls came in here and touched things. She left *marks* on them."

Matt kept his face blank. "What kind of marks?"

"Smudges."

If the girl had done real damage, he could have asked her to pay for it—or paid for it for her—and been done with the entire mess. Instead he had to reason with Jasper about smudges. "Could you wipe them off?"

The man reared back. "I don't think you understand."

Matt hid a grimace. "Maybe not."

"She besmirched my property!"

Matt had arrested a lot of people for a lot of crimes, but *besmirching* wasn't on that list. Did he explain to Jasper that nothing had been damaged? Did he fib and tell him he'd speak with Katy? What Matt wanted to do—call Jasper a two-faced hypocrite—wouldn't solve the problem. The man had a lot of nerve to accuse a cleaning girl of "besmirching" when he himself had visited prostitutes and possibly bribed Ben Hawks to cover it up. If Matt's hunch was correct, Jasper had done other things, too. He'd been one of the riders who busted out the windows at the Silver Slipper.

Annoyed, Matt tapped the counter. "Let me see the brush set."

"Of course."

Jasper stepped into the back office and returned with a box holding a silver-plated brush and comb. Sure enough, Matt saw a fingerprint on the handle. He also thought of blue ribbons and Pearl braiding Sarah's hair.

He looked at Jasper. "How much is this?"

The shopkeeper named a high but manageable price.

"Tell you what," Matt said. "Sarah likes pretty things, and she's too young to know about…besmirching."

"Of course."

"I'll give you half price for it."

"Half?" Jasper's nostrils flared.

"You said yourself it's damaged goods."

"Well, yes. But—" He clamped his lips. If he kept talking, he'd trip over his own greed.

Matt ran his palm over the bristles. They tickled. "That's fine quality."

"The very best."

"What's a fair price?" If Jasper believed the brush had been rendered worthless, he had no call to charge full price. On the other hand, he liked money.

The shopkeeper drummed his fingers on the counter. "I'll take off ten percent."

"Make it twenty."

"Fine," Jasper answered.

Matt slid a silver dollar across the counter. As Jasper put it in the cash drawer, he looked over the top of his spectacles. Matt saw questions in his eyes and prepared himself for another inquisition. Jasper never asked a direct question. His thoughts twisted like a lariat, going round and round until he tossed the loop.

The shopkeeper made a show of pushing up his spectacles. "I hear your daughter had a near miss with a freight wagon."

"That she did."

"I also heard a new woman in town came to her rescue."

Matt didn't care for Jasper talking about Pearl behind her back. Gossip ran fast and furious, and Jasper served on the school board. She didn't need word to leak that she had a baby out of wedlock. "That's right," he answered evenly.

"I hear she's pretty."

Matt thought so, but he shrugged.

Jasper tugged on his cuffs. "I'm looking forward to meeting her."

He wouldn't be so pleased when he learned about her son. Matt had no intention of spilling Pearl's secret. She deserved to handle the situation as she saw fit. "I'm in the woman's debt," he said simply.

"Do you recall her name?"

The shopkeeper sounded far too eager. Why the interest in Pearl? Matt had an idea and it turned his stomach. He didn't dare let the irritation show. The less Jasper knew before the school board meeting, the better off Pearl would be.

Matt worked to sound bored. "Her name is Pearl Oliver."

"Ah!" Jasper said. "Carrie Hart's cousin."

"Yes."

"A preacher's daughter."

"That's her."

Jasper's nose twitched as if he smelled cheese. "We need

a new church, a disciplined one. Her father might just be the man to lead it."

Matt thought Cheyenne had enough churches. He felt no call to worship a God who let men do what he'd done in Virginia, or who gave sweet girls like Sarah to women like Bettina. Matt didn't know which he loathed more—his own failure as a man, or God's failure to protect the innocent. He snatched up the comb and brush. "I've got work to do."

"One more thing, Deputy."

Matt met Jasper's stare. "What is it?"

"The Golden Order meets next week. I'll be mentioning today's vandalism. You should be there to explain what you're doing about it."

Matt would have rather punched a beehive, but Jasper's invitation served another purpose. If he attended the meeting, he could watch and listen. He'd see who had the biggest axes to grind. He wouldn't leave early, either. In his experience, the real business took place after the meeting when men shared cigars.

"I'll be there," he said.

As he left the shop, Matt thought of the letter in his pocket. He wanted to be at the school at twelve sharp. With a man like Jasper on the board, Pearl would need all the help she could get. The shopkeeper, he felt certain, would judge her as unfit because of her son. Matt had no such prejudice. People made mistakes. He'd made a bad one when he'd married Bettina, and a worse one during the war. No way could he judge Pearl for giving in to the oldest of temptations.

But Jasper would. A man who'd be offended by a smudge on a hairbrush would see an illegitimate child as the blackest mark a woman could have. The thought made Matt furious. A woman like Pearl deserved understanding, not judgment. She also needed protection from the likes of

Jasper Kling. Matt hoped his letter would be enough to give her a fresh start. If it wasn't, maybe he could help her find a job. Or maybe…his mind went down a road that led to a nice supper at the hotel and that horrible performance of *Romeo and Juliet*.

"Don't be a fool," he muttered. If he wasn't careful, he'd do something stupid like ask Pearl to supper. He had no business courting her. None at all. Keeping that thought firmly in mind, he whistled "Dixie" all the way to the sheriff's office.

Someone knocked on Pearl's bedroom door. Before she could say "Come in," Carrie cracked it open. "Hi!"

Pearl wished her cousin would wait for permission to enter. Toby had nursed and fallen sleep, giving her a moment of quiet. With the interview tomorrow morning, she'd been fighting an upset stomach all day. She'd been about to lie down when she'd heard the knock.

"Come in," she said belatedly.

Turning, she saw Carrie displaying the dress she'd ruined helping Sarah. To Pearl's amazement, the gown looked brand-new. Gone were the mud stains at the knees and bosom. It had been laundered and pressed into immaculate folds.

"You worked a miracle!" Pearl declared.

"Mrs. Dinwiddie helped." Carrie hung the gown in the wardrobe, then sat on the edge of the bed with a grin. "Guess what?"

Pearl sat at the vanity. "You bought a new hat at the dress shop?"

"Even better!"

"What could be better than a new hat?" Pearl teased.

Carrie's cheeks turned as pink as a June rose. "How about a *real* conversation with Matt?"

Envy raced through Pearl with a fierceness she'd never known. What would it be like to enjoy a man's attention… and Matt's attention in particular? She didn't know, but thoughts of him filled her mind with poignant regret. She pushed the images back because of Carrie, but she still felt ashamed of herself. She forced a smile. "That's wonderful."

"I saw him before school." Carrie put her hand over her heart. "He thanked me again for helping Sarah, but this time he really saw me. For an instant, I thought he'd ask me to supper. He didn't, but he wanted to. I could *feel* it."

Pearl knew all about feelings. They couldn't be trusted. "Are you sure?" she asked gently.

"I'm positive," Carrie insisted. "This is a start, a real one. I'm more excited than ever about that supper party."

Pearl's heart dropped to her toes. Carrie hadn't mentioned the gathering since they'd visited Miss Marlowe, and Pearl hadn't brought it up. Considering her own wayward feelings for Matt, the ones that came suddenly and unbidden, the idea of a dinner party had less appeal than ever. To hide her upset, she faced the mirror and pulled a pin out of her hair. "I don't know, Carrie. I'm still…" she shrugged.

Carrie stood behind her and removed another pin. "You're just like Matt. You need a push."

"I need time," Pearl said gently.

"You need courage." Carrie put her hands on Pearl's shoulders. "I'll invite Matt, of course. And Dan Cobb. He works with Matt. You'll like him."

"Carrie, no."

She didn't seem to hear. "Meg Gates will come. So will Amy Hinn. And the Hudson brothers. They work for the railroad."

Pearl couldn't bear the thought of a supper party. Men would flirt and women would ask questions. Every nerve in her body quivered, but her heart ached for Carrie. Her cousin loved Matt and needed Pearl's help. If Pearl agreed to the party, she could return a measure of the love she'd received.

"All right." She smiled at Carrie's reflection. "We'll do it."

Pearl decided to look at the bright side. She'd come to Cheyenne for a fresh start. At the party she'd make friends with Amy and Meg. As for the Hudson brothers, she'd be friendly without being forward. She'd wear her plainest dress and braid her hair tight. She'd be fine…really she would.

Carrie started to unravel Pearl's braid, but Pearl stopped her with a touch of her hand. "I'll do it."

"Let me," Carrie insisted.

"No." Pearl had to speak her mind. She didn't like anyone touching her hair, not even Carrie. "I'll do it later."

"Sure." Carrie sat back on the bed. "We have plans to make."

Together they planned the menu and set a date for the Saturday after next. With each minute, Pearl grew more anxious. Her only peace came from Carrie's excitement and the hope that tomorrow she'd be hired as a teacher.

Chapter Six

"Good morning, Miss Oliver."

Pearl looked up from the bench in the foyer of Miss Marlowe's School and saw Miss Marlowe herself. Her formal tone fit the mood of the day. So did the woman's attire. She stood before Pearl in the full regalia of a navy dress loaded with trim. Pearl stood and offered her hand. "Good morning, Miss Marlowe."

"Are you ready?"

"Yes, I am." She put iron in her voice, but her palms were damp inside her gloves.

Miss Marlowe indicated a corridor. "Follow me."

With their heels clicking in unison, they walked toward a fan of light indicating an open door. As voices filtered from the room, Pearl recalled the past hour. She'd been nervous and hadn't eaten breakfast. Toby had spat up twice. When she couldn't manage her hair, Carrie had stepped in and fixed it. Mercifully she hadn't argued about winding the braid in a tight coronet. Last, she'd helped Pearl into the blue dress and given her a hug.

Bolstered by the gown and Carrie's kindness, Pearl entered the conference room with a smile. The men stood and greeted her with solemn nods. The woman she surmised to be Lady Eugenia looked bored. When Miss Marlowe took a seat, Pearl did the same. No one would help her with her chair at a business meeting. As she sat, so did the men.

"Introductions are in order." Miss Marlowe indicated the man on her right. "This is my nephew, Nigel Briggs."

He nodded but said nothing.

Miss Marlowe turned to the woman. "This is Lady Eugenia, wife of Lord Calvin Anderson."

According to Carrie, Mrs. Anderson was married to the fourth son of an English nobleman. Carrie and Miss Marlowe hoped to earn her support, but her expression filled Pearl with doubt. Her brows were either permanently arched, or she didn't like what she'd heard from Miss Marlowe.

"Next we have Mr. Gates."

The banker, Pearl recalled. He served as chairman. In the event of a tie, he'd break it. Carrie described him as cold-hearted. Pearl hoped she wouldn't need his vote.

"And last," Mrs. Marlowe said. "May I present Mr. Kling."

Pearl recalled Carrie's hope that he'd respect her honesty. When he nodded at her, she smiled back.

Mustering her courage, she surveyed the faces around the table. "Good morning. I appreciate the opportunity to meet with you."

"It's our pleasure," Miss Marlowe answered. "Now, Miss Oliver, please tell us about your teaching experience."

Pearl folded her hands in her lap. "I taught Sunday School for four years. I love children and believe they learn best with kindness *and* discipline."

Lady Eugenia spoke next. "What of your education?"

"I earned a teaching certificate before leaving Denver."

"Yes, we know." Mr. Gates riffled through some papers. "We have your file."

Lady Eugenia looked unimpressed. "I was inquiring of your *formal* education, Miss Oliver. Have you attended normal school? Perhaps you've studied French and mathematics?"

"No, I haven't." Pearl doubted Miss Eugenia would support her. Regardless of Toby, she disapproved of Pearl's credentials. Even so, Pearl did her best to present her skills. "I attended a private school in Denver where I graduated with honors."

Mr. Briggs pursed his lips. "My aunt tells me you'll be teaching our youngest girls." He shot an annoyed look at Lady Eugenia. "I don't imagine they'll be learning French."

Pearl hoped she'd found a friend. She made eye contact with Mr. Briggs, but he looked annoyed by the entire proceeding. Instead of giving her a supportive nod, he scowled as if she'd ruined his day.

Mr. Gates gave Mr. Briggs a sour look, then turned to Pearl. "As you know, Miss Oliver, our teachers must have impeccable reputations."

She raised her chin. "Of course."

"You've provided three letters of reference. They speak well of you."

She said nothing.

"You're not married. Is that correct?"

"Yes."

"Yet you have a son." Mr. Gates raised his brows. "That implies poor judgment at best."

Pearl nearly shot to her feet and walked out. They'd been told of the circumstances surrounding Toby's conception. How dare he act as if she were a tart! She'd fought Franklin Dean, but he'd been stronger and cruel. Why couldn't

Mr. Gates see how vulnerable she'd been? Why did people doubt her integrity?

Lady Eugenia cleared her throat. "How old is your *son?*"

She said "son" as if Toby were a mongrel. She wanted to shout with indignation, but a show of temper would sabotage her dreams. Fighting to stay calm, she answered the question. "Toby is three months old."

Lady Eugenia sniffed. "I presume he's nursing. How do you expect to care for him?"

"The school has a lunch hour," she said carefully. "I'll make a quick trip home. We have a wonderful housekeeper, and my father lives with us."

The woman looked down her nose. "I see."

Pearl doubted it. Lady Eugenia had money and servants, not to mention a husband. She didn't have to worry about feeding her children or keeping them warm, but Pearl worried all the time. She desperately needed an income. She had to make this wealthy woman understand. "May I be blunt, Lady Eugenia?"

"I suppose."

"If my son gets sick, he'll need a doctor and medicine. Medicine costs money. So does food and clothing. I'm his sole support. Not only would teaching allow me to meet that obligation with honor, it's a worthy occupation." She took a breath. "I'm hardworking and responsible. You won't regret hiring me."

Nigel Briggs grimaced. "Your situation is...complicated."

"*And* dubious," Lady Eugenia added.

Pearl saw the position slipping through her fingers. No way would she surrender without a fight. With her head high, she addressed Mr. Gates. "May I speak frankly, sir?"

"Of course."

She scanned the faces around the table, gauging the expressions without guile. "It's true my son was born out of wedlock. As you know, I was attacked and a child resulted. I love my son very much. I also believe in the Ten Commandments. Among them is 'Thou shalt not bear false witness.' I could have pretended to be a widow. No one in this room would have known any better. But I will *not*... willingly...break God's commands."

Lady Eugenia frowned.

Miss Marlowe beamed a smile.

Mr. Briggs scratched notes with a pencil. Did she have his support or not? Pearl couldn't tell.

Mr. Gates, an experienced negotiator, blanked his expression. She wondered how many desperate men he'd turned down for loans.

Last she observed Mr. Kling. Behind his spectacles she saw a sheen of admiration. He'd squared his shoulders and looked approving of her stand for the truth. He held her gaze until she blinked, then he looked at Mr. Gates. "May I address the trustees?"

"Of course."

Mr. Kling folded his hands on top of the table. "Miss Oliver's circumstances are indeed troublesome. Above all, we must protect our girls from moral turpitude. Even the appearance of improper behavior can't be tolerated. Young minds are impressionable."

Pearl's heart turned to stone.

"Yet," he continued. "We must recognize a sad truth. We live in a sinful world. Miss Oliver is a victim of the vileness we hope to end by raising principled young ladies, who in turn will raise principled sons and daughters. I appreciate her truthfulness today. No matter how we vote, Miss Oliver deserves our respect."

Pearl's heart swelled with gratitude. Carrie had been right. He shared her values.

Miss Marlowe broke the silence. "Your candor is admirable, Miss Oliver. I want to express my support for giving you the position."

"Thank you."

Lady Eugenia stifled a yawn, a sure sign of disregard. Mr. Briggs said nothing, but his aunt had influence over him. Counting Miss Marlowe, Mr. Briggs and Mr. Kling, Pearl had three votes. Hope welled in her chest.

Mr. Gates cleared his throat. "You're excused, Miss Oliver. We'll discuss your application and take a vote."

She stood. "When might I hear?"

"We'll vote now," he said. "Wait in the foyer."

Pearl left the room, closed the door and returned to the bench she'd occupied before the interview. With her hands in her lap, she stared at the painting on the opposite wall. It was a landscape depicting mountains and a herd of sheep. *The Lord is my shepherd. I shall not want.* Her heart took comfort in the familiar psalm, but her mind relived the past ten minutes. Mr. Gates had told her to stay for the answer. Was that good or bad? A long wait meant intense discussion among the board members, maybe a split decision. A short one would signal—

"Miss Oliver?"

She saw Miss Marlowe and stood. "Yes?"

The woman gripped her hands. "I'm so sorry, dear."

Pearl went numb.

"The vote was two to three. I can't tell you how the others voted, but you know how I feel."

"Thank you," she murmured.

"The decision is positively foolish…" Miss Marlowe rambled on, but Pearl didn't hear the words. How would she support her son? She couldn't impose on Carrie forever.

Her cousin had championed her. Would the board hold it against her? Hot tears filled her eyes. "I have to go," she mumbled.

Hoisting her skirts, she ran out the door and down a dirt path. As the chill of autumn slapped her face, the sun beat on her back. The tears in her eyes acted like a veil, blurring her surroundings into a white haze. Almost running, she cut across a field of dry grass. Carrie's house was two blocks away, but Pearl couldn't go home until she composed herself. If her father saw her, he'd be upset. With her neck bent, she turned down an unfamiliar street and paced down the boardwalk.

She didn't see the man approaching from the opposite direction. She didn't see his boots or his badge. She didn't see anything at all until she plowed into a broad chest and looked into a pair of familiar green eyes.

Chapter Seven

Matt clasped Pearl's arms to steady her. As his fingers tightened on her sleeves, a trembling shot to his elbows. She dipped her chin to hide her face, but he'd already seen the sheen of tears. If she'd been Sarah, he'd have pulled her against his chest, held her and rocked her. The thought rocked *him*. He had no business comforting this woman, but neither could he bring himself to step back. "Are you all right?"

"I'm fine."

"You don't sound fine."

"I am," she insisted with a wave of her hand. "Everything's fine. Really, it is."

Except her voice had a wobble, and she'd lowered her chin another notch. The angle gave him a view of the top of her hat, the same one she'd worn to Carrie's house. No ribbons graced the brim. He couldn't see her blue eyes, but damp trails marked her cheeks.

Like most men, he found a woman's tears unnerving. He knew how to deal with anger, even violence. As a lawman, he handled fights every day. As a husband, he'd dealt with Bettina. When he'd left the Rangers, she'd pouted. When pouting didn't make him stay, she'd shouted at him. *You care more about the Rangers than you do about me!* Matt wasn't proud of himself, but he'd shouted back. The woman with him now wasn't pouting or yelling. Her tears came from a deeper place. As a lawman, he had a duty to protect her. All business, he lifted his hands from her shoulders. "What happened?"

She shook her head. "I need to get home."

"To the hotel?"

"No, to Carrie's house." Her voice cracked.

"I'll walk with you."

"No!" Her chin jerked up, revealing the stubborn set of her mouth. "I appreciate the offer, but I'm fine."

He wanted to respect her feelings, but she was heading toward Ferguson Street. Soon she'd attract attention she didn't want. He knew that for a fact, because she looked lovely in the blue dress that no longer had mud stains at the knees. If he didn't mind his manners, he'd be whistling "Dixie" again. He decided on a compromise. "I'll walk you as far as Dryer Street."

"It's not necessary—"

"It is," he insisted. "You're headed for a bad part of town."

"Please," she murmured. "Just go."

Matt put tenderness in his voice…and strength. "You know I can't do that. How about I buy you coffee?"

She pressed her hand to her mouth, but a sob escaped between her fingers. What had he done to make her cry? Confused, he searched the street behind her. His gaze shifted to the path that led to Miss Marlowe's School. The pieces of the puzzle slammed together. "You had the interview today."

She took a hankie from her pocket and dabbed at her eyes. "Obviously I didn't get the job."

Matt saw red. "Those fools—"

"It's over." She lowered the square of linen. "There's no use crying about it."

He admired her fortitude. Bettina would have moped for weeks. "I guess my letter didn't do much good."

"Oh, it did!" Her gaze rose to his face. "At the very least, it made me feel better."

"I'm glad. Now let me walk you home."

She grimaced. "I don't want my father to see me like this."

"We'll walk slow." He had no business sounding pleased, but he didn't mind escorting Pearl in the least. Aside from adding another good deed to his account, he enjoyed her company.

Worry whipped across her face, but then her eyes brightened as if she'd had a pleasing thought. Maybe walking with him wasn't so bad. Matt let his eyes twinkle. "How about it?"

"That would be nice," she answered. "If we walk slow, Carrie will be home for lunch. I'm sure she'd fix you something."

Matt didn't see what Carrie had to do with anything, but he liked the idea of walking slow with Pearl. He motioned for her to pass, then fell into step at her side. He preferred silence to chatter, but he sensed she needed to talk. If he'd misread her, fine. She could tell him to hush. "What was the vote?"

"Two to three."

He considered the five trustees. "I figure Miss Marlowe voted yes. Who else?"

"The vote was secret, but I think it was Mr. Kling."

"Jasper?"

"Yes." She looked up at him. "You're surprised."

"I know Jasper. You're mistaken."

"I'm sure of it." Her voice held authority. "Other than Miss Marlowe, he was the only trustee to speak kindly."

Matt couldn't believe his ears. Jasper had wanted a girl arrested for besmirching a hairbrush. He'd never give an unwed mother a chance to teach little girls. No matter what Jasper had said, Matt felt certain he'd voted against her. As he'd learned from Dan, Jasper Kling did one thing in public and another in private. The thought of Pearl trusting him put Matt on full alert. He wasn't in a position to enlighten her about Jasper's bad habits, but neither could he leave her thinking the man was her friend. He also wanted to know what Jasper had said during the interview. Considering the G.O.'s possible turn to violence, any comments by Jasper could be revealing.

They were across the street from Madame Fontaine's bakery. Instead of going to Carrie's house, Matt steered Pearl in to the brightly decorated café. "I'm buying you a piece of pie."

"But—"

"We have to talk," he said. "It's business."

She hesitated but allowed him to guide her into the café. Knowing she didn't want attention, and not wanting it himself, he led her to a table in the back. As he pulled out her chair, she arranged her skirt and sat. Matt dropped down across from her, then wished he'd taken a table by the window. The corner felt dark and intimate. It was too isolated for the two of them, yet he needed privacy for what he had to say.

She raised her chin. "What's this about?"

"Jasper Kling."

Her mouth tensed. "I don't gossip."

She had doubtlessly been the victim of wagging tongues in Denver. He could imagine the speculation. *The preacher's daughter! Can you imagine? Who do you think is the father?* Matt had no time for gossiping fools who judged others but didn't see themselves. In his line of work, people shamed themselves every day, just as he'd shamed himself in Virginia. Regardless of his personal failings or maybe because of them, he had to caution Pearl.

Madame Fontaine came to take their order. "Good morning, Deputy." She smiled at Pearl. "And to you, *mademoiselle*."

As Matt looked up, Madame Fontaine winked at him. "I see you've brought another darling girl this morning. Where is your Sarah?"

"In school."

"Ah…" She raised a brow. "So you and the *mademoiselle* have this lovely day to yourselves."

Pearl blushed to the roots of her hair. Matt didn't like Madame Fontaine's easy words, but it was the way of the French. Rather than correct her wrong impression, he asked Pearl if she'd like cherry pie. Still blushing, she answered primly. "Yes, please."

"Two slices," he said to Madame Fontaine. "Coffee for me and milk for the lady."

As the bakery owner left, Matt turned to Pearl. Even in the dim corner, her hair had a shine beneath the hat that matched her dress. He had to remember why he'd brought her here, and it wasn't to look at her hair. "I'd like to hear more about the interview."

"Why?"

"I'm concerned." He had to quiz her without revealing his suspicions about Jasper and the G.O., so he weighed his words carefully. "Jasper asked me about you."

"He did?"

"He heard about Sarah's accident." He told her how Jasper had asked her name and learned of her father's profession. "He seemed interested, if you know what I mean."

Her brows shot up.

"I just thought you should know." Leaning forward, he kept his voice low. "It's none of my business, but you're new in town. You're not aware of certain things." *Like Jasper's letters to the editor and his rantings at the Golden Order.*

"That's true," she said quietly. "But I know what I saw today."

"What did you see?"

Pride burned in her eyes. "He gave me respect. No one else even tried to understand. Except Miss Marlowe, of course."

Matt couldn't figure it out. Why had Jasper been kind to a fallen woman? "You must have impressed him."

"I told the truth," she said quietly.

He still couldn't make the pieces fit. Jasper never forgave anyone for anything. Matt didn't believe for a minute he'd supported Pearl. He might have *appeared* to support her for his own reasons—reasons Matt found repulsive—but he doubted he had voted for her. When it came to impropriety, Jasper had no tolerance for anyone.

A waitress brought the coffee, milk and pie. They ate in silence until Pearl set down her fork. "I don't understand. Why don't you like Mr. Kling?"

Because he keeps secrets. He's a hypocrite and liar. Matt wanted to enlighten her, but he had no business talking about Jasper. He shrugged. "I just don't."

Pearl sliced a bite of pie. "I do. He was kind to me today."

The more Matt said against Jasper, the more she'd defend him. He considered telling her about the besmirched hairbrush, but he didn't want to mention hair. Neither did he want to talk about hypocrites and hog ranches with a preacher's daughter. Annoyed, he stabbed at the pie. "I still think he voted against you."

"Why?"

Matt didn't want to go down that road, but she'd insisted. "They know about your son, right?"

"Of course."

If she could shoot straight, so could he. "Jasper's not one to overlook a person's mistakes."

Her brows hitched together. "What *mistake?*"

She hadn't gotten with child by herself. Did he have to spell it out for her? "You know what I mean."

She gasped in shock, then shot to her feet and raced to the door.

Matt didn't understand. Until now, she'd been candid about her situation. He hadn't said anything she hadn't acknowledged herself. He couldn't let her leave in a snit, so he slapped some coins on the table and went after her. Before he could catch up, she pushed through the door. It swung shut behind her, nearly slapping his face. By the time he'd gone through it, she gained half a block.

"Hold up," he called.

She hoisted her skirts and ran faster. He broke into a run. Chasing Pearl was getting to be a habit. When he reached her side, he jumped in front of her to block her path. She stopped short and glared at him through her tears. "Go away!"

He clasped her arms. "Pearl, I'm sorry."

"Leave me alone!"

"Whatever I said, I didn't mean to offend you."

"You said I made a mistake!" Fury blazed in her eyes. "I didn't! I didn't want—I pushed him—*I said no!*"

She broke into sobs and hunched forward as if she'd been socked in the belly. If he hadn't been holding her arms, she'd have crumpled to her knees in the middle of the street, a heap of helpless skirts and tears and that's when he understood… She'd been raped.

His heart caught fire. He wanted to kill the man who'd touched her. A noose and a tall tree…. A bullet to the man's brain. The violence carried him to Virginia in a haze of rage. He'd never take the law into his own hands again, but sometimes he thought about it. If anyone harmed Sarah— he clenched his jaw. If someone hurt his daughter, blood would run thick.

Right now, he needed to help Pearl. She'd straightened her back, but her eyes were still gleaming. "I'm tired of defending myself! I'm tired of being blamed and accused! I won't stand for it."

"Good."

She glared at him. "I don't want pity, either."

"I don't give it." Everyone in this world had a story to tell, including him. Most of those stories had lousy endings. "I don't feel sorry for you, Pearl. Not a whit."

"You don't?" She sounded steadier.

"No, I don't. But I'd like to kill the brute who hurt you."

"He's dead."

"Good." Matt wouldn't have to go to Denver and arrest someone. "You're alive. You survived."

"Yes." She seemed to breathe the word. "I did."

"I can see that." He saw everything about her and he liked what he saw. She was brave, smart and pretty to boot. "I jumped to a very wrong conclusion, and I'm sorry. I'd be grateful if you'd accept my apology."

"Of course."

Matt let his eyes twinkle. "You're a force when you're angry, Miss Oliver. I'm glad that fury's not directed at me right now."

In spite of his teasing, she looked bleak. "I'm not mad anymore. Just disappointed."

"So am I," he said quietly. "You'd be a wonderful teacher."

"Do you think so?"

"Sure." He smiled.

Pearl's eyes clouded. "Sometimes I wonder if the trouble will ever go away."

"I don't know," he said truthfully. "Something like that stays with a person, but it doesn't have to stop you from living. You're a good woman, Pearl. And a good mother. Some man is going to be honored to have you for a wife."

A whimper escaped from between her lips. She covered her mouth with her fingers, a gesture that made him wonder if she'd ever been kissed with true tenderness…if she wanted a husband…if she felt damaged or whole. He had no business thinking such thoughts, no call to hurt for what she'd endured. But he did. He wiped her tears with his thumb. "Feel better?"

"I do."

"Good."

Her eyes clouded again, this time with resignation, and he thought of the ribbons he shouldn't have sent, the ribbons he wouldn't take back for anything.

She lifted her chin and smiled. "I'm glad you and Carrie are friends."

So was Matt. Carrie had brought him closer to Pearl. He indicated the way to Carrie's house. "I'll walk you home."

"Thank you, Deputy Wiley."

The formality annoyed him. He'd called her Miss Oliver to show respect, not to put up a wall. "Call me Matt. We're friends now."

"All right, Matt."

She smiled shyly, then started down the boardwalk. After ten steps, she commented on the weather. Matt commented back. It was indeed a lovely day, but not as lovely as the woman at his side. It wasn't a matter of whistling "Dixie," either. She had his heart tied in knots. Not that it mattered.... No way would he court a blond-haired preacher's daughter. Not when he'd failed so badly as a husband. And not when he didn't respect her faith.

With that thought squarely in mind, he commented on the clouds. Pearl talked about the wind. And that was that.

Pearl hoped Carrie had already arrived for lunch. Asking Matt to share a meal with them was a small way to repay her cousin's kindness, though she'd had to swallow a surge of envy. She liked Matt far more than she wanted to admit. His apology had touched her deeply. So had the flash of anger when he'd understood the circumstances of Toby's conception. In that moment, Pearl had felt both safe and understood.

What if... But the question had no bearing. Matt belonged to Carrie and Pearl intended to help her cousin in every way she could.

To her pleasure, Carrie hurried down the front steps. When she saw Pearl with Matt, she hesitated, but only for a moment. "I haven't heard a thing! What happened?"

Pearl took a breath. "I didn't get the job."

"Oh no."

Carrie tried to hug her, but Pearl pulled back. Kindness would make her cry, and she wanted to keep the dignity she'd regained. She indicated Matt. "I invited Deputy Wiley for lunch."

With a winsome smile, Carrie faced him. "We'd love to have you."

"No, thanks," he answered. "I've got work to do."

"You still have to eat," Carrie insisted.

Matt smiled his appreciation. "I'll be fine, Carrie. Don't worry about me at all." He turned to Pearl. "Take care now."

"I will."

His eyes lingered a bit too long and her throat tightened. She couldn't let his friendship matter to her. She couldn't care about this man or want his attention. She had to help Carrie. "Are you sure about lunch? Martha's a good cook."

He looked pleased. "I wish I could, but Dan's waiting for me."

"Of course."

He gave Carrie a nod, looked at Pearl a last time, then walked away. Pearl wished he'd been friendlier to Carrie than he'd been to her. The circumstances were all wrong. She turned to her cousin. "I was upset after the interview. I ran into Matt—"

"You don't have to explain."

"But—"

Carrie looped her arm around Pearl's elbow. "Matt takes care of people. I'm glad he helped you."

He'd done more than *help*. He'd looked at her as if she were whole and pretty, as if he were interested in her. Pearl stomped the thought like a bug. "I thought you'd be home. That's why I asked him to lunch."

As they climbed the steps, Carrie sighed. Pearl felt both guilty for liking Matt and sad for Carrie because he hadn't been happy to see her. Hoping to make things right, she touched her cousin's arm. "Maybe the dinner party will open his eyes."

"I hope so."

So did Pearl, though she still dreaded questions and

looks. As they entered the house, she smelled the soup but had no appetite. More than anything, she wanted to hold Toby and grieve in private. "I'm exhausted," she said to Carrie. "Would you mind if I skipped lunch?"

"Not at all," she answered kindly.

After a quick hug, Pearl went upstairs. She told her father the bad news, pleaded a headache and went to her room. There she changed into an old dress, picked up Toby and moved the rocker to the window. With the sun warming her face, she rocked with her son in her arms, praying for the strength to endure the rest of her life.

"Why, Lord?" she whispered.

She hadn't asked that question in a long time. After the rape, her feelings had run amok. At first she'd been numb. She'd stopped praying and hadn't confided in a soul. When her monthly hadn't started, she'd begged God to let the cup pass from her lips. Instead he'd given her the grace to bear the hardship.

In those dark days she'd clung to God instead of questioning him. She'd accepted the situation the way she accepted bad weather. She didn't know why blizzards struck, but they did and somehow the snow, sometimes deep and treacherous, nourished the earth. God hadn't abandoned her. He'd given her good friends and a beautiful son. He'd also exacted justice on her behalf, both in Denver and on Calvary.

She hadn't been angry with God at all…until now. Why had He given her feelings for a man she couldn't have? Not only did Matt belong to Carrie, but Pearl had a deep fear of being a wife. Rocking steadily, she thought of her mother's favorite psalm. *I lift my eyes unto the hills from whence cometh my help?* Never before had the Lord let her down, but today she felt bereft as she thought of the next verse. *My help cometh from the Lord.*

Yes, but where was He?

Through the window she saw a puffy cloud. It reminded her of cauliflower, her least favorite food in the world, and surprisingly she found comfort. God knew her likes and dislikes, her needs and wants. He'd made *her.* He'd made Toby. In spite of the circumstances, she'd rejoiced at the child being knit in her womb. She'd rejoice now, too.

The rocker kept time as she spoke out loud. "Father in Heaven, I know you love me, and I know you'll provide. I need a job. Please open the right door."

Closing her eyes, she prayed for Toby and her father, then Carrie. Unbidden, Matt's face appeared in her mind and she recalled his expression when he'd turned down their lunch invitation. If he had any interest in Carrie at all, Pearl couldn't see it. Yet she'd seen something in his eyes. Loneliness? Yearning? She didn't know, but she'd sensed a deep-rooted longing. Bowing her head, she whispered, "Lord, Matt needs you, too. Draw him back into your arms. And Carrie.... She needs a husband. Bless them, Lord. Amen."

The prayer hurt, but she meant every word.

Chapter Eight

Two days after the interview, Pearl put Toby in the carriage and asked her father to accompany her on a hunt for "Help Wanted" signs. She needed a job and she intended to find one. Surely a decent shop would need a clerk. Her father had agreed to accompany her, and now they were on Dryer Street, the block filled with fashionable shops that included Kling's Emporium.

After discussing the interview with Carrie, Pearl still thought Mr. Kling had voted for her. Carrie thought Mr. Briggs had cast the other "yes" vote, but she hadn't seen the way he'd glared at Pearl across the table, as if she'd insulted him by wasting his time. Pearl had also considered Matt's comments about Mr. Kling's interest in her. Not likely, she'd decided. Like anyone, he'd been curious and had asked questions. A natural reaction, nothing more. As they neared his shop, Pearl glanced at her father.

"Let's visit Mr. Kling," she said. "I want to thank him for speaking up at the interview."

"Good idea," Tobias answered.

When they reached the shop, Pearl saw a collection of womanly whatnot in the window. "Such lovely things!"

Her father smiled. "You sound like your mother."

"I miss her."

"So do I, princess. She'd be proud of you *and* her grandson."

Bolstered by the memory, she lifted Toby out of the carriage. Her father held the door and together they stepped into a world of china and silk, silver trinkets and expensive clothing. As they approached the counter, Mr. Kling stepped out of his office.

His brows shot up. "Miss Oliver! This is a surprise. A nice one, I might add."

His enthusiasm reminded her of Matt's warning. Suddenly nervous, she forced a smile. "This is my father, Reverend Tobias Oliver."

The shop owner came around the counter and the men shook hands. "Good morning, Reverend."

"Good morning, Mr. Kling."

The man's gaze went to Toby, then rose to Pearl's face. "This must be your son."

"Yes."

"*And* my grandson," her father added.

Toby didn't have a father, but he had a good man in his life. Pearl and her father traded an affectionate look. Fortified, she turned to Mr. Kling. "I want to thank you for your support at the meeting."

"You're welcome." He made an awkward bow, then faced Tobias. "You raised a fine young woman, sir. I admire her integrity."

"Thank you," Tobias replied.

Behind his spectacles, Jasper's eyes looked huge. "I've been thinking about you, Miss Oliver. I understand your need for employment and happen to have an opening for a clerk. Would you be interested?"

Could her prayers be answered so easily? She wanted to take the job on the spot, but any position she accepted had to allow her to go home at lunch to nurse Toby. She'd also learned to ask questions before jumping into new ventures. "It's an appealing offer. What would I be doing?"

He laced his hands behind his back. "My clientele expects a high standard of service. You'd be assisting customers, arranging merchandise and making sure the shelves are *always* free of dust.

"And the hours?"

"The store opens at nine o'clock and closes at four. You'll have Sundays and Mondays off. Would that be acceptable?"

If Mr. Kling allowed her to go home at lunch, she wouldn't be away from Toby for more than three hours at a time. She'd have to hurry, but her father and Martha would help.

"If I can go home for lunch, the hours would be fine."

"I expect you to take exactly one hour."

She'd have plenty of time to feed Toby, but she had one more question. "And the salary?"

"Two dollars a week."

The amount was fair. Not generous, but adequate as long as they stayed with Carrie. Relief swept through her until she saw her father's tight expression. "Papa? What do you think?"

"I have a question for Mr. Kling."

"Of course," he replied.

As always, Tobias spoke with authority. "The trustees found my daughter's situation questionable. I have to believe you agreed with the vote."

"I did."

Pearl's heart plummeted. Matt had been right.

Tobias's frown deepened. "If you don't think my daughter is fit to teach, why are you offering her a position in your shop?"

"She's honest."

Tobias looked dissatisfied. "She also loves children. She'd be a fine teacher."

"You're a minister, sir." Mr. Kling's voice had a hint of condescension. "I'm sure you understand the implications. Her situation raises questions for impressionable school-girls. Appearances matter."

And they could be deceptive. Franklin Dean had been a wolf in sheep's clothing. Jasper didn't strike Pearl as a wolf, but neither was he a pillar of honesty. In the meeting he'd said one thing and done another. The man couldn't be trusted. Her gut told her to walk out of the store, but her next thought was more practical. He'd offered her good hours and a reasonable salary. She needed the job.

"I'd like to accept the position," she said to both men.

Her father hesitated, then nodded his agreement. Jasper acknowledged her with an awkward bow from the waist. "I'll see you tomorrow at nine o'clock."

"I'll be here."

Her father extended his hand. "Thank you, Mr. Kling."

As the men shook, the shopkeeper bobbed his head. "Please, call me Jasper."

"Then I'm Tobias."

Pearl sagged with relief. A job…. She had a job!

As she silently celebrated, the men made small talk. Her father and Mr. Kling discovered they both enjoyed chess, and they shared a deep concern for the moral climate of Cheyenne. Before they left the store, Mr. Kling invited her father to a meeting of something called the Golden Order and he accepted. Pearl welcomed her father's involve-ment. His heart condition limited his ability to work, but he needed a purpose. Joining the Golden Order would give him a chance to make friends in Cheyenne.

When they left the shop, she put Toby back in his carriage and hugged her father hard. "We're going to be fine, Papa. I know it."

"So do I, princess."

Today the nickname didn't bother her at all.

Matt didn't usually work Saturday nights. He claimed the privilege as a family man and left Saturdays to men without children. Tonight he'd enjoyed a quiet evening with Sarah. They'd played checkers—he let her win—then he'd read her a story and put her to bed. Knowing he wouldn't sleep, he sat staring into the fire, pondering his suspicions about the Golden Order.

If they'd crossed the line as he suspected, they had to be stopped. *How* was the problem. If he asked too many questions, the vigilantes would lay low. The problem would go away for a while, but they'd strike again without warning. Matt needed to set a trap. A trap needed bait, but he hadn't been in Cheyenne long enough to have the connections for an effective ruse. He needed a break but didn't see one coming.

Yawning, he banked the coals of the dying fire. As he headed down the hall, someone pounded on his door. He opened it and saw Dan. "What happened?"

"Someone beat Scottie Fife to a pulp."

Matt strapped on his gun belt. "Where did it happen?"

"Behind the Silver Slipper." Dan described how Scottie had been tricked into the alley. Instead of the customer he'd expected, he'd encountered five masked men in black derbies. "Doc says he'll live, but he's lost an eye."

"I want to talk to him." Matt punched into his coat. "Any witnesses?"

"Maybe. The girls are waiting for us."

Matt went to Sarah's room where he scooped her into

his arms. Blanket and all, he carried her across the street to Mrs. Holcombe's house. The widow would understand. He'd woken her up before. Tomorrow she'd remind him that Sarah needed a mother, as if he didn't already know it. As Dan knocked on her door, Matt called her name so she wouldn't be alarmed. She opened the door and he carried Sarah to the sofa, kissed her forehead and tucked the blanket around her shoulders. Bless her heart, she didn't wake up. He thanked Mrs. Holcombe profusely, then left with Dan.

As they neared Ferguson Street, the night turned rowdy with noise from a dozen saloons. A tinny piano played a rambunctious tune, and Matt heard female laughter from an upstairs window. Forced and empty, the sound depressed him. So did the plink of bottles as he and Dan passed one saloon after another, each with a name more tempting than the last.

When they reached the Silver Slipper, the noise died to silence. With Dan behind him, Matt pushed through the batwing doors into a room blazing with light. The customers had moved down the street, leaving behind the smell of whiskey and an abandoned Faro game. The six women who worked as dancing girls were huddled around a table.

Matt tipped his hat. "Good evening, ladies."

"Good evening," they murmured.

He'd have wagered a month's salary that not a single woman in the room had chosen this life. They'd fallen into it because of hunger and shame and only God knew what else. The rouge on their cheeks did nothing to hide the pallor of fear. Katy the cleaning girl sat on the fringe of the group. With her clean-scrubbed face, she looked more ashen than the others and twice as scared.

Matt surveyed the women. "Did anyone see anything?"

After a pause, a brunette named Lizzy raised her hand.

"Speak freely," he said.

"I saw their horses as they galloped off."

"I did, too," said another girl.

The dam broke and the women all started talking at once. Matt raised his hands. "One at a time, ladies."

After a couple minutes, he discerned there had been five attackers. In addition to wearing masks, the riders had chosen horses with no discernable markings. Sometime during the beating, one of the men had scrawled "God is not mocked" on the back door with white chalk.

"I'd like to speak to Scottie," he said to the group.

Katy pushed to her feet. "I'll take you."

Leaving Dan to continue with Scottie's girls, Matt followed Katy up two flights of stairs to a third story as ornate as a New Orleans hotel. Katy tapped on the door. When someone called for her to come in, she led Matt into a bedroom furnished from top to bottom with fancy things.

Matt made eye contact with the doctor. "May I speak to Scottie?"

"Only if you're quick," he answered. "I just dosed him with laudanum."

As Matt approached the bed, he saw the damage to the man's face. As Dan had said, he'd lost an eye. The remaining one was swollen shut, and bruises covered every inch of his face.

"Hello, Scottie," Matt said quietly. "What can you tell me?"

"Not much."

"Did you recognize anyone?"

"They got me down too fast."

"How about voices?"

Scottie swallowed painfully. "They're sly, Wiley. They didn't say a word.

Matt had to admire the group's discipline. They had a secret and intended to keep it.

When Scottie motioned for a glass of water, Katy stepped forward and lifted it to his lips. The gesture held tenderness, but Matt didn't think there was anything improper between the two of them. Katy had cared for her ailing husband before his death and had the demeanor of a nurse. When Scottie groaned, the doctor motioned for Matt to leave. As he headed for the stairs, he heard footsteps, turned and saw Katy following him.

"It's the men who shot out the windows, isn't it?" she asked.

"I think so."

Tears welled in her eyes. "I know Scottie's business is wrong. So do the other girls. We don't want to be here. It's just..." She shook her head.

"Sometimes there's not much of a choice," he said for her. He'd seen it too many times. A woman lost her way and couldn't make ends meet. Prostitution was a downhill slide that ended at places like the one Jasper Kling had been visiting. Matt had to wonder what would happen if the businessmen leading the Golden Order offered decent jobs to these woman? What if someone gave them a second chance?

Katy bit her lip. "I have enough money saved for train fare home. I'm leaving next week."

"That's good."

"I wish I could take Lizzy and everyone with me."

So did Matt. He couldn't make that happen, but he could stop the vigilantes. "Did you see anything else tonight?"

"I only remember the hats."

The black derbies claimed authority and made the group

known. Eventually they'd make a mistake, but how many people would suffer before they stumbled? Matt had to take action *now.* As he and Katy arrived in the main dance hall, he made eye contact with Dan. The deputy shook his head, a signal he hadn't gleaned any useful information. The two men bid good-night to the women and paced out the door.

As the bright light of the dance hall faded to black, Matt saw the answer to the problem with startling clarity. He and Dan had been *inside* the saloon. Now they were *outside* in the dark. They were also outside of the G.O. If they could somehow get *inside,* they'd have the information they needed to make arrests during the next attack.

"We need a spy," he said to Dan.

"A what?"

"Someone who can get inside the G.O." Matt picked up his pace. "They're not going to stop, and they're smart. We need to find a man they'll trust but who sees them for what they are. It's the only way."

Dan's brows lifted. "Who do you have in mind?"

Matt scanned faces in his mind, disregarding one after the other. If he approached someone favorable to the vigilante activity, he'd tip his hand to the Golden Order. On the other hand, the G.O. knew where everyone in Cheyenne stood on the issues of crime and Ferguson Street. "We need a newcomer to town. Someone they don't know."

"A wild card," Dan added.

"Exactly." Only one man fit that bill. Matt didn't care for ministers, but he liked Pearl's father. "What do you know about Tobias Oliver?"

"Carrie's uncle?"

"That's right."

"I haven't met him, but I expect I'll see him at church tomorrow."

"Good." Matt saw the pieces coming together. "See if you can get a feel for what he thinks of what's happening."

With their boots tapping on the wood, Dan chuckled. "I have a better idea. Come with me. You can talk to him yourself."

Matt answered with a laugh of his own. "Not a chance." He hadn't prayed since Virginia and he wasn't going to start now.

The men parted at the corner. Dan left whistling a nameless tune. Matt walked alone in the dark with only his thoughts for company. As he neared the edge of town, coyotes joined in a song that would haunt his dreams. Would he ever sleep well again? Maybe, if he could stop the Golden Order. With the wind pushing him, he hoped he'd found the answer in Tobias Oliver. A minister.... The irony nearly choked him. Matt had no faith in God and even less in men who claimed to know Him, but what else could he do? The G.O. had to be stopped, and Tobias Oliver offered his only hope. With a little luck, the man would be on their side, and soon Matt would sleep without dreams.

Pearl woke up in the middle of the night to the call of howling coyotes. As the endless wind stirred the cottonwood outside her window, she felt the restlessness in her gut. She'd been working for Jasper—that's how she thought of him now—for two days and she'd grown weary of his persnickety ways. Neither did she care for how he treated people. Wealthy patrons received the utmost respect. Customers of lesser means were made to feel uncomfortable until they left. Pearl would have quit, but she needed the money.

Unable to get back to sleep, she padded downstairs for a glass of water. To her surprise, she found Carrie sitting at a desk in the parlor with a pen in hand.

"You're up late," Pearl remarked.

Carrie smiled. "I'm writing the invitations to the dinner party."

Pearl's belly lurched, but she'd made up her mind to go through with the party for her cousin's sake. "Do you need any help?"

"I'm almost finished." She signed a note and set it aside. "That's the last one. I'll deliver them at church, or early in the week for anyone who's not there."

In spite of her good intentions, Pearl sighed.

Carrie looked up from the pot of sealing wax, saw Pearl's expression and spoke in a tone as gentle as cotton. "What's wrong, cousin?"

"Everything," Pearl admitted. "I don't like Jasper, and I hate being away from Toby so much. Teaching would have taken me away from him, too. But it's a noble occupation. In Jasper's shop, I'm dusting trinkets and kowtowing to people like Lady Eugenia. It feels all wrong."

"You could quit," Carrie said. "We don't need the money."

"*I* need it," Pearl insisted.

"That's pride talking." Carrie came to sit on the divan. "I've got more than enough for our needs. We're family, Pearl. Please don't feel beholden."

"But I do."

"You shouldn't." Carrie sounded brusque but in a good way. "Do you know how lonely I'd be without you and Toby? Do you have any idea how wonderful it is to have Uncle Tobias telling stories at supper?"

Pearl said nothing, but she knew what Carrie meant. Meals were a joy. The three of them traded stories and they all loved Toby. Pearl missed her friends at Swan's Nest, but she'd found a connection just as true with Carrie. "We *do* get along, don't we?"

Carrie gripped her hand. "We're sisters now. Don't ever forget it."

"I won't."

With a gleam in her eye, Carrie tightened her grip. "Since we're sisters, I'm going to say something you probably don't want to hear."

Pearl hesitated. "What is it?"

"There's more than one way for you to solve your money problem. I know you've been hurt, but a husband—"

"Carrie, no."

"Why not?" she said gently.

Pearl didn't know what to say. How could she explain the helplessness of being attacked, the fear that shook her bones? It was like describing a toothache to someone who'd never had one. Knowing Carrie couldn't understand—and being glad for that innocence—Pearl skipped over the most primal reason for her doubts and focused on a lesser one. "I have an illegitimate son. What man would want us?"

"A good one," Carrie insisted.

"I don't know."

"I do." Her cousin's face lit up. "I can't wait for you to meet Dan Cobb. He's funny and sweet, and he loves children. He'll—"

"Carrie, no."

"Why not?"

"I'm not ready." Except her mind had conjured up a picture of Matt. She'd tasted cherry pie and remembered his hands on her arms, steadying her as he gazed into her eyes. If it hadn't been for Carrie, she'd have worn the blue ribbons every day. Matt made her feel brave, but thoughts of other men sent tremors down her spine. She had to stop Carrie from getting ideas. "I want you to promise me something."

"What is it?"

"No matchmaking."

Carrie laughed. "I won't push, I promise. But that's not going to stop Dan and the Hudson brothers from noticing you."

Pearl went pale. "I hope they don't."

"Look at yourself!" Carrie chided. "You're *much* prettier than I am."

"That's not true."

"I'm being honest." She lifted her chin. "I'm pretty enough, but you're like sunshine. Any man would be glad to marry you."

Pearl didn't want *any* man. She wanted—*Stop it*. She had to stop thinking about Matt. For Carrie's sake, she'd be friendly at the dinner party, but she wouldn't wear her best dress. She'd braid her hair tight and she'd get to know Amy and Meg. As for Dan and the Hudson brothers, she hoped they'd sense her reluctance and leave her alone.

She managed a small smile for Carrie. "I'm not interested in a husband, but *you* are. If Matt has a lick of sense, he'll see that you're pretty and smart and just plain good."

Carrie blushed. "Thank you."

Eager to change the focus, Pearl grinned. "Now we have a party to plan."

Together they planned the menu, including the desserts they'd make themselves. Carrie decided to buy a new gown. Pearl would wear navy blue and no ribbons in her hair. With a little luck, Matt would notice Carrie at last and Pearl could be happy for them both. Never mind her own rebellious thoughts. They belonged with the ribbons in the back of a drawer, destined to be forgotten with all of her impossible dreams.

Chapter Nine

"Daddy, this is for you," Sarah said as she came down the steps from Miss Marlowe's School. "It's from my teacher."

"Thank you, darlin'." Matt tucked the small envelope in his shirt pocket, then swung Sarah into his arms. He figured the note was about his daughter's schoolwork, or maybe she'd been talking too much. He'd read it tonight in private, then remind her not to chatter like a magpie.

Sarah had other ideas about the note. She tugged the envelope out of his pocket and shoved it under his nose. "The paper's pretty. Open it now."

"Nope," he said.

"Yes!" She wiggled against him. "Miss Carrie asked me to give it to you special."

"She did?"

Sarah nodded. "It's an invitation." She stretched the unfamiliar word into a serious matter indeed.

Perhaps Carrie had planned a class event. The sooner he knew if he had to rustle up cookies, the better off he'd be. He set Sarah down and reached for the letter. "In that case, we better see what it says."

Matt popped the wax seal, read the invitation to a supper

party on Saturday evening and grinned. Dan had received the same invitation yesterday at church, and he'd nearly busted his buttons at the prospect of socializing with Carrie. Matt's buttons were busting, too. He hadn't seen Pearl since the day of the interview. The party would give him a chance to see how she was doing. It would also give him a chance to chat with Tobias Oliver. On Sunday Dan had been impressed with the man. Not only did he have a level head, he'd already attended a meeting of the Golden Order. They'd agreed Matt would chat with the minister at the next opportunity, drop a hint about their suspicions and possibly ask for his help.

Pleased with the turn of events, especially the prospect of an evening with Pearl, Matt swung Sarah back into his arms. Giggling, she hugged him hard. He was about to set her down when he noticed Carrie watching them from the top of the steps.

"Hi, there," he called with a stupid grin on his face. "I got the invitation."

Carrie's eyes went wide, then she hurried toward them. The exercise must have been a bit much, because her cheeks were blazing pink. He almost asked if she was feeling all right but decided to keep his concern to himself. She'd probably had a hard day with a dozen girls as lively as Sarah.

She looked at his daughter and smiled. "You did a good job delivering the invitation. Thank you."

Sarah hugged his neck. He squeezed her tight, set her down, then looked at Carrie. "Thanks for including me. I'll be there."

"Oh good!"

"Dan's looking forward to it." He hoped she'd take the hint about his partner. Dan would like nothing better than sitting next to Carrie during supper. With a little luck, Matt would end up next to Pearl.

When Carrie got tongue-tied, Matt hoped it was because of the mention of Dan. Stammering, she told him the other folks who'd be attending. He knew and liked them all.

"I best be going," he said. "See you Saturday."

"Wait!" Carrie called after him.

She'd sounded urgent. "What is it?"

"I was wondering…" She bit her lip. "Did you know Pearl's working for Jasper Kling?"

"She's *what?*"

"She's clerking at his shop. I was about to visit her. Would you and Sarah like to go with me?"

Sarah tugged on his hand. "Can we go, Daddy? Please?"

"Sure, darlin'."

He sounded at ease, but his gut had done a somersault. He couldn't stand the thought of Pearl working for Jasper. Yesterday he'd had another run-in with the two-faced hypocrite. It must have been Pearl's day off, because he hadn't seen her when Jasper summoned him to deal with three of Scottie's girls. The problem had started when Katy visited the shop. Predictably, he'd called her a Jezebel and ordered her to leave. When she'd run back to the dance hall in tears, Lizzy and two other women had shown up in skimpy dresses.

Jasper wanted the women arrested for trespassing. Matt had told them to leave, but he'd refused to toss them in jail. Instead he'd given them a warning, and the women had left with a wink and an offer he'd definitely refuse. Jasper had been less obliging. He'd called Matt a milksop and said he'd take care of the problem himself. How, he didn't say, but Matt had his suspicions. If men in black derbies attacked Scottie or the dance hall again in the next few days, he'd have another sign of Jasper's involvement, which in turn pointed to the Golden Order.

Having Pearl in Jasper's store made Matt's hackles rise. He swung Sarah up to his hip so he could move faster. "Let's go."

Carrie moved to his side and the three of them walked the five blocks to Jasper's shop. Carrie chattered as much as Sarah, but Matt barely heard a word. His mind was on Pearl and Jasper's nosy questions about her. He'd tried to warn her about the man, but she'd been too trusting for her own good.

When they reached the front of the shop, Matt saw new items in the display window. Yesterday it had held womanly whatnot. Today he saw men's neckwear, a walking stick and a black derby…the same hat worn by the men who'd beaten up Scottie Fife. A hat in the window… Matt couldn't think of a better way to summon the elite of the Golden Order. Men could come idly to the store, exchange information and go on their way.

His nerves burned like fire at the implication for Pearl. She'd see who visited the shop. She'd learn their names. She'd have knowledge that would make her a valuable witness and put her at risk. Matt couldn't stand the thought of Pearl being in harm's way.

He held the door for Carrie, vaguely aware of her passing but keenly aware of Pearl balanced on a ladder in the middle aisle. Unaware of them, she flicked a feather duster along the top of a cabinet while humming "Three Blind Mice."

Sarah wiggled out of his arms. "Miss Pearl!"

Startled, she turned too quickly. She grabbed for the cabinet to steady herself, but the glass front offered no purchase. She swayed to the right, then the left. Her knees buckled, and she toppled off the ladder.

Matt charged forward to catch her. So did Carrie. Being taller and faster, he beat her by three steps. As he gripped

Pearl's waist, she twisted and grabbed his shoulders. He lifted her off the riser and guided her to the floor, setting her down with a gentle bounce. Their eyes tangled the way they had after the failed interview. If they'd been alone, he'd have risked a teasing smile. When Pearl blushed, he wondered if she'd had the same thought.

She broke the spell by mumbling "Thank you" and stepping back. Before he could reply, she turned to Carrie. "Matt just saved me from an embarrassing fall. I'm glad you stopped by."

"Me, too," Carrie said brightly.

Sarah plastered herself against Pearl's skirt. "I'm sorry, Miss Pearl. I made you fall."

Matt's heart clenched at his daughter's woeful tone. Sarah had the misguided notion that bad things were her fault. She thought she had to be good to make people love her. That if she never acted up, she'd never be hurt again. He attributed the notion to Bettina's departure, which he blamed on both himself and God. How could the Almighty fail a little girl the way he'd failed Sarah?

Matt opened his mouth to correct his daughter, but Pearl had already dropped to a crouch. "You didn't make me fall, Sarah. You were happy to see me, and I'm happy to see you."

"Really?"

"You bet." She smiled so brightly Matt felt sunshine.

As she straightened, Sarah's head bobbed up. Her braids, more than passable in his estimation, flicked against her shoulders. "Are you *really* happy to see me?"

"Oh yes!" Pearl patted the child's head. "Your braids look pretty today."

"My daddy bought me a special brush." Sarah leaned closer to Pearl as if to share a secret. "He knows how to fix braids now."

Pearl smiled. "I can see that."

Matt's eyes flicked to another blond braid, the one circling Pearl's head like a crown. No ribbons today. Not a single comb or a fancy curl. Even without adornment, her hair was beautiful. Instead of pushing the awareness aside, he let it unfold into a simple fact. If it weren't for his flaws and their differences, he'd already be courting her. For a cynic like himself, such feelings for a godly woman weren't wise.

Smiling too brightly, Pearl looked at Carrie. "What can I do for you two?"

Two? Matt didn't like the implication. If Pearl thought he had feelings for Carrie, he'd have to set her straight.

"Table linens," Carrie answered. "I want new ones for the party. Matt's agreed to come. Isn't that nice?"

Pearl smiled at him. "I'm glad."

So was he. When he smiled back, her cheeks turned pink and she turned away. "The linens are over here." Pearl led the way to another aisle.

Matt had no interest in napkins but he wanted a closer look at the men's hats. "Where's Jasper?"

"At the bank," she answered.

He ambled to the corner displaying men's attire. Matt didn't care for fancy clothing. He owned a suit for funerals and a pile of store-bought shirts. As for hats, he wouldn't get caught dead in a derby. Thinking of the hat in the window, he looked for others on the shelf but didn't see them. Why would Jasper advertise an item and not put it out? He took it as another sign that the derby was a signal, not an advertisement. He wanted to share the information with Dan before the man left the office, so he crossed the store. "Ladies?"

They both turned.

"I just remembered something." He kept his voice even. "Would you mind keeping Sarah for me?"

"Of course," they said in unison.

Pearl sealed her lips.

Carrie grinned. "I'll take her home with me. You can stay for supper."

Supper would give him a chance to speak with Reverend Oliver. He'd also be able to quiz Pearl about Jasper. Matt wanted to say yes, but he had a bad feeling about the black hat. If something happened tonight on Ferguson Street, he needed to be ready. "Thanks, but no to dinner. I'll get Sarah in an hour."

Sarah scampered to him for a hug goodbye. Matt lifted her, kissed her nose and told her to be good. As he set her down, Jasper came through the door. His small eyes went to Pearl, lingered, then skittered to Matt. He blanked his expression but not before Matt caught the ogle he'd given Pearl.

The shopkeeper stared at him. "Good afternoon, Deputy."

"Jasper."

The man turned to Carrie. "Miss Hart, it's a pleasure. I suppose you've come to visit Pearl."

Since when did Jasper get to use Pearl's first name? It made sense since she worked for him, but Matt didn't like it.

Carrie smiled. "I came to buy table linens."

"They're from Boston," Jasper said with pride. "Pearl can help you. She's learning quickly."

Pearl thanked him for the compliment, but she sounded tense. Matt wondered if Jasper had been overly friendly with her. She'd hate that kind of attention, and he hated the thought of it on her behalf. Looking at Jasper, he made a silent vow. Every day he'd drop by Jasper's store to keep an eye on Pearl. The black derby, too. Matt excused himself and left the store. He'd be back, though. And he'd be watching.

To Pearl's relief, Jasper retreated to his office and closed the door. She wrapped Carrie's napkins in brown paper and gave Sarah a piece of candy. After they left, she put a penny in the till to pay for it. She didn't want to be accused of stealing or being careless. Her duties included dusting the store twice a day, so she picked up the duster and went back to work.

Her nerves felt as twitchy as the ostrich plumes flicking the invisible dust. She'd never been good at hiding her feelings, and she feared Carrie could see her reaction to Matt. When he'd caught her from falling, he'd lifted her up and floated her to the floor. She'd felt weightless in his arms. His muscles had bunched beneath her fingers and she'd felt safe. Not frightened. Not panicky...until she'd remembered Carrie.

Pearl didn't know what to make of the unexpected visit. She figured they'd met after school, but who had suggested a visit to Jasper's store? Pearl would find out tonight, but in her heart she already knew. Matt hadn't come to the shop for Carrie's sake. He'd come to see *her*. Catching her had been an act of duty, but his hand had stayed on her waist after she'd landed. His eyes had lingered on her face and she'd seen a question in his eyes.

What if...

"Stop it," she said out loud. What if pigs could fly? What if she could kiss a man without fear pressing into her throat? She flicked the duster over a shelf holding women's shoes. To distract herself, she admired a pair of ivory kid boots. She touched the buttery leather and wished she could afford to buy them. She yearned for all sorts of things, all beyond her reach.

"Pearl?"

She turned and saw Jasper. He'd left his office and closed the door behind him. Maybe he'd leave for the day. She lowered the duster. "Yes, Mr. Kling?"

"Call me Jasper," he said as he approached her. "I insist."

"It's a habit."

They'd had this conversation before. As an employee she didn't mind being addressed as Pearl, but she didn't have to surrender the polite distance of a man's surname. He'd approached her for a reason, so she asked, "What can I do for you?"

His lips pulled back in what might have been a smile. "I'd like to invite you to have supper with me."

Blood drained from her face. She needed to make a polite excuse, but she couldn't think of one. She opened her mouth, closed it, then managed to say, "Hmm."

Jasper's eyes gleamed behind his spectacles. "With your father, of course. We'd need a chaperone."

If she'd had any doubts about his intentions, the mention of a chaperone would have laid them to rest. She had no interest in being courted by this man. Her reaction had little to do with his small eyes and pointed chin. His demeanor put her off. So did the way he treated people. She had to nip his interest in the bud. "Thank you, but I can't accept."

"You're shy," he said kindly.

She said nothing, but her cheeks flushed. Not from embarrassment but anger, though Jasper wouldn't know the cause. She hoped he'd take the hint and leave. Instead he shifted nervously on his feet. "I want you to know, Pearl. I admire how you conduct yourself."

She said nothing.

"Your father, too." He pushed up his spectacles. "He spoke eloquently at the Golden Order meeting. We're glad to have him."

Pearl had to blank her surprise. Her father had come home from the meeting shaking his head. He agreed with the group in principle, but he'd been put off by the vitriol. He didn't plan to go back, and he'd been particularly critical of Jasper's ranting about Ferguson Street. Tobias hated sin as much as the next man, but he knew the folly of a superior tone and refused to throw stones at anyone.

Jasper had no such humility. Pearl had to discourage him, or else she'd be fending off his advances every day. Still holding the duster, she searched her mind for something true that would send him on his way. She settled on the obvious. "I very much appreciate having employment, sir. But you need to know, I'm not interested in…personal attention. I've made a decision to serve the Lord as a single woman."

Jasper gripped her free hand. "God bless you, Pearl. You're as faithful as Paul, the greatest of the Apostles."

She pulled back instantly. Jasper let go, but his eyes stayed on her face. Clutching the feather duster, a poor weapon at best, she stood like a deer sensing danger. Had she overreacted? She didn't think so, but she couldn't be sure. Jasper had an odd manner, but he'd simply complimented her dedication to God.

She had to respond or else she'd rouse his curiosity. "Thank you for understanding," she finally said.

With an awkward bow, he went to the display window. Pearl resumed her dusting, but she couldn't stop trembling. She didn't trust her first reaction, but her second one to Jasper echoed the same uneasiness. She glanced at his back. He'd put out the men's accessories just yesterday. Now he appeared to be removing them. The effort struck her as odd, but she had no desire to question him.

To her relief he finished arranging the new display—fine china and silver goblets—then went back to his office and closed the door. Pearl continued her dusting, but she couldn't shake off her nervousness. She read the *Cheyenne Leader* every day, so she knew about Scottie Fife's beating. The riders had worn black derbies like the one in the window.

She considered mentioning the coincidence to Matt, but she didn't want to visit him at the sheriff's office. She didn't want to think about him at all. He belonged to Carrie. Even if he'd been free, Pearl had no real hope for a courtship.

She tried to pray for Matt and Carrie, but her temper flared. Today she'd felt the sweet awareness of Matt protecting her from harm. She'd touched Sarah's braids and thought of the ribbons stashed in her drawer. How much more disappointment could she stand? And now she had Jasper to worry about.

Where are you, Lord?

She didn't know. The Lord had made Heaven and earth, but it seemed He'd forgotten a frightened woman in Cheyenne.

Chapter Ten

An hour before the supper party, Matt dragged the straight razor over his jaw, cut himself and grimaced. Fatigue made him clumsy, and the week had been brutal. Since he'd seen the derby in Jasper's window, he'd split working nights with Dan and the other deputies. When he slept during the day or in the wee hours of the morning, his dreams were vivid and intense. He could cope with the smoky images from the war. The shame fit like a pair of old boots. What he couldn't abide were the dreams that followed. Last night he'd seen Sarah and Pearl with matching hair ribbons and he'd jolted awake.

Dabbing at the cut, he thought about his visits to Jasper's shop. He stopped by twice a day now. Jasper assumed Matt was after "besmirchers." In truth he was watching over Pearl. Sometimes he'd bring Sarah, and he'd listen as the two of them jabbered about everything from braids to books to dolls. He could get used to having a woman around. So could Sarah, and that presented a problem. No matter how he felt about her, he was the same man who'd failed Bettina.

He looked at his reflection in the shaving mirror. "Be smart, pal. Don't go hurting anyone."

Someone tapped on the bedroom door. "Daddy?"

"What is it, Sarah?"

"Who are you talking to?"

"No one."

"But I heard you!"

"Hold on, darlin'." He put on his shirt. "Come in."

She opened the door, then looked around the room. "I heard you talking to someone. I *know* I did."

"I know. Pretend you didn't."

"If I had a mommy, you could talk to *her.*"

"Sarah—"

She huffed with an air of a full-grown woman. Did all five-year-olds do that or only his daughter? Since getting to know Pearl, Sarah talked constantly about mothers and babies. Yesterday she'd told him she wanted a baby brother as cute as Toby. Matt understood Sarah's needs, but there was only so much a single father could do.

He finished with his tie, put on his coat and lifted her to his hip. "Want to play horsey?"

"Yes!"

He galloped her into the kitchen where Mrs. Holcombe was dishing up supper. She liked being an adopted grandma, and he couldn't have managed without her. He kissed Sarah goodbye, put on his hat and left through the front door. He'd left his horse tied to a hitching post, so he climbed into the saddle. He usually boarded the gelding at the livery, but tonight he wanted to be ready to ride. If the Golden Order struck, he'd be there quick.

He rode two blocks to Dan's house and dismounted. Before he knocked, Dan opened the door. Bay rum wafted in a cloud. Matt fanned it from his nose. "You smell like a girl."

Dan grinned. "So do you."

It was true, almost. Matt had splashed something minty on his jaw, but he hadn't bathed in it. "You ready?"

Dan put on his hat and closed the door. "Dinner with Miss Carrie Hart? You bet I'm ready."

Matt felt the same way about Pearl but wished he didn't. Tonight he'd be wise to focus on the other business at hand, which meant carving out a private talk with Tobias. From his conversations with Pearl, he'd learned the minister had attended a G.O. meeting and found the gathering troublesome. When Matt had mentioned the vigilante attacks at the Silver Slipper to Pearl, she'd reacted with outrage and said her father felt the same way. Matt was fairly certain he could trust Tobias. Whether the man would volunteer for a risky mission remained to be seen.

Dan mounted his roan and they rode to Carrie's house. Instead of thinking about how to approach Tobias, Matt found himself wondering if Pearl would wear his ribbons. Soon he'd see for himself. The thought shouldn't have pleased him, but it did.

As she considered what to wear to the party, Pearl was tempted to use Toby as an excuse to stay upstairs. He had the sniffles and had fussed when she'd put him down, but he'd fallen asleep and was breathing evenly in his bed. She'd made arrangements with Mrs. Dinwiddie and Hattie, the serving girl they'd hired for the night, to keep a close eye on him, but she planned to sneak upstairs herself for a few peeks.

Considering Matt would be at the dinner party, she'd need those respites. She couldn't bear the thought of an evening in his presence. Every time he visited her at Jasper's store, she liked him more. Her feelings for the man were in a jumble.

She liked him.

She feared what she felt.

Most of all, she felt guilty for coveting her cousin's beau... except he didn't belong to Carrie. The more Pearl spoke with Matt, the more clearly she saw his feelings. He liked Carrie, but she'd never be more than Sarah's teacher. Pearl didn't dare think about what he felt for *her*. She only knew she had to put Carrie's feelings before her own. That meant putting on a brave smile for tonight's party and hoping her cousin wouldn't be hurt.

What it *didn't* mean was flirting with Dan or the Hudson brothers. Instead she'd get to know Meg and Amy, and she'd be friendly to Mrs. Griffin, the widow Carrie had asked to serve as chaperone with Tobias. If her plan failed, she'd retreat to the kitchen with Mrs. Dinwiddie and the serving girl. With that duty in mind, she lifted a navy blue gown with narrow sleeves from the wardrobe. As she checked the dress for wrinkles, Carrie pushed through the bedroom door.

"You can't wear that!" she declared.

"Why not?"

"It's depressing!"

Carrie usually spoke more gently. Pearl attributed her shrill tone to nerves. "It's fine." Although she had to admit, the color *was* a bit gloomy. The last time she'd worn the gown had been to a funeral.

Carrie shoved the dress back in the wardrobe. As Pearl reached to take it back, Carrie pushed through her dresses, a mix of grays, blues and drab browns and pulled out the gown Pearl had worn to Josh and Adie's wedding. As she held it out, her face lit up. "This is perfect!"

"Carrie, I can't."

"Why not?"

Because Matt will notice me instead of you. Because

I'll feel pretty and alive and I'll want things I can't have. "I just can't."

"But it's beautiful!" Carrie held the dress to her chin. Powder blue with an overskirt and white ribbon trim, the gown reminded Pearl of her friends at Swan's Nest, especially Mary who had ordered her to hold her head high. What would it be like to slip into the shimmering folds? To slip her arms into the sleeves that puffed and narrowed at her wrists? She ached to feel pretty, but not with Matt at the supper table. She'd want to smile at him, maybe flirt. She couldn't. Not when he belonged to Carrie. Not when she feared men and marriage.

Carrie shoved the dress into her arms. "You've *got* to wear this one."

She didn't understand. "But why?"

Her cousin looked close to tears. "If you wear that dreary navy blue, I'll look like a strumpet."

She had a point. A week ago they'd gone shopping. Carrie had selected a pink taffeta gown with oodles of ruffles. Pearl thought the dress was overdone and she'd said so. Carrie had loved it. Pearl hadn't pressed the point because she'd doubted herself. What did she know about fashion these days? She hadn't cared about looking nice for a long time. But she cared tonight.... She cared because of Matt.

The admission left her deeply disturbed. If she said yes to her cousin's request and wore the dress, she'd be risking Matt's attention. If she said no, Carrie would look silly in the rose-colored ruffles. As Pearl weighed the choice, she touched the sleeve of the silky dress. It warmed with her touch and she knew. She wanted to look pretty tonight. Not for Matt or Carrie, but for herself. "You're right," she said. "The silk is prettier."

With Carrie's help, Pearl put on three petticoats and

slipped into the shimmering gown. When she looked at herself in the mirror, she saw the woman who'd caught Adie's bridal bouquet and boldly come to Cheyenne for a second chance.

"You look perfect," Carrie said. "Now let's fix your hair."

Her crowning glory...the white mane that had attracted Franklin Dean. Her breath hitched at the memory, and her stomach knotted. Blinking, she flashed back to the buggy ride and the terrible memory of being trapped. She yearned for the safety of the navy blue, but she couldn't explain the reason to Carrie without more upset. Trembling, she sat at the vanity. "Put it in a coronet."

Carrie huffed. "And hide your pretty hair?"

"I like it that way."

She put her hands on Pearl's shoulders and pressed to keep her in place. "I have an idea."

"Don't—"

Carrie had already loosened Pearl's braid. As the white-gold strands brushed her nape, she recalled her mother putting up her hair for the first time. She'd been fourteen and confident. She wanted to be confident again. "All right," she said. "Make it pretty."

"You won't be sorry."

Carrie went to work with a brush and a comb. Ten minutes later Pearl had the loveliest chignon she'd ever worn. The style struck her as the perfect mix of beauty and restraint. She liked it.

"Thank you, cousin." She meant it.

"One more thing."

When Carrie opened the drawer holding Pearl's hair ornaments, Pearl went pale. She didn't want her cousin to notice Matt's ribbons.

Pearl lifted a comb from the drawer. It was made of

mother of pearl and had been a gift from her parents on her fourteenth birthday. She treasured it. "How about this?"

"It's too fancy."

She selected a comb made of bone.

"It's too plain."

Just as Pearl had feared, Carrie dug past her everyday ribbons to the blue ones. She set all of them on the vanity, then selected the palest blue.

"This one's perfect," she said. "It matches your eyes."

Pearl didn't want to wear one of Matt's ribbons not only because of what he'd think, but because of what they meant to her. The ribbons were a memory, an impossible dream. If she wore one tonight, they'd become as ordinary as her others. She wanted to tell Carrie to put them back, but her cousin would fuss and Pearl would have to explain. Resigned, she let Carrie fashion a blue bow above her ear.

Carrie stepped back. "You look beautiful, cousin."

She *felt* beautiful. For the first time in a year, she felt the lift that comes with a pretty dress, the pleasure of silk on her skin. She owed Carrie for this moment, so she stood and smiled. "Now it's your turn."

They went to Carrie's room where they repeated the ritual of petticoats and looking pretty. The pink dress made Carrie look like a blooming rose, a bit overblown but still lovely. Carrie bit her lips to make them pinker. "I hope Matt likes my dress."

"So do I." She meant it, but her wayward mind went to her own blue gown. As she put the finishing touch on her cousin's hair, someone knocked on the door.

"Come in," Carrie called.

The serving girl they'd hired for the night stepped into the room. "Your guests are arriving, Miss Hart. I've seated Mr. Cobb and Mr. Wiley in the parlor like you said."

"Thank you, Hattie."

With a nod, the girl left. Carrie looked at herself in the mirror, pinched her cheeks until they glowed, then bit her lips for the third time. They were beginning to look like overripe plums. Pearl touched her shoulder. "Carrie, stop."

"Stop what?" Carrie's voice quavered.

"Stop biting your lips." Pearl took her hand. "You look beautiful. Matt will see you for the woman you are, or he won't. If he doesn't, he's a fool."

"If he doesn't, I'll die."

"No, you won't," Pearl said gently. "We don't always get what we want, but the Lord gives us what we need."

Carrie's eyes misted. "You sound like my mother."

"Mine, too."

The women hugged, then Carrie took a breath. "I'm ready."

Together they walked down the stairs. As they entered the parlor, Matt and another man stood to greet them. They both looked polished in dark coats and string ties, but the resemblance ended with their clothing. Matt looked weary and had dark crescents under his eyes. The fellow she guessed to be Dan had a cheerful air. Brown eyes twinkled below his straight brows, and he had an easy smile. He looked rested and ready for a good time.

"Good evening," Carrie said to the men. "Matt, you know Pearl, but I don't think Dan does." She hooked her arm around Pearl's waist and nudged her forward. "Dan, this is my cousin, Pearl Oliver. Pearl, this is Deputy Dan Cobb. He's Matt's partner."

Dan held out his hand. "The pleasure's mine, Miss Oliver. Welcome to Cheyenne."

"Thank you, Deputy."

As the four of them sat, someone knocked on the door.

The maid answered and the Hudson brothers walked in. As the servant took their coats, Tobias came down the stairs and issued a jolly hello. Amidst the chatter, Mrs. Griffin arrived with Amy Hinn and Meg Gates.

Pearl tensed every time Carrie introduced her, but the knots in her stomach loosened as she settled into small talk with Meg and Mrs. Griffin. On the other side of the room, Carrie angled into a conversation with Matt, Dan and her father. Dan looked charmed, but Matt's brow furrowed. When he shot Pearl a look from across the room, she realized she'd been staring at him. She looked away, but not before his eyes found the ribbon and he smiled.

Just like that, they'd shared a secret. Pearl hated herself for enjoying the moment, but she couldn't help it. For the first time in a year, she hadn't turned into jelly because a man had noticed her. She'd been pleased. But now she felt guilty. If she couldn't keep her eyes to herself, the night would be long and tense.

"Pearl?"

She turned and saw Amy Hinn, another teacher at Miss Marlowe's School. Glad to be distracted, Pearl made room for Amy on the sofa. As they chatted, Garth Hudson brought them each a cup of punch. Judging by the look in his eyes, Amy wouldn't be single for long.

The parlor was buzzing with conversation when Pearl heard a faint whimpering from the top of the stairs. Toby had woken up because of his sniffles. As she pushed to her feet, the whimper turned into the wail of a cranky baby. Pearl hurried in the direction of the stairs, but she didn't have to go up them. Hattie was approaching the parlor with Toby propped on her shoulder.

"I'm so sorry, miss," she said to Pearl. "I tried to calm him, but he won't have nothin' to do with me."

"It's okay, Hattie." Pearl whisked Toby out of the girl's arms and into her own. "He doesn't know you, that's all."

Hattie gave Pearl the towel she'd had over her own shoulder. "Take this, miss. He'll drool on your pretty dress."

Pearl cared more about Toby than the gown, but she appreciated the girl's thoughtfulness. Holding Toby with one arm, she draped the towel over her shoulder. "I've got him. You can go back to helping Mrs. Dinwiddie."

Hattie curtsied and slipped out of the room. Pearl took a step to follow her, but someone gripped her arm. She turned and saw Carrie.

"You can't leave," her cousin whispered with a hiss. "I need you here."

"But—"

"I'll hold him," Carrie said in a voice that carried over the shrieking. "I love babies!"

She'd made the comment for Matt's sake, not to help Pearl or even Toby. Pearl resented it, but only Toby mattered. She had to calm her son. "I need to rock him back to sleep. Go take care of our guests."

Carrie reached for the baby. "Let me try," she said too loudly.

Rather than cause a stir, Pearl let Carrie take her wailing son. If he settled, she'd be relieved. If he didn't, she'd follow her original plan.

Carrie settled the baby in her arms, carried him into the parlor and made a show of rocking him. To Pearl's consternation, her son reared back and screamed even louder. She'd heard enough—more than enough—and followed Carrie with the intention of rescuing Toby. As she approached her cousin, so did Matt. They traded a look, one that linked them as parents, then Matt spoke in the tone of a man accustomed to being obeyed. "This boy needs his mama."

Carrie, suddenly speechless, let him lift the baby without an argument. He propped Toby against his shoulder, patting the boy's back as he carried him to Pearl. To her utter shock, Toby wiggled his bottom against Matt's arm, reared back, stared at him and stopped crying.

"Silence is golden," joked one of the Hudson brothers.

Amy smiled. "Matt's got a special touch."

Pearl thought so, too. Matt turned sidewise so that Toby could see her. Instead of reaching for her, the baby batted at Matt's jaw and grinned. It was the biggest smile she'd ever seen. Matt smiled at her to share the moment, then made a cute face at her son. "Hello, there, Toby."

The boy answered with a grunt.

Matt bounced him on his arm. "I thought you wanted your mama, pal."

Yes, but he also wanted a father. As her son looked at Matt with awe, Pearl could barely breathe. The sight nearly broke her resolve to keep her distance from this man. Toby needed a father, and Matt had a knack. Sarah needed a mother, and Pearl wanted a daughter. They'd make a perfect family...except Pearl couldn't bear the thought of being a wife, and Matt didn't want one.

It all seemed crazy and unfair, even more so when Toby put his head against Matt's neck and popped his thumb in his mouth. Matt hummed a tune he'd probably sung to Sarah at bedtime. A hush settled over the room as everyone watched and waited for Toby to fall asleep. When the baby's breathing deepened to indicate a steady slumber, Matt looked at her and whispered, "Want me to carry him upstairs?"

The thought of going upstairs together, as if they were a family, sent shivers down her spine. Whether from fear or hope, she couldn't say. She also had to think of appearances and Carrie's reaction. Her cousin would feel left out if Pearl accepted Matt's offer. She was about to decline when her father approached.

"Let's all go," Tobias said with a smile.

As if he were herding sheep, Tobias motioned for her to lead the way. The three of them went up the stairs and turned into Pearl's bedroom, dimly lit by a lamp on her vanity. Matt spotted Toby's cradle in the shadows and went to it. Pearl stepped to his side, neatened the bedding and lifted the coverlet.

As gentle as snow falling, Matt placed Toby on his tummy. Pearl covered him with the blanket, then patted his back until he settled again. As she lifted her hand, she turned and saw Matt watching her with stark admiration.

"You're a wonderful mother," he said in a hush.

But could she be a good wife? She didn't know and she doubted it. Besides, Carrie had feelings for Matt. Pearl would never betray her cousin's trust. Afraid her emotions would show, she mumbled, "Thank you."

Her father must have seen her consternation, because he motioned them both to the door. "Let's go before he wakes up again."

"Good idea," Matt whispered. He smiled again at Pearl, then rested his hand on Toby's back. "Sleep tight, little boy."

The sight of Matt's fingers, strong and masculine, filled Pearl with the longing to be together as a family. With her heart aching, she kissed her fingers and touched her son's head. As she moved, her shoulder brushed Matt's bicep and he didn't move. The moment felt natural and right, but all wrong at the same time.

Turning abruptly, she led the way to the hall and hurried down the stairs. Needing to calm herself, she detoured away from the parlor and headed to the dining room to light the candles.

As she lit the first one, she saw the card with her name and frowned. Someone had switched her seat with Meg's and she knew who'd done it. Yesterday she and Carrie had disagreed about the seating plan. Carrie wanted to be next to Matt and across from Pearl. Pearl wanted to be on the opposite end of the table, next to her father and as far from Matt as she could get. The change put Pearl directly across from him. Annoyed, she lifted the place card. Before she could switch it back with Meg's, Carrie glided into the room with their guests. To avoid a scene, Pearl left the cards alone.

As she looked up, Matt flashed a smile and approached to hold her chair. "May I?"

Why yes, Deputy. Thank you. Instead she schooled her features. "I have to check something in the kitchen." She indicated the seat next to Carrie. "You're across from me."

Matt looked amused…and challenged.

To avoid him, Pearl slipped through the side door. She asked Mrs. Dinwiddie for extra butter, then went back to the dining room. As she'd hoped, Matt was helping Carrie. Dan, seated on her right, held her chair and she sat.

She tried to avoid Matt's gaze, but he seemed just as intent on gaining her attention. When a smile tipped his lips, she turned to her father who was helping Mrs. Griffin with her chair. A widow of two years, she was wearing mauve with silver brocade. She looked vibrant. So did Tobias. Pearl had never seen her father smitten, but he had that look tonight. The realization put a lump in her throat. Everyone at the table, except her, could chat with the opposite sex with ease. Most men frightened her. Matt didn't, but he belonged to Carrie.

When Tobias sat at the head of the table, Pearl cleared her throat. "Father?"

"Yes, princess?"

She hid a cringe. "Would you say grace?"

"Of course."

The Lord already knew Pearl appreciated the food on the table. She needed provision of another kind, so she asked God for peace, good will and the discipline to keep her eyes off Matt Wiley. He provided those mercies right up until dessert.

Chapter Eleven

Matt should have seen the trouble coming, but he'd missed the signs. If he'd been alert, he'd have realized Carrie liked him...a lot. Enough to bump his foot under the table. Enough to brush against his arm every time she passed the potatoes.

Dan must have noticed her interest, because he'd shot daggers at Matt all through the meal. Matt had shot back a few of his own. Twice Dan had made Pearl smile at a stupid joke. When she'd tipped her head with pleasure, jealousy had ripped from one side of Matt's chest to the other. He wanted Pearl to look at *him* that way, but that was crazy. He had no business courting any woman, especially a preacher's daughter. To add to his frustration, Carrie had honed in on his conversation with Tobias. Matt had planned to invite him for a cigar after dessert, but he hadn't gotten the chance. Considering Carrie's persistence, he doubted he would.

The entire evening had been filled with frustration. Instead of leaving tonight with Tobias as a new ally, he'd have to figure out another way to speak with the man. He also had to make his position clear to Carrie without hurting her feelings. As for Pearl, he hadn't been able to take his eyes off her. If he slept at all tonight, he'd be dreaming of Cinderella with ribbons in her hair.

He'd had about all he could take when the maid came through the kitchen door carrying a serving plate in each hand.

"Dessert's here!" Carrie said brightly.

Matt joined the others in admiring the sweets. One plate held a chocolate cake. It looked simple and tasty. The other tray showed off cream puffs dusted with sugar. Tasty or not, they were too complicated for his simple ways. He had his heart set on the cake, but Carrie put a pastry in front of him.

"I made the cream puffs," she said proudly. "It's a family recipe."

Matt tried not to scowl at the pastry. After Pearl and Carrie finished serving the desserts, everyone lifted their forks. He tried to slice a bite of the cream puff, but the filling squished out the sides. He sawed with his knife but got nowhere. When he pushed harder, the pastry shot off the plate and landed in his lap.

Dan laughed out loud.

Pearl pressed her napkin to her mouth, but her eyes were dancing. Matt figured the joke was on him. If it made Pearl smile, he didn't mind. As their eyes met, his lips curved into a smile.

Carrie gasped. "Oh no! They're overbaked!"

Muttering apologies, he wrapped the mess in his napkin and stood to take it to the kitchen. As he turned, the tablecloth came with him and he realized he'd caught it in the napkin. Chocolate cake landed in Carrie's lap, and coffee spilled all over the pink dress. Pearl and Amy jumped up to steady the candles. Everywhere Matt looked, he saw sloshing coffee and crooked plates. He also had custard on his coat.

"Sorry," he muttered.

Dan cackled. "Man, you're a klutz!"

"Thanks, buddy." Matt sounded wry, but he meant it. Someone had to put the levity back into the evening and he couldn't do it. Carrie was close to tears, and Pearl looked nearly as upset as she darted around the table to help Carrie. He almost said he'd pay for all the laundering, but the words shot him back to the day they'd met. A lot had changed since that moment. Blond hair no longer made him crazy, and he felt a tug in his heart he'd never expected to feel again…a tug he didn't want to feel. Not only had he been a terrible husband, he also knew the sting of a woman's betrayal. Except Pearl would never betray anyone. She had a good heart, too good for the likes of him.

The women were all furiously blotting the dress, so he wadded the napkin and carried it to the kitchen. With the meal done, the cook had left. The hired girl was alone with a basin of steaming water and a mountain of dishes.

As the door clicked shut, she looked up and saw the blotch on his coat. "I'll get you a towel, sir."

"Thank you."

She opened a cupboard, saw the empty shelf and excused herself. "I'll be right back."

Matt dumped the cream puff in a garbage pail without regret. He didn't care for cream puffs. He liked chocolate cake, blue ribbons and women who took care of others. Sighing, he found a rag, dabbed at his coat and made an even bigger mess.

The door opened and Pearl entered with the plate of chocolate cake in one hand and the leftover cream puffs in the other. She set the desserts down, then glanced at him with a mix of mirth and worry. The spill didn't bother her at all, but she cared about Carrie and her cousin had been terribly embarrassed. He shook his head. "Sorry about the mess."

"It's all right," she answered. "We can clean it up."

"Maybe."

She tipped her head. "What do you mean?"

"I have a bigger mess than a cream puff." He looked Pearl in the eye. "Tonight meant a lot to Carrie, didn't it?"

She said nothing.

"More than I knew, I'm afraid."

When her eyes widened into moons, Matt knew a simple truth. Not only couldn't Pearl Oliver tell a lie, but she also couldn't keep a secret, either. He hadn't imagined Carrie's flirting. She'd set her cap for him, and she'd set it hard. His stomach churned and not from the meal. Not once had he thought of Carrie as more than Sarah's teacher. It was Pearl who filled his thoughts and made him crazy. The thought of coming between these two good women upset him.

He shook his head. "I didn't know she'd gotten ideas. I thought—"

"Your coat's a mess," Pearl said. "I'll get a damp cloth."

She turned her back, a sign she wouldn't talk about her cousin. Out of respect, he said nothing as she dampened a dish towel at the sink. With her eyes still averted, she handed it to him. "Here."

The awkwardness irked him. They hadn't done anything wrong. He valued Pearl's friendship and didn't want to lose it. Being stubborn, he let the towel dangle between them. When she finally looked at him, he indicated the flap of his coat. "I'll make it worse. Would you mind?"

She hesitated, then came closer. With her eyes on the coat, she put one hand behind the smear and dabbed at it with the towel. When she bent her neck to get a better view, he smelled her flowery soap. He told himself to look away from her ivory skin. He didn't have to see the ribbon above her ear. He didn't have to touch it. He could do the right thing and step back, except stepping back felt all wrong. He cared for Pearl and knew she had scars. He wanted her to feel pretty again, so he touched the silky ribbon above her ear.

Startled, she looked up. She didn't pull away, but her eyes had a wild shine and she looked ready to bolt.

"Sorry." Matt lowered his hand. "I thought I recognized the ribbon."

"You did, but it's just a ribbon." Her voice came out high and thin, as if she were trying to convince herself more than him. He thought of Sarah's reaction when she'd caught him talking to himself. He'd told her to pretend she hadn't heard, but she had. Matt wanted to pretend he didn't know Pearl's thoughts, but he did. She liked him as much as he liked her. She also loved Carrie and felt loyal to her cousin.

She turned abruptly to the wash basin. "That's the best I can do."

Matt glanced down. The coat looked new.

Pearl rinsed the towel, then went to work scraping the plates. Matt wanted to talk some more, but he had no business being with Pearl until he squared things with Carrie. He didn't know exactly how he'd do it, but he'd find a way to protect her dignity.

He headed for the door. "Thanks for your help," he said to her back. "I better talk to Carrie."

The dishes stopped rattling, but Pearl didn't turn. "She's upstairs. Everyone went home."

Matt stopped at the door. He and Pearl were alone. The serving girl would be back, but they could sit in the dining room. They could share a piece of chocolate cake. He could talk to her in the candlelight and no one would know, which was why he had to leave. He knew from experience that secrets had dangerous consequences. "Tell Carrie I said thanks for supper."

"Of course."

As he opened the door, she pivoted. "Wait. I have something for Sarah."

She dried her hands, then cut two generous slices of cake and put them on a plate. After wrapping the dessert with a towel, she handed it to him. "There's a piece of you, too."

"Thank you." With the cake in hand, he paused at the door. "Good night, Pearl."

"Good night, Matt."

He shut the door behind him, but he couldn't block the echo of her voice in his mind. He'd be hearing it when he ate that chocolate cake, and he'd be touching that blue ribbon in his dreams. As soon as he could, he'd square things with Carrie, but then what? He couldn't deny his feelings for Pearl, but neither could he court a preacher's daughter. With the cake in hand, Matt left with his stomach in a knot. He had some thinking to do, and he'd doubtlessly be doing it all night long.

Pearl helped the serving girl clean the kitchen, then she climbed the stairs and tapped softly on Carrie's door. The quiet sobbing ceased, but Carrie didn't call for her to come in. Knowing the need for privacy, Pearl extinguished the wall sconce and went to her room. There she lit a lamp, checked on Toby and sat at the vanity.

Her eyes went to the ribbon above her ear, the one Matt had touched. She'd ignored him all through supper, but then the cream puff had skittered and she'd seen the shock on his face. She'd wanted to laugh with him, and that's when she'd admitted a frightening truth. If it weren't for Carrie, she'd be willing to go down a dangerous path.

What if…

She closed her eyes to block the fearful yearning, but she saw Matt's face. She recalled his Texas drawl and the minty scent of his skin. From the day they'd met, she'd fought her feelings. She'd prayed. She'd stifled her thoughts and denied her dreams. She'd done everything she could to fight her fear of men *and* to protect Carrie, but she couldn't stop her heart from leaping when Matt looked into her eyes. She couldn't stop herself from yearning for the things she deeply feared. A husband…affection…a father for Toby.

Pearl wept into her palms. Her friends at Swan's Nest would have understood. Adie had lived with a secret and knew the cost. Mary knew how to fake a smile. Bessie, a nurse, would have made tea and listened to her woes. Caroline, the victim of a forbidden love, would have cried with her.

Lifting her face, she stared at her reflection in the mirror. Tomorrow she'd be a friend to Carrie. But how? What could she say? She'd stopped Matt from talking, but she knew what he'd been about to say. He didn't have feelings for Carrie and never would.

Would her cousin accept the truth? Pearl hoped so, but love couldn't be easily denied. She knew, because she felt the seeds of it growing in her own heart. The seeds had to be plucked out, so she lifted her hand to her hair and loosened the ribbon. She pulled it free, laid it flat on the vanity, then rolled it tight. As the silk warmed with her touch, she placed it in the back of the drawer, far from the ribbons she wore every day.

She'd never forget this night. When he'd touched her hair, she'd almost swooned and not from panic. The panic had come an instant later. Had it started because of his touch? Or when she thought of Carrie? She didn't know. The way things stood, she'd never find out. It hurt, but a small thought gave her comfort. Because of Matt's touch, the ribbons were special again.

Chapter Twelve

Matt set the cake on the counter and asked Mrs. Holcombe to stay a few more hours. The revelation about Carrie and the private moment with Pearl had left him tense, and he couldn't shake a feeling of dread. If the Golden Order planned to strike, tonight seemed likely. Full of Saturday night revelers, Ferguson Street made an appealing target. When Mrs. Holcombe agreed to stay, he changed clothes and climbed back on his horse.

As he rode across town, the wind sent leaves skittering down the street. The air was rarely still in Cheyenne, and tonight the rush matched his mood. Pearl had him all stirred up. So did the black derby Jasper had removed from the display window. A message had been sent, and Matt was worried. With each attack on the Silver Slipper, the G.O. had become bolder. Broken glass had become broken bones. Neither could he forget Jed Jones. The man's thievery had led to a broken neck.

Brokenness…Matt knew all about it. Shuddering, he thought back to the night his own life had been shattered. Good intentions had gone awry and he'd done the unthinkable on a humid night in Virginia. Riding down the street now, he recalled arriving at Amos McGuckin's farm with his men. He remembered the haze of the smoky torches, the orange glow against an inky sky. He blinked and smelled smoke. He coughed, and his eyes burned. It was too real to be a dream. Fire bells cut through the night and he knew... the Golden Order had gone from breaking bones to burning down buildings.

Six blocks away the sky took on an orange glow. Matt kneed his gelding into a gallop. If he hadn't been at Carrie's party, he'd have been patrolling Ferguson Street when the fire started. He might have seen the riders running off at a gallop.

Nothing struck fear in the citizens of Cheyenne like fire. The wooden buildings stood side by side and were as dry as tinder. As the crowd in the street thickened, he slowed his horse. A block away he saw the Silver Slipper being swallowed alive by flames. Like an animal breathing its last, the building roared as the roof collapsed into flaming rubble. He hoped no one was inside, because there would be no survivors.

As he passed through the crowd, he spotted a cluster of women from Scottie's place. Scottie, still bruised and using a cane, stood apart from them. A black patch covered his damaged eye. Matt rode over to the saloon owner and dismounted. "What happened?"

Scottie stared at the flames. "They killed her."

Matt's belly knotted. "Who?"

"Katy."

An oath spewed from his lips. Where was God when the Golden Order set the fire? Why hadn't he saved the sweet, innocent woman who only wanted to go home?

Scottie pounded the ground with his cane. "She didn't deserve to die."

"I liked her," Matt said simply. "I'm sorry."

"You're *sorry?*" The female voice came out of the dark.

He turned and saw Lizzy sweeping in his direction. Ashes were clinging to her skimpy gown, and soot had painted shadows on her face. Matt didn't blame her for being angry. Being sorry wouldn't bring Katy back to life anymore than Matt could change what had happened in Virginia. He steeled himself for a lambasting, maybe a slap across the jaw.

Lizzy shuddered. "I couldn't find her. I looked *everywhere*. She-she—" The woman burst into tears.

The women crowded around her like a flock of nervous birds. A scrawny blonde glared at him from over her shoulder. "We were already out when we saw her in the window. She must have gone back for Scottie, but I'd helped him downstairs."

Scottie surveyed the pile of smoldering timbers. "I'd like to kill those—"

"Me, too!" Lizzy cried.

Matt felt the same way, but he wouldn't give in to the anger. "I figure this is arson."

Scottie snorted. "Good work, Deputy."

Matt ignored the sarcasm. "Did you see anything?"

"What do you think?" Scottie stared at him with his one good eye.

Matt turned to the women. "Ladies?"

A blonde raised her voice. "I saw them."

"Who?" Matt asked.

"The men in black derbies." She started to weep. "They had torches and were threatening to burn us out. Sparks were flying everywhere. I ran to get the others…and Katy." The girl broke into sobs. Lizzy hugged her tight and glared at Matt.

"What are you going to do to stop them?" she demanded. "Katy was just plain good. She was going home. She—"

Matt cut her off. "I know."

A redhead glared at the remains of the Silver Slipper. "I lost everything. The picture of my baby—" She burst into tears.

"They should hang for this!" Lizzy cried.

Matt tended to agree. Anyone playing with fire on a windy night deserved to swing high and fast. The thought gave him pause. If he wasn't careful, he'd become what he loathed.

His gaze narrowed to the dying embers. An innocent woman had died a horrible death, and it had happened on his watch. With his blood flowing hot and bitter, he got down to business. Tonight that meant linking the men in black derbies to the members of the Golden Order. The masked riders had disappeared into the night, but someone could be observing on their behalf.

Matt surveyed the crowd. Most of the men had joined the bucket brigade, but they were losing the battle with the spreading flames. A second saloon had turned into a flaming skeleton, and the dance hall next to it would soon follow. Matt spotted the fire marshal, Bill "Crawdad" Pine, manning the steam engine. The city had invested a fortune in the fancy equipment, but the wagon had arrived too late to save the Silver Slipper. Judging by the wind, the rest of the block would suffer the same fate. All the businesses were of a tawdry nature, but that didn't ease Matt's conscience. An innocent woman had died tonight. Considering the extent of the blaze, he feared others had died with her.

He studied every face in the crowd. Most of the people were strangers or regulars on Ferguson Street, but a particular man—Chester Gates—didn't belong. The banker lived on the other side of town. Why was he speaking to the fire marshal? Looking at him now, Matt recalled his interest in the prime land purchased by Scottie Fife. If the G.O. forced Scottie to sell the property, Gates would cash in. Sensing trouble, Matt led his horse toward the men and called a greeting.

Crawdad answered in the Louisiana drawl that had earned him his nickname. Matt nodded at Gates but spoke to the fire chief. "I hear this is arson."

"I'd say so," Crawdad remarked.

Gates coughed against the smoke but said nothing.

Matt watched him carefully. "A girl died tonight. Whoever set the fire will stand trial for murder."

"Murder?" Gates had a face of stone, but his voice betrayed his nervousness.

Matt decided to push. "You got here fast, Mr. Gates. Did you see anything? Maybe men in black derbies?"

"Not a thing, Deputy." The banker schooled his features. "I was working late. I heard the fire bells and came to help. You can't have too many men on a bucket brigade."

Liar.

The banker rubbed his chin. "Any idea who did this?"

"Not a one." Actually Matt had five. Their names were Chester Gates, Jasper Kling and three other members of the Golden Order.

"Fires are serious in this city." Gates glanced at Crawdad. "That new steam engine seems to have worked."

"It's a help," the chief replied.

The talk turned to the need for more wells and pipes from the river. The shift away from who had started the fire seemed natural, but Matt's instincts said otherwise. Most people quizzed him unmercifully when it came to crime. Gates didn't want to talk to him, but he'd come to see the Silver Slipper burn. Matt felt certain the G.O. had started the fire, but he couldn't take action without hard evidence. He hoped that would change when he spoke with Tobias. Tomorrow was Sunday. Matt didn't attend church, but Tobias did and so did Dan. If Dan happened to run into the minister, the two of them could talk. It was late, but his friend wouldn't mind being woken up considering the need.

Matt said goodbye to Crawdad and Gates, then rode to Dan's place. He knocked on the door, calling his friend's name so he wouldn't come out shooting.

Bleary-eyed and haphazardly dressed, Dan invited him inside. "You better have a good reason for being here."

"I do." Matt tossed his hat on a chair. "The Silver Slipper just burned to the ground."

Dan came fully alert. "I'd call that a good reason."

"Five other saloons went with it."

He winced. "Any deaths?"

Matt told him about Katy. "I'm tired of waiting for a break. You're going to church tomorrow to talk to Tobias Oliver."

Dan shook his head. "*You're* going."

"No way."

"Come on, Wiley." Dan raked his hand through his hair. "You know the man better than I do. Bite the bullet and sit through a sermon."

Not a week passed that Dan didn't try to prod Matt into taking Sarah to church. It was good-natured jesting and Matt didn't mind, but he'd drawn a line for himself. No way would he sit through a sermon. "You know my answer to *that*."

"I do," Dan replied. "I also see the perfect place to speak with Reverend Oliver."

Dan had a point. Matt hated the thought of hymns and hallelujahs, but he'd do anything to stop the Golden Order. He also liked the idea of seeing Pearl. He had no right to

such a thought, but holding Toby had stirred him up in powerful ways. The boy made him want to be a father again,
to have a son who'd maybe someday wear a badge or be a
soldier. Even more important, Matt knew how much a boy
needed a man to teach him things. Toby had his grandfa-
ther, but the old man wouldn't live forever. No one did.

As the thought settled, Matt flashed to the fire and the
need to stop the Golden Order. "I'll go to church," he said
to Dan. "But just to see Tobias."

Dan grinned. "Don't look so scared. God's not going to
fall off his throne at the sight of you in church."

Matt glared at him.

Dan's expression hardened in return. "Talking to Tobias
is smart. We agree on *that*."

Matt heard the dangling thought and scowled. "What
don't we agree on?"

"The way you treated Carrie at supper." Dan's voice lost
its sleepy pitch. "You laughed at her, and then you walked
out."

Matt stared in disbelief. "The Golden Order is burning
down buildings and you're worried about my *manners?*"

"I'm telling you to wise up about Carrie."

"Me?" Matt couldn't believe his ears. "You're the one
who likes her."

"But *you're* the one she wants."

Matt saw an answer to both their problems. "So change
her mind. Sweep her off her feet."

Dan scowled at him.

"I'm serious." Sweet Carrie and Iowa Dan…. They fit
like bread and butter. "Ask her to supper. I bet she'll say
yes."

At the sight of his friend's gaping mouth, Matt almost
laughed. He knew the feeling, because he felt that way
about Pearl. It was like standing on a bluff looking at rich

land that stretched for miles. It could be his, but only if he took a chance. Could he be a husband again? He didn't know, but the thought wouldn't go away.

Dan eyed him thoughtfully. "Do you think she'd say yes?"

"You won't know unless you ask."

"I suppose." Dan wandered to the window. "Just promise me one thing."

"What is it?"

"That you'll be gentle with her." He turned and looked at Matt. Dan had a soft side, and it showed. "After you ran off to the kitchen, I tried to help her. She cares for you, Wiley. Why, I don't know. But she does."

Matt had seen the look, too. "I didn't know—"

"You do now." Dan's voice came out rough. "If you hurt her, we'll be having words."

Matt had hurt enough women already. "I'll speak to her as soon as I can, and I'll be gentle about it." Maybe he'd see her tomorrow at church. Exactly how he'd approach Carrie, Matt didn't know. Did a man tell a woman he wasn't going to say what he hadn't ever said? The thought gave him a headache.

Dan heaved a sigh. When he looked at Matt, his brows hitched together. "This Golden Order mess has me worried."

"Me, too."

"Reverend Oliver will be at risk. If Jasper suspects us, so will Pearl."

"I know."

"What are you going to tell him?"

"Everything." Matt shared Dan's fear. "The man deserves to know what he'd be getting into. If he has any doubts, we'll look elsewhere."

A smile tipped on Dan's lips. "So you're really going to church?"

"I'm going to see Tobias," Matt corrected.

"You'll see Pearl, too."

"So?"

"You like her, don't you?"

"It doesn't matter what I like," Matt countered. "She doesn't belong with a heathen like me."

Dan laughed out loud. "Who says you're a heathen?"

"I do."

His expression turned thoughtful. "For a heathen, you spend a lot of time being mad at God."

"I do not." Except he felt the old fury now. If God was good, why had Katy burned to death? Why hadn't the Almighty stopped Matt and his men from lynching Amos McGuckin? Matt knew what *he'd* do if he were God. He'd erase that night in Virginia. He'd change Pearl's past, too. He'd give her Toby, but she'd have a husband who loved her. And Sarah would have a mother who'd never leave.

He glared at Dan. "I don't want to talk about this stuff."

His friend shrugged. "Suit yourself."

"I will."

If he could stop the Golden Order, maybe he could forgive himself for having once been like them. And if he could forgive himself, maybe he could forgive God. One thought led to another and he imagined sleeping like a baby and waking up with Pearl at his side. A wife…a mother for Sarah…a father for Toby. Tomorrow he'd go to church and he'd see Pearl. He couldn't help but hope she'd be wearing his ribbons.

Chapter Thirteen

Pearl tapped on Carrie's door, waited for her cousin to answer and stepped into the stuffy bedroom. Propped on pillows, Carrie looked as pale as the bed sheets. Pearl sat on the edge of the mattress. "Church starts in an hour," she said gently. "You need to get dressed."

Carrie sniffed. "I can't."

"Tea will help."

"*Nothing* will help." She blew her nose into a hankie. "I didn't sleep a wink. There's no way I can manage a Sunday school class."

Carrie and Amy shared responsibility for teaching the girls. "They need you, cousin."

"I know." She sighed. "Would you fill in for me?"

Pearl loved the idea, but she couldn't let Carrie wallow in self-pity. "You'll feel better if you go to church."

Carrie dabbed at her eyes. "I can't do it. Not today."

Pearl understood the desire to hide. She'd walked around with a pregnant belly and no husband. People, especially children, could be cruel. If Carrie lost her composure at church, people would gossip. She couldn't hide forever, but she didn't have to face her problems today. Tomorrow would be soon enough.

Pearl absently smoothed a wrinkle out of the sheet. "Do you remember when we first met? You told me not to cry because I'd get puffy?"

Carrie nodded.

"You're more than puffy," Pearl said gently. "You're as sodden as Toby gets."

Her cousin sniffed. "I'm a mess."

"Don't worry. I'll help Amy."

"Thank you!" She gripped Pearl's hand. "I don't know what I'd do without you."

"You'd be fine."

"I'd be miserable," she insisted. Biting her lip, she gave Pearl a look full of love. "I don't know what I'd do without you, cousin. I can talk to you about anything."

Pearl felt the same way…almost. She'd never tell Carrie about the ribbons, but she wanted her cousin to know she'd had a private conversation with Matt. "We need to talk about last night."

Carrie groaned.

"I know it's hard," Pearl said. "But someday you'll laugh about it."

"Maybe, but will Matt?"

"I think so." Pearl thought of the ribbons. Would he forget touching her hair? She wouldn't, but she had to try.

Carrie set a wadded hankie on the nightstand. "I tried so hard, but he ignored me all evening. He kept looking across the table at—at—"

Pearl's heart stopped.

"At Dan!"

Blood stained Pearl's cheeks, but she had no reason to be ashamed. She couldn't stop her wayward feelings, but she'd behaved honorably.

Carrie sighed. "Maybe he was worried about something."

"Maybe."

"I just don't know," Carrie said with a moan. "I thought Matt and I had a lot in common, but last night he seemed like a stranger."

Pearl refused to hide her unexpected meeting with Matt. "I talked to him afterward. We were in the kitchen."

"What did he say?"

Pearl wanted to protect her cousin, but she couldn't distort the truth. "I don't think he realized how you felt until last night."

"Really?"

"I'm sure of it." Pearl described the conversation without mentioning the ribbons or the cake. Some things were private. Others had to be said with the hope of sparing her cousin more hurt. "He likes you, Carrie. But he doesn't seem...interested."

Tears welled in her eyes. "I feel like a complete fool."

"You're not."

"Yes, I am." She stared at the ceiling. "I still care for him."

"I'm sorry. I know it hurts."

Carrie's faced stiffened into a mask. She bit her lips, but the pain showed in her eyes. "I need...a moment. Would you leave me alone for a bit?"

"Of course."

Pearl headed for the door. As she turned the knob, Carrie called out to her. "Wait! I didn't ask about you."

"That's all right."

"But I want to know." Carrie put on a brave smile. "Who did you like best? Grant or Dan?"

The truth froze on Pearl's tongue. She liked Matt. "I'm not interested in courting. You know that."

Carrie hugged her knees. "*I* like Dan. After Matt ran out, he made everyone feel at ease. Even me."

"He's nice."

A smile touched Carrie's eyes. "I think he likes you."

"That's funny," Pearl answered. "*I* think he likes *you*."

"*Me?*"

Pearl saw a chance to boost Carrie's spirits. "He had his eyes on you all night. Didn't you notice?"

"I was too busy watching Matt. And Matt was watching…" Carrie's eyes turned into saucers. "Matt wasn't watching Dan! He was watching *you*."

"Oh, Carrie." Pearl could barely breathe. "He's yours. I know that. I'd never— It wouldn't be right. I'd—"

Carrie leaped out of bed and ran to Pearl. For a terrible moment, Pearl thought her cousin would slap her face. She hadn't meant to get in the way of Matt's affections. Truly, she hadn't. "Carrie, I—"

"Oh, Pearl." Just like the day they'd met, Carrie wrapped her arms around Pearl's waist and hugged her. Emotions swamped them both. Upset. Anger. Jealousy…and love. Their feelings collided and mixed until Carrie stepped back.

"Listen to me, Pearl."

"I'm so sorry. I—"

"This isn't your fault."

"But—"

"*It's not your fault,*" Carrie repeated. "I know what you did for me. You didn't want to have the party, but you put up with it for me. When you asked Matt to lunch, you did it for me."

Pearl bit her lip. "That's true."

"Every time you've had the chance, you've pointed him in my direction." Carrie's face clouded with disappointment. "If Matt doesn't have feelings for me, I'd be a fool to want him for a husband."

"But you care for him."

"I do." Tears welled in her eyes. "I care enough to want him to be happy."

"Oh, Carrie."

"I want you to be happy, too. Now go." She sounded unsteady. "This hurts too much right now. I need to be alone."

"But—"

"Please." The word broke into pieces.

Pearl knew how it felt to fall apart. Aching for Carrie, she left the room and closed the door. As soon as she stepped into the hall, pressure built in her throat and chest. She'd expected Carrie to berate her. Instead she'd offered compassion. If Carrie gave her blessing, Pearl could wear Matt's ribbons.

What if...

The thought stopped her cold. She had no business thinking of Matt as more than a friend. Even if Carrie's feelings for him changed, or if she stepped back, Pearl still lived with a profound fear of intimacy.

Shaking inside, she hurried to her room. She had to finish getting ready for church, so she sat at the vanity and looked at herself in the mirror. She'd already put her hair in a braid and wrapped it tight. Today it pulled at her scalp and gave her a headache. Feeling confused, she touched the braid. For the first time in a year, she wanted to be pretty. She didn't dare touch Matt's ribbons, but she had others.

Pleased and nervous, she opened the drawer and selected a strand of yellow satin. Instead of putting it in her hair, she looped it around the crown of her hat, tied a fancy bow and pinned the hat in place. It felt good to feel pretty and even better to feel brave. Satisfied, she changed Toby into a blue baby gown, then carried him downstairs where her father was waiting with the baby carriage.

Tobias smiled at her. "You look lovely, princess."

"Thank you." Today she felt like a princess.

"Where's Carrie?"

"She's not well."

"I see." Tobias didn't need an explanation. He'd witnessed the cream puff fiasco. "I hope she feels better soon."

"Me, too."

She put Toby in the carriage, and they left the house. As she expected, her father set a fast pace. Tobias refused to *ever* be late to church. Pearl was secretly pleased. His face had a healthy glow and he wasn't out of breath. She would never understand the symptoms that made her worry about his health. They came and went like changes in the weather.

Enjoying the moment, she smiled at him. "I'm excited about teaching."

"I would be, too."

Her father loved being a minister and had led Colfax Avenue Church for many years. He'd given it up to accompany her to Cheyenne. "You miss it, don't you?"

"I do, but I'm slowing down."

"Not today, you're not!" Pearl laughed as they raced past a bungalow. They were practically running.

Tobias got a faraway look in his eyes. "I used to charge into church like a man on fire. Now I'm sitting on my laurels. I'm useless."

"Papa! Don't say that."

"It's true, Pearl. What am I good for these days?"

Looking up at him, she spoke in a scolding tone. "For one thing, you're the world's best grandpa. Toby and I need you."

"If you say so."

"I do."

He patted her arm, but she was still worried about him. Tobias couldn't handle rigorous work, but he needed to do more than watch his grandson. As they turned the corner, she saw the church and felt hopeful. People were milling by the stone steps and speaking excitedly. Pearl spotted Amy and her mother. As they approached, Amy waved. "Did you hear? Half of Ferguson Street burned down last night."

Pearl shuddered. "What happened?"

Amy told them about the devastation and the suspicion of arson. When she finished, her voice turned somber. "A cleaning girl died. Her name was Katy. Sometimes she came here to worship."

Pearl had seen Katy looking in the window at Jasper's store. He'd shooed her away, then related a story about a smudge on a hairbrush. He'd told Pearl to turn away anyone from Ferguson Street.

Mrs. Hinn tsked her tongue. "The men who set that fire have to be stopped."

"I quite agree," Tobias replied.

"Miss Pearl!"

She turned and saw Sarah holding her daddy's hand. Pearl waggled her fingers in greeting, then let her eyes drift to Matt. He was dressed for church in the coat she'd wiped clean. She hadn't expected to see him. Would he think of last night and touching the ribbon? It was too soon for such thoughts, but she couldn't help it.

His eyes met hers and he removed his hat. "Good morning, Pearl."

"Good morning, Deputy."

As he greeted Tobias and the Hinns, Sarah tugged on Pearl's dress. "Do you like my hair?"

She saw a perfect braid. "You look lovely."

The child spotted the baby carriage and squealed. "You brought Toby!"

"That's right."

"He's wearing blue," she said with authority. "That means he's a boy."

When Toby made a noise for attention, Pearl picked him up. If people wanted to judge her, so be it. She proudly showed Toby to Sarah, who thought he was even more special than Annie, her doll. Pearl didn't mean to glance at Matt, but her eyes had a will of their own. The pleasure in his gaze stole her breath. So did the lazy smile on his lips. His eyes flicked to her hat. Was he looking for a blue ribbon? She didn't know, but he frowned slightly at the yellow bow on her hat.

Oh, the fun of making a man wonder! Pearl had to suppress a smile. She couldn't remember ever feeling this way.

Mrs. Hinn broke into her thoughts. "Tell us, Deputy. Is it true those men in derby hats set that fire?"

"Yes, ma'am," he answered. "There were witnesses."

Tobias scowled. "Such a tragedy."

Pearl thought about the hat Jasper sometimes put in the window. In the time she'd worked for him, he hadn't sold a single one. Considering his clientele—businessmen and railroad executives—the coincidence seemed odd. Was there a connection to the men who burned down the Silver Slipper? It seemed likely. Later she'd mention her worry to Matt.

Amy broke into her thoughts. "The whole city could have gone up in flames. One girl died, but there could have been more."

Mrs. Hinn huffed. "Arson's no way to fight sin!"

Pearl's gaze stayed on Matt. Instead of looking at

Amy, he had his eye on her father. "What do you think, Reverend?"

Tobias stood a bit taller. "I find Ferguson Street as distasteful as any God-fearing man, but burning it to the ground won't solve the problem. As the saying goes, 'Hate the sin, love the sinner.'"

Amy and her mother started talking at the same time. As Tobias answered them, Matt turned to Pearl. "I don't see Carrie."

"She's ill."

"I'm sorry to hear it." Except he didn't sound sorry. He sounded relieved. "I'll see her at school, then."

He held her gaze for a moment too long, a sign he wanted her to understand his intentions. Tomorrow he'd clear the air with Carrie. Before Pearl could ponder what that meant for her, the church bell rang a familiar call to worship. She put Toby in the carriage and told Amy she'd be taking Carrie's place. With Sarah in tow, they left for Sunday school class.

As they walked away, she heard Matt speaking to her father. "We have something in common, sir. Perhaps we could talk after the service?"

"Of course."

Why would Matt want to speak with her father? Pearl had no idea, and she wouldn't ask. Once a minister, always a minister. Tobias wouldn't breathe a word of his conversation with Matt. Unless… She thought of the way Matt had looked at her today. Was the conversation about her? Did he want to court her? At the thought, she could barely breathe.

What if… The question dangled like a ripe apple. Afraid to touch it, she walked with Amy and Sarah to teach Sunday school.

Chapter Fourteen

On Monday afternoon, Matt picked up Sarah from school and took her to Mrs. Holcombe's house. He'd been hoping for a word with Carrie, but she'd left before he could signal her. He intended to tell her, as gently as possible, that he appreciated her friendship but had no romantic inclinations.

Pearl presented a different challenge. The yellow ribbon had irked him. He wanted her to wear *his* ribbons. The yellow bow looked pretty, but the blue ones stood for something between them. Just what, Matt didn't know. He only knew he had to make things right with Carrie before he thought too much about Pearl. Not only did he owe it to Carrie, but he also wanted to spare Pearl the awkwardness of knowing the truth when Carrie didn't.

Eager to get the job done, he decided to visit Carrie at her house. First, though, he wanted to speak with Dan about his conversation with Tobias. Not only had the minister agreed to help, but he also had a fire in his belly for the cause of justice. It matched the one that burned in Matt, causing him to wonder why Tobias felt so strongly. He'd wanted to ask, but questions would lead to more questions. If Matt quizzed Tobias, the man would quiz him back. Matt had no desire to tell anyone in Cheyenne about his mistakes.

When he reached the sheriff's office, he opened the door and instantly smelled trouble. Instead of stale coffee, he smelled sugar and spice. His gaze landed on a plate of baked goods on his desk. Expecting to see Dan, he turned to his friend's desk. He saw Dan all right. And Carrie. They were seated across from each other. Matt had to make himself clear to her, and he had to do it today.

"Good afternoon," he said as he hung up his hat. "I hope Sarah's not in trouble."

Carrie stood and smiled. "Not at all."

She gave Dan a look. The two of them must have done some talking, because Dan headed for the door. "I'll give you two some privacy."

Matt appreciated the gesture, but being alone with Carrie bothered him. What if she started to cry? He hated it when women cried. What if she screeched like Bettina? Thoughts of his former wife reminded him that he'd been a rotten husband. He was doing Carrie a favor by keeping his distance. He'd be wise to do the same favor for Pearl.

As the door closed, Carrie stood. "I need to explain myself, Matt. I hope you don't mind."

"Not at all."

"About last night…" She bit her lip. "I'm afraid I made a fool of myself."

He hadn't expected her candor. Relieved to face the awkwardness, he saw a chance to do right by her. If he struck the right tone, he could save Carrie's pride. He indicated the chair by Dan's desk. "Have a seat. I need to say a few words."

"No, you don't." She stayed on her feet. "I understand."

"You're a good woman, Carrie. It's just—"

"I know." She managed a smile. "I didn't realize until last night, but Pearl's a very lucky woman."

Had he been that transparent? Apparently, although he didn't consider Pearl lucky. He'd ruined Bettina's life. He liked Pearl a lot, but she'd have been wise to run from him.

Carrie raised her chin. "I'm admittedly interfering here, but I want you to know something about her."

Matt refused to talk behind her back. "I don't—"

"She's a wonderful woman," Carrie insisted. "I know she was standoffish at the party, but she has a good reason. If you talk to her, you'll see how sweet she is. She loves children, and…" She bit her lip. "I'm babbling again."

As long as he lived, Matt wouldn't understand women. He'd expected Carrie to throw a tantrum, to blame him for breaking her heart. Instead she'd come to fight for Pearl. The gesture touched him more than anything she could have said or done. It had taken courage and generosity, a generosity of spirit he didn't often see in females. Bettina hadn't possessed it. Carrie had it in abundance and so did Pearl.

A thought came to mind and it wouldn't let go. Maybe he hadn't been such a bad husband after all. Maybe he'd married the wrong woman. He'd have stuck it out forever if Bettina hadn't left, but he'd realized shortly after the wedding they were mismatched. She hadn't been strong enough for marriage to a lawman, and he'd been unable to compromise more than he had. Their marriage had failed, but not because of him.

Carrie managed a dignified smile. "I brought cookies to make up for the cream puff. They're from Pearl and me. You can share with Dan."

Her kindness touched him. "Thank you."

"You're welcome," she said.

"I mean for more than the cookies." With things settled between them, Matt could be generous, too. "You've been a friend to Pearl and a wonderful teacher for Sarah. Today you've been a friend to me, too. I appreciate it."

"It's the right thing to do." She looked close to tears, so he said nothing. Today she'd given everyone their dignity. She deserved to keep hers.

He lifted a cookie off the plate and took a bite. "It's good," he said with a full mouth. "Oatmeal raisin is Dan's favorite."

"He just told me."

Good for Dan. Matt decided to give his friend some help. "He likes cream puffs, too. His mama makes them at Christmas."

"So do I."

Matt took the interest in her eyes as a good sign. As Carrie headed for the door, he went ahead of her and held it wide. As she passed, she gave him a last lingering look. "Goodbye, Matt."

"Goodbye, Carrie."

As she passed through the door, he saw Dan watching them from down the street. Matt had a good mind to shout at him to walk Carrie home. If Dan didn't ask her, he didn't deserve to call himself a man.

Carrie saw Dan, too.

And Dan saw Carrie.

They met in the middle of the boardwalk, exchanged a few words and then walked together in the same direction. Good, Matt thought. They were fine people who deserved happiness. Pleased, he stepped back into the office and wrapped some cookies in a napkin for Sarah. Not only had Carrie given her blessing to Matt's interest in Pearl, but she'd also opened his eyes to the truth about his first marriage. It had failed, but not because of him.

His mind went down a road that ended with a mother for Sarah, a woman with blond hair and blue eyes that sent beams of light into a dark world. That, he realized, was the problem. Pearl's heart brimmed with love for God and goodwill toward people. Matt simmered with bitterness and loathing. Pearl needed a man who shared her faith, not a heathen like himself.

Even so, the longing in his heart couldn't be denied. Could he become the man she deserved? He didn't know, but he saw a ray of hope. If he could stop the Golden Order, maybe he could forgive himself for what he'd done. Maybe he could stop hating the Almighty for allowing good men to go bad. If Matt could sit in church without knotting his fists, he could court Pearl without guilt. Everything depended on his ability to stop the Golden Order, and that mission depended on Tobias Oliver.

Matt saw a certain irony. For a man who didn't care for God or ministers, he was in a peculiar state of need. Whether he liked it or not, he had to depend on Tobias. He could only hope the man was more reliable than his God.

Pearl was arranging women's shoes when her father walked into Jasper's shop. It was Wednesday. He'd visited yesterday, too. Instead of chatting with her, he'd struck up a conversation with Jasper about the fire on Ferguson Street. Today they planned to have lunch together. Pearl found the friendship troubling. Her father needed friends, but he had nothing in common with the shopkeeper. When she'd mentioned his visit to the shop over supper, he'd brushed off her concern and changed the subject.

Tonight she'd speak to him again. In the few weeks she'd worked for Jasper, she'd lost what little respect she had for the man. Only the paycheck kept her working for him.

Her father offered a smile. "Hello, princess."

"Hello, Papa."

"Is Jasper here?" He patted his belly. "I'm ready for lunch."

Jasper stepped out of his office. "It's good to see you, Reverend." The men shook hands as if they were old friends. "You're right on time. I appreciate punctuality."

"I do, too."

So did Pearl, but she didn't watch the clock like Jasper. The one on the wall read 11:55 a.m. He'd be back at exactly one o'clock.

Jasper indicated the door. "I hope you don't mind. I've invited Chester Gates to join us."

"Not at all," Tobias replied.

Pearl respected Mr. Gates even less than she respected Jasper. He'd visited the store twice. Both times he'd acted as if they'd never met. She could understand that he'd voted his conscience, but ignoring her was rude.

As the men left, she went back to arranging the shoes. She placed the first pair on the shelf and aligned the toes an inch from the edge. Jasper insisted on perfection. Once he'd measured her work with a ruler. As she arranged the next pair, the bell over the door jangled. She turned and saw Matt. As he took off his hat, his eyes darted around the store. "Is Jasper around?"

"He just left with my father."

The tension left his face. "Good. I'd like a word with you."

Her heart sped up. "About what?"

"The cookies."

Pearl felt the warmth of a blush. Last night she'd had a heart-to-heart with Carrie. Not only had Carrie given Pearl her blessing when it came to courting Matt, but she'd also decided to play Cupid. Without telling Pearl in advance, she'd visited Matt and delivered cookies as a gift from both of them. Pearl had protested that he'd get the wrong idea. Carrie had looked at her as if she'd lost her mind, then she'd told Pearl to be brave. Considering Carrie's graciousness, how could Pearl do otherwise?

Looking at Matt now, she felt a quickening of her pulse. "Carrie baked them."

"I know," he said. "She came to see me."

"She told me."

"Just so you know, things are square between us." His eyes took on a twinkle. "Maybe she'll take a shine to Dan."

"I hope so!" Pearl could easily hope for love for Carrie, but what about herself? Looking at Matt, she felt a quickening in her pulse. Should she encourage him? What did a woman do when a man interested her? Blinking, she thought of her offer to braid Sarah's hair. Matt had mastered the art, but there were other things a little girl needed to know.

With her cheeks warm, she smiled. "How's Sarah?"

"Just fine."

"She's growing up fast." Butterflies swirled in Pearl's belly. "I seem to recall I offered to braid her hair. You've gotten good at it, but maybe I could show her a different way to fix it."

Matt's expression didn't change, but the air in the shop turned thick. Pearl felt foolish. "Never mind. I was just thinking—"

"No." He waved off her objection. "She'd like that. She likes Toby, too. Maybe we could all go for pie after church."

He looked as surprised at the invitation as she was. Were they talking about their children or the possibility of more than friendship? She searched for the answer in Matt's eyes and found confusion and hope, a mix that matched her troubled thoughts. She had feelings for him, but she also had doubts about her ability to be a wife. She felt safe with Matt, but until now he'd belonged to Carrie. The thought of being courted by a man still terrified her, and those feelings came in a rush.

Her throat closed with apprehension. Abruptly she turned back to the shoes. "I can't. Not this Sunday." *Not ever.*

"Maybe during the week," he suggested.

Pearl shook her head.

Silence hung like a sheet, but it did nothing to hide her nervousness. Her pulse started to race, and she landed back in Denver in Franklin Dean's buggy. If she'd never been attacked, she could say yes to Matt. She wouldn't have this fear. She wouldn't be trembling as she arranged shoes in a store owned by a hateful man.

Matt touched her shoulder. "Are you all right?"

"I-I'm fine."

How had she gotten into this mess? She didn't want to discuss her fears with Matt. "If you'll excuse me, I have to get back to work."

As she nudged a shoe into place, Matt touched her shoulder. His touch couldn't have been gentler, but she startled like a deer and bumped into the shelf behind her. She would *not* let Matt see the painful memories, the fearful reaction she had to fight. She turned quickly back to the shoes. She moved one, then another. When Matt didn't budge, she finally looked at him. "Do you need something else?"

She saw knowledge in his eyes and felt transparent, as if her fears were marbles on display in a fragile glass bowl. Slowly, giving her time to retreat, he raised one hand and touched the braid wrapped tightly around her head, mimicking the touch they'd shared in the kitchen. She told herself to stay still, but her legs stepped back on their own.

She forced herself to look at him, but she couldn't find her voice.

Matt stared into her eyes. "I think I understand. You're not over being attacked, right?"

"Yes," she murmured.

"You live with bad memories." The lines around his mouth tightened into crevasses and his drawl thickened. "It's like walking through a field of gopher holes. If you step the wrong way, you fall and you break all over again."

Looking into his eyes, she saw scars as vivid as her own. "You know what it's like."

"I do."

Aching for them both, she raised her chin. "I hope we can still be friends."

"Sure," he said gently. "I'd like that."

She'd told the truth, but it tasted like a lie. She wanted more than friendship from Matt. She wanted to give him everything he needed. She just didn't believe she could. When she took a breath, so did he. He mentioned the Indian summer, and she agreed the weather had been too warm. She asked about Sarah, and he told a funny story. When they'd both relaxed, he said, "I better get going."

Pearl felt a fresh pang of loss. Someday Matt would marry, and Sarah would finally have a mother. Pearl couldn't be that woman, but she could brighten the child's day.

"Wait," she said. "I have something for Sarah."

She went to the storeroom and knelt beside a newly arrived crate from New York. It held an assortment of chapbooks. She picked out a story about a shepherd boy and took it to Matt. Later she'd put money in the till to pay for it.

She handed him the gift. "This is for Sarah."

"Thank you. She'll enjoy it."

They traded goodbyes and Matt left. Pearl intended to go immediately to the cash box to pay, but two women walked in as Matt was leaving. They needed help with draperies. After they made a purchase, Mrs. Gates came to look at china. Not for a second did Pearl forget the money she owed. Jasper would fire her instantly if he thought she'd stolen from him. As soon as the store emptied, she reached in her pocket for some coins.

As she took a nickel in change, Jasper came through the door. She startled like a rabbit. "Mr. Kling!"

She had no cause to feel guilty, but the circumstances condemned her.

His brows arched. "Hello, Pearl."

"I was making change for myself." She felt foolish. "I bought one of the chapbooks. I gave it to—to a friend. I would have paid right away, but we had customers. I—"

"Don't fret, Pearl." For once, he looked sympathetic. "You're as honest as the day is long. I know that."

"Oh." She felt vindicated but frightened at the same time. Jasper sounded too friendly. Nervous, she resorted to formality. "Thank you, Mr. Kling."

He looked down his nose. "I *do* wish you'd call me Jasper."

If she declined his offer, she'd antagonize him. If she said yes, she'd be compromising her need for distance. She settled on a simple truth. "Thank you, sir. But I'm not comfortable—

"Jasper," he repeated. "Say it."

Blood rushed to her cheeks, turning them red with a mix of anger and fear. She looked him in the eye. "I can't, sir. It wouldn't be proper."

He looked pleased. "I understand."

She doubted it.

"Pearl?"

She put her hands on the drawer. As she closed it, it squeaked. "Yes?"

"I respect your father greatly. I admire you, too." His voice dropped low…or did it? He hadn't twitched a muscle, but she felt trapped behind the counter and had to work to breathe evenly. Silently she prayed he'd disappear into his office. Instead he tipped his head. "You're affected by what I've said."

"I'm fine," she said too quickly. "It's—it's a warm day."

"Stay here."

He brushed by her, went to the back room and returned with a glass of water. She took it and drank, but she felt like a princess being poisoned.

"Better?" he asked.

"Yes, thank you." As she set the glass on the counter, she thought of the things Franklin Dean had taken from her—purity and innocence, confidence in herself and in the goodness of people. He'd been killed in Denver when he'd attempted to murder the man who'd revealed his hypocrisy to the people of Colfax Avenue Church. Was Jasper a danger like Franklin Dean, or was it in her head? Considering the circumstances, it seemed likely the unease was in her head.

Instead of leaving, he stood with her. "Your color's back."

"I'm fine now."

He smiled again. "I'm *very* glad."

Pearl didn't like his tone. Neither did she like her father befriending this man or Carrie putting Pearl's name on cookies. She was mad at Matt, too. Why did he have to be handsome and kind, a man with a Texas drawl and an adorable little girl who needed a mother? Why couldn't she say yes to supper and risk a kiss? It wasn't fair. Pearl wanted to shout at God, too. How much did He think she could endure? She didn't dare break down in front of Jasper. Squaring her shoulders, she went back to shelving shoes. She knew life could be much harder than what she'd just endured, but she didn't think it could feel any more forgotten.

Chapter Fifteen

At nine o'clock on Thursday morning, a time when Jasper Kling was sure to be at his store and Chester Gates would be counting his money, Matt just happened to walk by Madame Fontaine's bakery. He just happened to see Tobias Oliver seated at a table in the back, the same one Matt had shared with Pearl. The man just happened to be eating breakfast, and Matt just happened to stop for a cup of coffee.

The old adage—hide in plain sight—was the option the men had chosen when they happened to meet at church. For the third Sunday in a row, Matt had taken Sarah to the morning service. Each time he and Tobias had exchanged terse bits of information. Matt had gleaned the names of ten suspects, and he'd spoken with all of them. He'd earned some hard looks, but that came with the job. If things went as he hoped, Tobias had been invited for cigars after last night's meeting.

The sooner Tobias earned the trust of these men, the sooner Matt could bring them to justice. And the sooner he stopped the Golden Order, the sooner he could think about Pearl as more than a friend.

Their meeting at the store had stayed with him for days

now. He wanted more than small talk from her, but he had nothing to give in return. To protect her feelings, he'd stopped visiting the store. He still walked by and looked in the window, but he'd asked Dan to go inside to speak with her. His friend didn't mind a bit. Carrie visited Pearl every afternoon, and Dan and Carrie often left together. Yesterday he'd bought seats for *Romeo and Juliet* and he'd planned to ask her Sunday at church.

Matt wished his own problems were so easily solved. He pulled up a chair across from Tobias. "Good morning, Reverend."

"Good morning," Tobias replied.

"Any news?"

His eyes glinted above the scrambled eggs. "I shared a nice cigar with Chester Gates last night."

Matt sipped his coffee. "Anyone else?"

Tobias gave him five names. In addition to Gates and Jasper, he'd met with Troy Martin, Howard Moreland and Gibson Armond. Martin and Moreland both had ties to the crimes committed by the men in derbies. It took Matt a minute to place Gibson Armond, then he remembered. He owned a freighting company. Recently he'd complained about outlaws hijacking his loads. He was also the man who had almost run over Sarah.

Matt took a sip of coffee, then looked at Tobias. "I don't suppose they offered you a derby?"

"Not yet." He spoke in a hush. "But last night was an interview of sorts."

"What did they talk about?"

"Martin and Moreland complained about horse thieves. They both have axes to grind. Mostly, though, Jasper carped about Ferguson Street." Tobias buttered a slice of bread. "If you ask me, the man has an unhealthy hatred of the place. It makes me wonder if he's hiding something."

Matt thought of Jasper's visit to the hog ranch. His secret hadn't leaked, but the man lived with the threat of it. "He wouldn't be the first," Matt said.

"Nor will he be the last."

"What did Jasper say?"

Tobias shook his head. "He said the fire was God's punishment for the lowest of sins. I'm not one to judge, Deputy. But Jasper has some extreme ideas. He seems sensible enough in public, but he's a different man behind closed doors. Frankly, he scares me."

He scared Matt, too. When he'd asked Tobias to gather information, he'd expected there to be some risk. Now he worried he'd asked too much. "Sir, you don't have to do this. You can still get out."

"Why would I do that?"

"Because you're right about Jasper." Matt lowered his voice. "He's got a secret and he'll do anything to keep it. Once you accept that derby, there's no going back. If they think you're double-crossing them, you'll pay."

Tobias gave him a hard look. "Is my daughter in danger, too?"

"Possibly."

"Then I better move quick," he replied matter-of-factly. "These men have to be stopped before someone else dies."

Matt didn't understand his commitment, his willingness to risk his life. And Pearl… If Jasper suspected Tobias, he'd watch her like a hawk. Matt wished he'd never concocted this crazy scheme. "You don't have to be the one. I'll find someone else."

"Over my dead body."

"Sir?"

Tobias glared at him. "My daughter was raped because good men in my church turned a blind eye to hypocrisy. I was one of them. If I don't stop these men, who will?"

Matt understood. He, too, had failed to stop something terrible. "You're making up for what happened to Pearl."

"That's not it." The man's eyes seemed to catch fire. "My slate's clean because of what Christ did on the cross. I don't have to fix my own mistakes."

Matt wished he felt the same way. "Unfortunately some of us do."

"Are you among them, Deputy?"

A flaming arrow hit Matt, and it hit him hard. His eyes glinted. "With all due respect, reverend. That's none of your business."

Tobias chewed the bacon as if he didn't have a care in the world. Matt wanted to be nonchalant, but he felt as if he'd tripped in one of the gopher holes he'd mentioned to Pearl. His temper flared. "You're a nosy old man, aren't you?"

Tobias chuckled.

Matt didn't see the humor. "Everyone in Cheyenne has regrets. So what? A man learns to live with what he's done."

"But it gets old, doesn't it?" Tobias chewed the bacon for a long time. "All that worry, not sleeping. I had a rough time before Pearl and I reconciled. What I'm wondering, Wiley, is this: Are you stupid or gutless?"

Matt's eye narrowed. "Neither."

"It has to be one or the other." Tobias could have been talking about the weather. "You're either afraid to face up to what you did, or you think you can fix it on your own. The first choice is cowardly. The second is naive."

"I'm no coward."

Tobias smiled. "That means you're stupid."

Weren't ministers supposed to be meek and mild? Matt glared at him. "What are you getting at?"

"You asked why I'm willing to risk my life to stop the

Golden Order. I'm asking you the same question." Tobias softened his voice. "If I'm going to accept that black derby, I need to know what's got you working so hard. If they can, they'll use it against us both."

The man had a point. Matt wasn't ready to confess, but Tobias deserved an answer. He fortified himself with a slug of coffee, then looked the minister in the eye. "All right. Here it is. During the war I was a captain in Hood's Texas Brigade. We fought Grant in northern Virginia."

"I've heard of Hood's Army." Tobias sounded respectful. "You saved General Lee's life. Lost a lot of men doing it."

"That we did." Matt wished he could feel proud, but the heroism of the day had died on Amos McGuckin's farm. "Something ugly happened after the battle. I was responsible." From across the table, the men locked eyes. Matt had cowed outlaws, thieves and killers, but today he looked away first. "That's all I'm saying."

"It's enough," Tobias said quietly. "I won't ask you again, but I'd like you to do something for me."

"What?"

"Read the psalms."

Matt snorted. "That's poetry." Even when he'd been a believer, he'd preferred stories about vengeance and war. Sometimes he'd laughed at the Book of Proverbs, especially the verses about fools. The psalms had always struck him as whining.

Tobias took a pencil and a slip of paper from his pocket, jotted a few words and handed the scrap to Matt. "Here."

The note read Psalm 127. "What's this?"

"Your homework."

"This isn't Sunday school."

"Maybe not, but I'll be a minister until I die." He put

the pencil back in his coat. "That's my requirement for accepting a black derby. You read Psalm 127."

The old man had him over a barrel. "I hope it's short."

Tobias chuckled. "It's five verses."

"I guess I can tolerate it." He pushed up from the chair. The irony of what he had to say wasn't lost on him. "I'll see you in church."

"I'll be there," Tobias replied.

Matt left the bakery and walked three blocks to the sheriff's office. He stepped inside, didn't see Dan and decided to get his "homework" out of the way. His partner kept a Bible in the bottom drawer of his desk. Sometimes Dan read it at night. More than once he'd handed it to a man locked in a cell. Matt took the book from the drawer, thumbed his way to Tobias's psalm and read it. The part about the Lord building a house didn't hold his attention, but the rest of the verse described a man like himself, a night watchman guarding a city. The lawman in the psalm didn't get enough sleep, either. Matt could relate, though unlike the watchman in the psalm, he felt no desire to call on the Lord for help.

The next verses were about children and he liked them. Matt enjoyed being a father. Until recently, he hadn't thought about having sons. Now thoughts of sons made him think of Pearl and Toby. The thought stirred him in a new and good way, but his talk with Tobias had brought old bitterness to the surface. He felt tainted by it, unfit for female company. He'd been crazy to invite her for pie after church. It was a good thing she'd said no. Matt had nothing to give a preacher's daughter.

Feeling dreary, he drummed his fingers on the cover of the Bible and wished again he could sleep at night. He didn't want to ask Tobias's God for help, but neither did he want to be like the watchman in the Bible, trying in vain to stop evil. Matt hadn't thought a prayer in years, but he thought one now.

I don't deserve mercy, Lord. I don't deserve a family or even a good night's sleep, but I'm asking you to stop the Golden Order.

"Amen," he said out loud. He closed the book and put it back in the drawer. As he slid it shut, Dan strode into the office. The men traded a look but neither spoke. Matt had to give Dan credit for being wise. Some things were personal for a man. Others were downright humbling. Reading psalms counted as humbling.

Dan scratched his neck.

Matt yawned.

Silence stretched until Dan poured coffee for himself. "Nice day, isn't it?"

"Yep."

And that's all they said. It was all Matt *could* say, at least for now.

For the hundredth time, Pearl looked out her bedroom window at the moonlit street. Leaves skittered with the endless wind, but nothing else moved. The nearby houses were dark with sleep and quiet beneath the November sky.

The clock chimed eleven times and she sighed. Her father still wasn't home. He'd gone to a special meeting of the Golden Order, though why he'd become involved with the contentious group, Pearl couldn't fathom. Her father believed in pouring oil on troubled waters. The Golden Order was more inclined to put a match to tinder, yet he'd become a supporter. Why? Tonight she intended to find out.

But first he had to come home.

She was close to marching to the meeting hall herself when a fancy black carriage rolled down the street. Franklin

Dean had driven a similar brougham all over Denver, and she'd ridden in it many times. Like the one coming down the street, it had a hard top, square glass windows and ornate lamps on the sides. A driver sat on the high seat, guiding two matched grays as they clopped down the street.

When the carriage halted in front of Carrie's house, the driver jumped down and opened the door. To Pearl's astonishment, a man wearing a black derby climbed out and shook hands with another man she couldn't see. As the carriage departed, he turned up the walkway and she saw her father's face. Pearl knew what the derby meant. He'd become involved in something ugly, but why? Chills erupted on her skin like blisters. They popped and stung until she pressed her hands to her cheeks in horror.

She listened to the creak of the front door, then her father's footsteps as he climbed the stairs. After his bedroom door closed, she raced down the hall, barged into his room and shouted in a whisper, *"Are you out of your mind!"*

He looked at her as if she were a stranger. "I thought you'd be asleep."

"Asleep? How am I supposed to *sleep* when you're running around Cheyenne in the middle of the night!" She started to pace. "The Golden Order! Papa, you said yourself they're a bunch of troublemakers!"

"It's not what you think."

She pointed at the derby he'd set on the bed. All the pieces came together. The vigilantes and the Golden Order were one and the same. "If it's not what I think, why are you wearing *that?*"

"Calm down, princess."

"NO!"

Between her father's news and Jasper's prissiness, she'd had enough aggravation to last a lifetime. Adding to the upset, Toby had screamed half the evening with colic. Most irritating of all, Matt hadn't visited the store in days. He'd walked by and looked in the window, but he'd sent Dan inside to talk to her. Even Dan had annoyed her. He'd asked her if Carrie liked stage plays. Of course Carrie liked stage plays! So did Pearl. She also liked Matt, who had forgotten about her.

She put her hands on her hips. "I don't understand, Papa. If that hat means what I think, you've lost your mind."

"I most certainly haven't," he replied. "But neither do I have to answer to you."

"But—"

"I'm your father, Pearl. Not a child."

"Papa, I'm worried about you."

He walked to her side and spoke as if sharing a secret. "I know how this looks, Pearl. I'm asking you to trust me."

"I want to, but I'm scared." With good cause, she thought. "What are you doing?"

He shook his head.

She had only begged once in her life. She'd pleaded with Franklin Dean to stop unbuttoning her dress. She begged now because she feared losing her father. "Please, Papa. Tell me what's going on."

The clock ticked a dozen times. She bit her lip, but a cry rose to her throat. She put a hand over her mouth to hold it back, but it escaped in a whimper.

Her father stepped to her side. "Don't cry, Pearl. It's not what you think."

"Then what is it?"

"I'm helping Matt Wiley."

In a hushed tone, he told her about Matt's suspicions regarding the Golden Order. "I agreed to join because I'm in a unique position to help. It's the right thing to do."

Her body went limp. "But Papa, your health isn't good."

"It's good enough."

"But the danger! If they find out you're double-crossing them, they could—" She sealed her lips. The men in masks were accountable to no one but themselves. If her father exposed their crimes, he'd be a Judas and they'd kill him.

Tobias squeezed her hand. "I know the risks, Pearl. I also believe God called me to this task."

"But why?"

"Because I'm in the right place at the right time." He lifted their joined hands in an oath of sorts. "You know the story of Esther. She was made queen 'for a time such as this.' I believe I'm in Cheyenne for this very purpose."

"You're here for Toby and me." She hated the risk, the danger. "If something happens to you—"

"If it does, you'll be fine." His eyes filled with sadness. "I'm an old man, Pearl. I won't be around forever. You need to find a husband."

"How can you say that?" He knew her fears. She felt betrayed.

"It's true."

"Maybe I don't *want* to get married."

His brows arched. "That may be the first lie you've ever told me."

Her cheeks turned rosy. She *had* lied. She almost wished he'd call her "princess" so she could be a child again instead of a woman with adult problems.

Tobias looked pleased. "Deputy Wiley's a good man. He's troubled, but that comes with the badge."

She'd seen the pain for herself. "I know."

Her father looked into her eyes. "Do you love him?"

Until this moment, she danced around the question without answering it. She *liked* Matt. She *cared* for him. She worried about him and wanted him to be happy. But love? That meant desiring him the way a wife desired a husband. She had those feelings for him, but they terrified her.

"I don't know," she murmured.

"I didn't ask if you were afraid," Tobias said. "I asked if you loved him."

Her insides shook with a potent mix of hope and fear. "I do," she admitted. "I love Sarah, too."

"Be strong, Pearl." He spoke in his preacher's voice, the one that seemed to move mountains. "I don't know what's lurking in Matt's past, but I *do* know the Lord won't leave him twisting in the wind. The Lord won't leave you either."

"I want to believe that." She took a breath. "I *do* believe."

"So do I, daughter.... So do I."

Chapter Sixteen

Meeting Tobias at the bakery had risks, but it could be explained as coincidence. Matt made a point of visiting often. If a member of the Golden Order saw them, the encounter wouldn't be out of the ordinary. At church on Sunday, Tobias had indicated he'd accepted a derby and wanted to meet. The news had made up for the misery of sitting through a sermon, but it hadn't eased his worry about Pearl. She'd been tense and had watched her father like a hawk.

Neither had she been happy to see Matt, though she'd been delighted to see Sarah. As the females compared dresses, the men had arranged today's breakfast meeting.

As Matt pulled out the chair across from Tobias, he recognized Nicholas Hamblin seated by the window. The man owned a sawmill and went to all the G.O. meetings. He didn't say much, but he'd listened. He plainly recognized Tobias.

Matt kept the subject light. "Nice weather, isn't it?"

"Excellent."

He looked for another bland topic. "How's your grandson?"

"Just fine." A beaming grandpa, Tobias told stories until

Hamblin left. Tobias relaxed but only for an instant. "Stay alert, Wiley. The G.O. doesn't like you."

"That's no surprise."

"They're making plans." His voice dropped an octave. "Be careful, son."

"What kind of plans?"

"The kind that could make your daughter an orphan."

The blood drained from Matt's head. He'd faced death a hundred times during the war, but never had he felt the apprehension he felt now. If he died, who'd love his little girl? Who'd read her stories and braid her hair? He didn't dare sip his coffee. With his jittery hands, it would have sloshed down his shirt. "What are they planning?"

"That's still being decided."

"By the five men you mentioned?" Matt wanted to know his enemies by name.

"The same."

While eating his meal, Tobias told Matt about the meeting. Matt had kicked a beehive when he'd questioned members of the G.O., and now they wanted him gone. Troy Martin and Gibson Armond had called him soft. They wanted his badge but not his life. Howard Moreland had suggested a tree and a short rope. Gates had kept his own counsel. Jasper had gone into a tirade about Matt failing to lock up prostitutes, then he'd sided with Moreland.

By the time Tobias finished, Matt felt as if the walls had sprouted eyes and were watching his every move. His nerves had never been stretched so tight.

"Tell me," said the old man. "Did you read that psalm?"

Matt couldn't believe his ears. "The G.O. wants me dead, and you're bringing up poetry?"

"Sure."

"That's crazy."

"It's not crazy to me," Tobias replied.

Matt felt as if someone had blindfolded him, spun him in circles and told him to find his way home. He'd met with Tobias to stop the Golden Order, not to bare his soul. Matt didn't want to dawdle over trivia, so he shrugged. "The psalm was nice. Now let's get down to business."

"That's what I'm doing." Tobias buttered a biscuit. "What struck you as 'nice' about that little piece of poetry?"

"I didn't think much about it." Actually, he'd read it two more times. He'd thought a lot about the verses, particularly the one about the watchman.

"Take a shot," Tobias insisted.

Matt gave up. He wouldn't spill his secret, but he'd crack open the door. "I liked the first verse," he admitted. "About the watchman."

"Me, too." Tobias pushed back his plate. "I've never worn a badge, but I had a church to run. Without God's help, I'd have been sunk ten times over."

Matt saw a chance to steer the conversation. "Do you think we're sunk when it comes to the G.O.?"

"We'll get to that," Tobias said lazily. "I'm more interested in how you're sleeping."

"Fine." He'd lied and felt bad. "Actually, terrible."

"You look it."

"Thanks." Matt sounded droll.

"I have another verse for you." Tobias spoke as if he were reading a bedtime story. "'The sun shall not smite thee by day, nor the moon by night.' I used to wonder why we needed protection from the moon, then Pearl left and I couldn't sleep worth spit. Those nights were rough. My own daughter needed understanding, and I failed to hear her side of the story. I pressured her to marry the man who attacked her." Tobias shook his head. "Can you imagine anything so stupid?"

Matt recalled his own failings. "I'm afraid so."

"Some nights, I thought I'd lose my mind." Tobias paused to let the words sink in. "I think you know what that's like. Next time you can't sleep, try telling God how you feel."

"No way," Matt said. "My problems are my own business."

"You're wrong."

Matt huffed. "Not only are you nosy, you're meddlesome."

"I've walked the road you're on." He raised one brow. "What you feel now, it affects everyone around you, especially Sarah."

He'd voiced Matt's deepest fear. "You don't know that."

"I know about guilt. It's why you're going after the Golden Order so hard. You've got an ax to grind, not with them but with yourself. Am I wrong?"

If they'd been alone, Matt would have spilled his guts because Tobias understood. He felt a bond with the man…a minister of all confounded things.

Tobias heaved a sigh. "Speaking of guilt, I have a burden myself."

"What happened?"

"Pearl saw the derby."

Matt stifled a groan. Ignorance provided protection. A woman couldn't reveal what she didn't know. "What did you tell her?"

"Everything." Tobias raised his hand in a sign of defeat. "I know. I should have kept quiet."

"What did she say?" Matt asked.

"She's not happy, but she knows to keep quiet." Tobias hunkered forward. "I don't mind saying, I'm eager to end this charade."

So was Matt. If he could finish with the Golden Order,

maybe he could sleep at night. Maybe he could settle matters with the Almighty and not want to throw punches when he went to church. "It won't be long, sir."

"I hope not."

Matt made a decision. The more pressure he put on the Golden Order, the sooner they'd come after him personally. When they took aim, he'd fire back with both barrels. Dying wasn't an option. He needed to take care of Sarah.

Tobias stood. "We should meet before Sunday."

Matt thought about the coming week. Carrie had invited the girls from her class to a tea party on Thursday afternoon. When he picked up Sarah, he'd be able to speak with Tobias. "I'll see you after that party Carrie's having."

"Sounds good."

Tobias put coins on the table and left the bakery. Matt waited ten minutes, then pulled his hat low and headed for the sheriff's office. As he crossed the street, his neck hairs prickled. Any minute men in derbies could gallop down the street. A bullet could find his head and he'd be gone. As a lawman and a soldier, he'd faced his enemies head-on. The men in the Golden Order were devious. They didn't play by the conventional rules. They made up their own.

Stepping on the boardwalk, he thought about the watchman in the psalm. Matt could take care of himself, but today he'd have welcomed an all-seeing partner, someone smarter. Someone who'd keep Sarah safe, heal Pearl's heart and give Matt a decent night's sleep.

On Wednesday morning, a week after she'd seen her father in a black derby, Pearl went to work as usual. She'd grown accustomed to Jasper's persnickety ways, but today he'd been especially attentive. He'd struck up four conversations in the past hour, each one as bland as the last. When he'd gone to his office, he'd left the door ajar so he could hear her every step.

He'd also brought her a croissant from the bakery. She'd accepted it but hadn't taken a bite. Every time Jasper came out of his office, he looked at the roll sitting on a plate on the counter. Hoping he'd leave her alone, she'd finally taken a nibble, thanked him and turned back to the ledger.

"Pearl?"

She startled as he stepped out of his office. "Yes?"

"I have an errand to run." He pushed his spectacles higher on his nose. "I'll be back shortly."

"Of course." She still hadn't called him Jasper and she wouldn't. Neither had she called him "sir" or "Mr. Kling" because she knew he'd challenge her.

She averted her eyes until she heard the bell over the door, then she looked up and saw him pass by the display window. Breathing a sigh, she closed the ledger and rubbed her neck. She'd never been good at keeping secrets, and she found her father's deception exhausting. She wanted to go home and cuddle Toby until she forgot everything except his smile. She wanted to see her father, too. She still worried about his health, but she had to admit he looked well these days. He walked every morning at sunrise and sometimes at dusk. He had a spring in his step and a purposeful air about him.

Pearl wished she felt as confident. Not only did she worry about her father's involvement with the G.O., she couldn't stop thinking about Matt. She prayed every night for wisdom, but she felt no peace.

As she refocused on the ledger, the bell jangled above the door. She looked up and saw two women, both fancily dressed in bright colors. She didn't recognize them, but their revealing gowns belonged on Ferguson Street. In spite of their clothing, both women looked sad, even bitter. Pearl wondered if they'd known Katy. Jasper would want her to order them out of the shop, but she couldn't do it. Pearl knew how it felt to be scorned, so she refused to be unkind. If Jasper objected, so be it.

"May I help you?" she said brightly.

A brunette with frizzy hair gave her a snide smile. "We're just browsing." She turned to the shelf holding hand mirrors.

Pearl had admired the mirrors herself. She especially liked a white cloisonné edged with pink roses. The second woman, a redhead thanks to henna dye, smiled with sealed lips. Pearl wondered if she had bad teeth. Pearl smiled at her. "You've picked my favorite one. Aren't the roses pretty?"

"Oh yes!"

The girl's lips parted enough to confirm Pearl's suspicions. Her front teeth were the color of ash. No wonder the woman had sealed her lips. Pearl refused to add to her embarrassment. "A matching brush set just arrived. It's in the back."

The dark-haired woman eyed her with suspicion. "You work here?"

"I do."

The redhead looked at the brunette with a question in her eyes. They hadn't been expecting courtesy. Pearl enjoyed the surprise. "If you'd like, I'll get the brush."

The brunette huffed. "You shouldn't, not if you want to keep your job."

The woman clearly knew Jasper's ways. If he walked in, he'd be furious. Pearl decided to take that chance. "I'll be right back."

As she turned, she saw Jasper passing the display window. As her stomach clenched, the women straightened their spines to the point of arching them. They reminded

her of cats lying in wait for a mouse. Jasper's warning had
come soon after the incident with Katy and the hairbrush.
Belatedly she realized these women hadn't come to look
at mirrors. They'd come to retaliate for Katy's death by
making Jasper furious.

As he pushed through the door, his eyes went down the
brunette's flashy dress, up to the redhead's cleavage, then
across to Pearl's face. The mix of loathing and lust in his
gaze turned to confusion. The confusion hardened into the
arrogance she'd seen in Franklin Dean.

Jasper paced toward them, inspected the shelf, then
blocked the aisle so the women couldn't leave.

"Pearl!" he ordered. "Get the sheriff."

"But Mr. Kling," she protested. "They didn't do anything
wrong."

His gaze narrowed to her face. "A mirror's missing."

Pearl looked at the shelf. The cloisonné mirror hadn't
been replaced. She looked at the redhead. Wide-eyed, the
woman turned to her friend, who said nothing.

"It was just here." Pearl had been with the women every
minute.

"I'm telling you," he insisted. "The mirror's been stolen."
He glared at the women. "Empty your pockets!"

The women stayed smug and silent. The cats had riled
the mouse, and the mouse was roaring. Pearl sensed a trap
about to be sprung. She opened her mouth to suggest they
look for the mirror on other shelves, but Jasper shouted at
her.

"Get Deputy Wiley!"

She raced out of the store, turned the corner and crossed
the street, dodging a buckboard going in one direction and
a rider coming in the other. Hoisting her skirts, she stepped
on to the boardwalk and burst into the door of the sheriff's

office. She saw Dan at the far desk. At the sight of her, he jumped to his feet. "What's wrong?"

"It's Jasper, he—"

The door opened behind her and Matt strode inside. He must have seen her running down the street, because he looked ready for a fight. "What happened?"

"It's Jasper," she answered, panting for breath. "Two women came into the store. They were friends with Katy. He's furious."

"Stay here." He looked at Dan. "Let's go."

"No!" Pearl cried. "I have to go back. Jasper thinks the women stole a mirror, but they didn't."

"How do you know?" he asked.

"I was with them the whole time." She told him about offering to fetch the comb and brush set. "Just as I turned, Jasper walked in."

Matt frowned. "Sounds like they were waiting for him."

Dan grabbed his hat. "I'm going with you, Wiley."

When Dan opened the door, Pearl walked through it. Matt followed her, but he didn't look pleased. As the three of them crossed the street, he guided her with a hand at her back. Dan brought up the rear. When they reached Jasper's store, Matt turned the knob on the front door. It didn't budge. Jasper had locked the women inside. Pearl knew how it felt to be trapped. To keep from crying out, she bit her lip.

Matt rapped on the door. "Jasper, open up."

Ten seconds passed before the key turned in the lock. Jasper cracked open the door, saw Matt, then opened it wide. "It's about time you got here."

Matt walked in with Pearl and Dan at his back. She looked past him to the two women, standing by the shelf with the mirrors. The brunette wore a smug expression. The redhead fidgeted with a hankie.

Matt removed his hat. "Good afternoon, ladies."

"They aren't *ladies*," Jasper replied. "They're Jezebels!'

While matching the shopkeeper's stare, Matt set his hat on the shelf. A gentleman removed his hat in the presence of a lady, and that's what he'd done. Jasper glared at the hat, then at Matt.

Ignoring him, Matt turned to Dan. "Would you take the ladies outside? I'd like to speak to Mr. Kling alone."

"Sure thing," Dan answered.

The women moved to follow Dan, but Jasper stretched his arm across the aisle. "They'll stay. So will Miss Oliver." He turned his beady eyes on Pearl. "You witnessed the theft, didn't you?"

If Pearl told the truth, she'd lose her job. If she supported Jasper's lie, she'd lose her self-respect. "No, sir. I did *not*."

Jasper's eyes narrowed to slits. "I believe you're mistaken, Pearl. These two *prostitutes* were looking at the mirrors. Now one of the mirrors is missing."

"I was with them the entire time."

"But you turned your back," Jasper said, leading her. "When I came through the door, you were looking away."

"Just for an instant."

He glared at her. "I saw the redhead put something in her pocket."

"This should be easy to solve." Matt struck a relaxed pose. "You're Jenna, aren't you?"

"Yes, sir."

"Would you mind showing me what's in your pockets?"

The girl looked to her friend. The brunette gave an imperceptible nod, as if to give the girl permission to speak. She looked at Matt, then indicated the shelf behind her. "I set the mirror here."

Pearl immediately saw the white cloisonné on the second highest shelf, out of sight but not unreasonably so. Matt picked it up and showed it to Jasper. "Is this the missing mirror?"

He grumbled. "Yes."

Matt put it back in its place. "Looks to me like no harm's been done."

Jasper's face flushed red. "That woman *meant* to steal it. If I hadn't come back, the mirror would be gone."

"I doubt it," Matt answered. "I think these ladies came here to make you mad. It's payback for chasing Katy out of your store."

And maybe for the fire, Pearl thought. Did the women suspect Jasper? It seemed possible.

Jasper glared at Matt, then at the women who were smirking. Pearl wished they'd stop mocking Jasper. No way would he tolerate such disrespect. If they pushed him, she felt certain the Golden Order would cause trouble.

Matt picked up his hat. "I have a suggestion for you, Mr. Kling. Call it even and send the women on their way."

Pearl had never spoken up to Jasper, but she had to speak now. "Mr. Kling?"

"What is it?" he snapped.

"What these women did was wrong." She shot them a look meant to scold, then focused back on Jasper. "Even so, the Bible tells us to forgive. If you leave them alone, they'll leave you alone." She looked at the women again. "Isn't that right, ladies? If Mr. Kling forgets today's incident, you will, too."

The women traded a look, then the brunette spoke to Pearl. "I suppose we—"

Jasper cut her off. "There will be *no* compromise. Right is right, and wrong is wrong." When he turned to Pearl, a chill shivered down her spine. "Thank you, *Miss* Oliver, for your opinion. We'll speak when this incident is over."

Pearl had no doubt she'd just lost her job. How would she provide for Toby and her father? She didn't know, but she had an even bigger fear. Would Jasper suspect her father's true motive for joining the G.O.?

Matt spoke in a too-reasonable tone. "I'll talk to the women, Jasper."

"Don't bother."

"It's my job and I'll do it." Matt looked straight at him. "No one's going to get away with anything while I'm wearing this badge. You can count on it."

If she hadn't known Matt's true motives, his tone might have passed for sincere. Instead she heard a threat. He suspected Jasper of wrongdoing, and he'd let the man know. He'd made an enemy today and so had she. Even worse, their enemy had the power to call her father's bluff. Trembling, she prayed for God to help them all.

Matt struck a casual pose. "You know how it is, Jasper. Women like these are trouble."

The shopkeeper's face flushed red.

Matt smirked. "Some men just can't keep their hands to themselves. A few have been known to head out to the hog ranch. Seems to me that's pretty low. They don't think anyone sees, or that anyone knows. But people see. And they talk." Matt tsked his tongue. "It's a crying shame what some men will do."

Jasper looked close to choking on his own tongue. Matt turned and spoke calmly to the women. "Ladies, you've had your fun. I expect this nonsense to stop." He turned to Jasper. "When a real crime is committed, I'll handle it. Until then, this incident is over."

Dan indicated the door. "Ladies."

They gave Jasper haughty looks, then sauntered down the aisle. Matt followed without giving Pearl a second glance. She watched him leave, hoping he'd turn to her but knowing he wouldn't. The more distant they appeared, the safer she and her father would be. She hated being alone with Jasper, but she worked for him, at least for a few more minutes. Standing tall, she faced him. "I know you're angry, but I had to tell the truth."

"Yes," he said, sounding cold. "You would."

"I don't believe they intended to steal. Deputy Wiley's right. They're provoking you."

"They shouldn't do that." He clipped each word. "Neither should *you*. I trust you've learned a lesson today."

"Sir?"

"You're naive, Pearl." His spectacles magnified his eyes. "I'm not ending your employment, but I *am* disappointed in you."

She wanted to quit, but she had to protect her father. If she antagonized Jasper, she might cast doubt on his loyalty to the G.O. As disgusting as it tasted, she had to eat crow. "Thank you, sir."

He looked down his pointy nose. "Women of that ilk are the doorway to a man's sin."

In front of her eyes, Jasper's countenance changed from mild to murderous. His mouth tightened into a sneer, deepening the corners into black lines. Perspiration gave a shine to his pasty skin, and his small eyes narrowed into black beads. In the most primitive of ways, he reminded her of Franklin Dean. If it weren't for the risk to her father, she'd have walked out of his shop and never returned.

Love for her father made her strong. She didn't dare speak, but she would *not* be cowed. She wouldn't.

Jasper gave her a suspicious look. "Do you understand me, Pearl?"

She stared hard but only for an instant. She couldn't win this battle with impertinence, so she lowered her voice. "Yes, sir."

"Let's get back to work."

She stepped to the counter and opened the ledger. Jasper went to the storeroom, fetched a black derby and put it in the window. Pearl knew what it meant. So would her father. So would Matt. The Golden Order would meet and make plans. Soon they'd make a move. Silently she prayed her father and Matt would stop the violence before it reached someone she loved.

Chapter Seventeen

Once upon a time, a little girl named Sarah brought home a fancy invitation to a tea party. Like all the other little girls, she wanted a pretty new dress to wear. Unlike the other little girls, she didn't have a mama who could make one for her. She had only a daddy. He loved her very much, but he couldn't spin straw into gold or even fix her hair very well. The little girl needed a mama and she needed one now.

"Deputy Wiley?"

Startled out of the daydream, Matt saw Mrs. Gardner, the owner of the dress shop where he'd brought Sarah to be measured. "Yes?"

The woman smiled. "Take a look at your little girl." With a sweep of her hand, Mrs. Gardner indicated Sarah.

Instead of her usual pinafore, she was wearing a cloud of pink ruffles. She looked almost grown up. A lump the size of Texas pushed into Matt's throat, and he wondered if he'd ever swallow it down.

The dress hunt had started when Sarah brought home an invitation for Carrie's annual tea party for her class. Sarah had heard the girls talking about going with their mothers. He couldn't meet that need, but he could buy his daughter something pretty. The tea party served another purpose. After yesterday's trouble at Jasper's store, the black derby had gone up. When he picked up Sarah from the party, Matt could talk to Tobias unnoticed.

Sarah curtsied for him. "Do I look pretty?"

"You're beautiful, darlin'." He winked at her. "You look like a real princess."

When she grinned, he thought about her baby teeth starting to come loose. Someday he'd be in this shop buying a wedding gown. Dazed, he turned to the clerk. "How did this happen? I thought she was just getting measured."

"I made this dress for the Andrews girl. Her mother changed her mind." Mrs. Gardner smiled at Sarah. "It's a perfect fit."

"Can I have it, Daddy?"

"You sure can." He didn't ask the price. He'd have paid a month's salary for the smile on his little girl's face.

As she ran to hug him, the door opened and in walked another princess. He hadn't spoken to Pearl since the trouble at Jasper's store and he wanted to know how she'd been. He stood a little taller. "Hello, Pearl."

"Hello, Matt."

Sarah did a twirl. "Do you like my new dress?"

"It's beautiful!"

Pearl oohed and aahed for a solid minute, making the womanly sounds Sarah missed so much. Looking at her with his daughter, with their matching hair and smiles, Matt had to admit to another failure, one that didn't trouble him as much as it should have. In spite of keeping his distance, he'd fallen for a blond-haired preacher's daughter. He'd do anything for this woman…even go to church.

The thought shook him to the core. He didn't belong in church, not when he had no love for God and even less respect for Him. Whatever feelings he had for Pearl, he had to deny until he could sleep at night. When that would be, Matt didn't know. Everything depended on Tobias and the Golden Order.

As Sarah scampered off to change, Pearl pushed to her feet. "It's nice to see you, Matt."

It was nice to see her, too. More than *nice*. He wanted to put his arms around her. He wanted to save her from the gopher holes and buy ribbons for her hair. He couldn't do either of those things until he put the members of the Golden Order behind bars. Until then, they were both in danger. If he showed his feelings for Pearl, she'd be at a greater risk from Jasper.

"How are things going?" He hoped she'd read between the lines. *How's Jasper treating you?*

"Okay, I think."

He heard what she didn't say. *I'm not sure what's going on. I'm uncomfortable.*

"I haven't seen your father lately." *Has the Golden Order met?*

"He's fine," she answered. "Nothing new."

At least nothing Tobias had shared with Pearl. Unless the old man sought him out, Matt would have to wait until Thursday for news. He didn't like being in the dark, but he couldn't risk drawing attention to Tobias. The G.O. could ride any day. The episode in Jasper's store had lit the fuse. Whether the fuse was long or short, Matt didn't know. Neither did he know where it ended.

Sarah came out of the back room and went to Pearl. "Miss Carrie's having a tea party. All the other girls have mommies. Will you go with me?"

Matt's heart hitched. Carrie had assured him she'd give Sarah extra attention, but it wasn't the same as having a mama of her own. If Pearl accompanied her, Sarah would be thrilled. The choice would also bring them closer to being a family. Matt wasn't ready for that closeness, but he couldn't deny his daughter. He gave Pearl a meaningful look. "If you could, I'd be obliged."

"I'd like to," she answered. "But I have to work."

"Could you leave early?" he asked. The less time she spent with Jasper, the better.

As Pearl looked down at Sarah, so did Matt. In his daughter's eyes he saw a familiar look, the one that pleaded for a mother's love. It broke his heart. It must have broken Pearl's, because she crouched to put herself at eye level with Sarah. "I'd *love* to go. I might be a little late, though. Would that be okay?"

Sarah nodded solemnly. "But just a little late, okay?"

"I'll do my best."

Pearl straightened, then tipped the child's chin. "I need to speak with your daddy. How about looking at the dolls?"

"Okay."

Sarah went to a glass cabinet at the front of the store. Pearl followed the child with her eyes, then turned to Matt with a nervous look. He wanted to reassure her with a touch of their hands, but he couldn't. He settled for a half smile, the one that didn't quite hide his feelings. "Are you all right?" he said in a hush.

"I just wanted to say, I—I miss you."

"I've missed you, too." The words were out before he could stop them.

As a blush stained her cheeks, she diverted her gaze to the dolls. Something had scared her and he knew what it was. What she felt for him terrified her. He understood, because he had similar doubts. Pearl probably feared the physical side of marriage. Matt was afraid he'd disappoint her with his dark moods. They were a mismatched pair, especially when he thought of church and God and the peace he didn't feel. As much as Sarah needed a mother, he couldn't court Pearl until he settled matters with the Almighty.

"Deputy Wiley?" Mrs. Gardner had set Sarah's dress, wrapped in brown paper, on the counter. "That will be $3.50."

He opened his billfold, paid and slung the dress over his shoulder like a sack of flour. It weighed next to nothing and he felt ridiculous. At the sight of him, Pearl chuckled and Sarah laughed with her. Surrendering to a grin, Matt hiked the dress up on his shoulder as if it weighed a hundred pounds. "Are you ready?" he said to Sarah.

"Yes, Daddy."

"Good." He looked at Pearl. "We'll see you at the party."

"I'll be there."

He gripped Sarah's hand and headed for the door. He didn't know what the future held, but he hoped Sarah would someday have a mother, and he wanted that woman to be Pearl.

Pearl left the dress shop with the lace she'd come to purchase and hurried home. She arrived ten minutes late and met with her father's wrath. "You're late," he scolded as she stepped through the door.

"I had to stop at the dress shop."

"But, Pearl, we agreed. You come straight home *and* on time."

Because of the trouble with Jasper, they'd decided she'd leave the shop at precisely four o'clock. Never would she be alone with him behind a locked door. Considering Jasper's extreme punctuality, leaving on time wasn't a problem. On the other hand, she resented being treated like a child. She set the lace on the table and removed her hat. "I'm sorry I scared you, Papa. It was only a few minutes." She slipped out of her cloak and hung it on a peg. "I saw Matt at the dress shop. He was buying something for Sarah."

Tobias huffed. "He should have walked you home."

"He couldn't."

They both knew why. Matt had to keep his distance, but she couldn't help but wonder how it would feel to share his life. She hadn't meant to say that she missed him, but she didn't regret the confession. He'd taken her hand and she'd felt safe. In that moment, she'd seen love in his eyes. Could she kiss him without panicking? Could she be the loving wife she wanted to be?

She didn't know and was afraid to find out. Neither did she know *how* to go about such a discovery. She couldn't walk up to him and suggest a kiss.

Her father sighed. "I'll be upstairs."

Pearl took the hint. If she wanted to talk about Matt, he'd be waiting. "Thanks, Papa, but I need to check Toby. Is he in his cradle?"

"Carrie has him. They're in the parlor."

Pearl walked into the front room where Carrie was swaying with Toby in her arms and humming a lullaby. Toby looked sleepy, so Pearl greeted Carrie in a hush. "Hi."

"Hi," she whispered. "He's almost asleep."

The women stood in companionable silence until Toby's eyes closed. Satisfied he wouldn't wake up, Carrie laid him in the basket and turned to Pearl. "I'm glad you're home. I've got something to tell you."

"Good or bad?"

"Good, I think." She bit her lip. "Or maybe not. I'm not sure."

"What happened?"

"Dan asked me to the theater."

Pearl spoke to Dan almost every day at Jasper's store. He never failed to ask about Carrie, a sign he had feelings for her. The situation was complicated because of Carrie's affection for Matt. She'd stepped aside for Pearl, but that didn't mean her feelings had died.

"What did you say?" she asked carefully.

"I said yes." Carrie dropped down on the armchair. "But I'm confused. I *thought* I was in love with Matt. I didn't think I'd ever get over it, but Dan's been wonderful. When we talk, I know he's listening. And when he smiles..." Carrie put her hand on her chest. "I didn't know a man could look so shy and purposeful at the same time."

Pearl sat on the divan near Toby and rested her hand on his back. She felt the beat of his heart and silently thanked God for turning loss into gain. For the next several minutes, the women talked about men, babies and courtship. The more they spoke, the more sure Pearl felt that Carrie had found the right man in Dan Cobb.

"Now it's your turn." Carrie's eyes twinkled. "Has Matt come to his senses and visited you at the store?"

"Not lately."

"I don't see why not." Carrie sounded like an irate mother hen. "I know he cares for you. I saw it when I spoke with him. He's being thick-headed."

No, Pearl thought, he was protecting her. Carrie didn't know about Jasper, her father and the Golden Order, and Pearl saw no need to tell her about the plan. Secrets were a burden, not a gift. She didn't want Carrie to worry about guarding her words. "He has his reasons," she finally said. "He and Jasper don't get along."

"That could be it," Carrie agreed.

"I *did* see him today." Pearl couldn't stop her heart from fluttering. "He was buying a dress for Sarah for the tea party. She asked me if I'd go with her."

"I hope you said yes."

"Of course." She couldn't disappoint Sarah. "I love that little girl as if she were my own."

"And Matt?" Carrie said gently. "Do you love him, too?"

Her body tensed at the prospect of admitting her feelings. If she told Carrie how she felt, she might hurt her cousin all over again.

"It's okay." Carrie came to sit next to her. "He wasn't right for me. I know that now. But I do think he's right for you, and you're right for him."

Pearl stroked Toby's back through the blanket. "Marriage scares me."

"Me, too." Carrie shivered but not with dread. "My mother said love made marriage the most special place in the world. I didn't understand, but I do now. When I'm with Dan, I'm starting to feel like we belong together."

Pearl felt the same way with Matt. Could she overcome her fear of the physical part of marriage? A kiss would tell her what she needed to know, but when would it happen? How could she test the waters without embarrassing herself with Matt? She didn't know, but today she had the faith to hope.

Chapter Eighteen

Pearl looked out the window of Jasper's store and saw a smattering of raindrops. She'd asked Jasper for permission to leave early for the tea party and he'd given it, but he'd also asked her to dust the shelves before she left. The coming storm gave her an excuse to put off the tedious chore. Not only did she want to keep her promise to Sarah, she was also tired of Jasper's company. All day she'd felt his eyes on her back. Was he deliberately crowding her, or was she overreacting? Pearl didn't know, but she'd had all she could take of his strange ways.

Eager to leave, she went to his office. Through the open door, she saw him dipping a pen in ink. "Mr. Kling?"

"Pearl!" His arm jerked and the ink spattered. His brow furrowed with annoyance.

"It's starting to rain. May I leave now?"

"Is the dusting finished?"

"No, but I'll come early tomorrow."

The pen hung in his hand, dripping ink on the ledger sheet. She knew he'd heard her. He heard everything. She tried again. "The rain's getting worse."

"Yes, a storm." He set down the pen.

A gust of rain hammered the window. The glass

shook but didn't break. Her belly clenched. "I need to get home."

"But you'll catch your death," he said smoothly. "Wait out the storm here. I'll walk you home when it's over."

"No thank you," she managed. "I have a-a commitment." She didn't want to mention her promise to Sarah. "My father's expecting me."

"Tobias and I are friends." His eyes glittered behind his spectacles. "He'd expect me to watch out for you."

No way would she be alone with Jasper in a store closed for business, especially not in a rainstorm. She wanted to walk out, but she couldn't risk antagonizing him. All week she'd worried that Jasper had begun to suspect her father. If she reacted now, she'd be denying her father's seeming trust of him. She had to behave as normally as possible. "I really do have to leave." She tried to sound regretful. "If you'll excuse me—"

"Just one thing."

Ignoring him, she went to the storeroom where she kept her cloak. The size of a bedroom, it held crates and a hodge-podge of unsold items. Two windows let in light, and a third beam came from the doorway. As she reached for her hat, something cut off the light from the door. She turned and saw Jasper with his hands on the doorframe, blocking the way out.

"Stay," he said in a silky tone. "I'll look out for you."

"I can't." She forced a smile. "If you'll excuse me, I have to get home."

He stepped into the room, cornering her by a shelf holding women's shoes. Rain turned into a torrent against the glass, and the light dimmed to a smoky haze. She smelled the starch in his shirt and the thickness of his breath. In his eyes she saw a gleam magnified by his spectacles…the same gleam she'd seen in Franklin Dean's eyes when he'd purposely taken a wrong turn on that buggy ride. Sweat beaded on her brow and her stomach recoiled. She needed to think, but she'd been reduced to a bundle of reactions. Fight or flee... She didn't know.

Jasper smiled at her.

She wanted to look away, but she feared turning her back. She settled for taking a step to the side. Her foot caught the corner of a crate and she lost her balance. As she reached for a shelf to steady herself, Jasper gripped her elbow.

"I've got you," he said.

Pearl pulled away from him, but he didn't let go of her arm. Darkness pressed from the ceiling and walls. She thought of the leather hood of Franklin Dean's buggy, the way it blocked the sun. Her pulse pounded in her ears, blurring all conscious thought except for one truth. Not even for her father's safety could she risk another minute in Jasper's presence. She jerked out of his grasp and ran out of the storeroom.

"Pearl! Wait."

As she raced to the front of the store, she realized she'd left her cloak and hat in the storeroom. She didn't dare go back for them. Silently she prayed Jasper hadn't already locked the front door. She gripped the knob and it turned. The door opened and she fled into the rain. Wanting to vanish from sight, she sped across the street, ruining her shoes in the puddles and staining her stockings. Rain drenched her hair and face. Mud clung to the hem of her gown, weighting her down.

She wanted to go home, but the house would be full of little girls and their mothers. Neither did she want to see her father until she'd regained her composure. Desperate for a dry place to hide, she slipped down an alley and took cover under a staircase. Shivering, she huddled next to a stack of wood and a barrel that smelled of food scraps. Bowing her head, she sobbed with the freedom given only by privacy.

When he fetched Sarah from the tea party, Matt deliberately arrived late. He wanted a few words with Tobias, and he didn't want to have them in front of ten talkative women and a bevy of little girls. He also needed to see Pearl. Since the day at the dress shop, he'd questioned key members of the G.O. Every one of them had complained about Scottie's girls shopping on Dryer Street. Would Jasper punish Pearl for her kindness to the two prostitutes? It seemed all too possible.

The dreary weather didn't help his mood. Dark clouds had rolled in from the west and turned Cheyenne into box-like shadows. Expecting a storm, he'd put on an oilcloth poncho that hung to his knees. It protected his clothing and his gun belt, but it didn't shield his gut from constant churning. With his nerves tight, he walked up the steps to Carrie's house.

Before he could ring the bell, she flung open the door. "Oh! You're not Pearl!"

"She's not here?"

"She's late. She missed the party." Carrie clipped the words. "She said she'd be here. She promised Sarah. Something's wrong. I feel it."

So did Matt. No way would Pearl break her word to a child. He had to get to Jasper's store. If the G.O. had discovered the ruse, Pearl would be in danger.

"I'm going after her," he said to Carrie.

"Hurry!"

As Matt turned from the door, Tobias strode into the foyer and lifted his coat. "I'm going with you."

The old man looked ashen. "It's raining, sir. Stay here."

Tobias glowered. "Do you think I care about getting wet?"

"No, but you can't help me."

"But—"

"Sir, with all due respect, you'll be in the way."

The men traded a look, then Tobias accepted the decision with a nod. "Bring her back, Wiley. If something happens to her I'll—"

"I know." If something happened to Sarah, Matt wouldn't be able to stop himself. The wail of a baby—Pearl's baby—cut through the air from a back room. Toby wanted his mama, and Matt wanted to find her. He looked past Carrie to Tobias. The men exchanged a glance only a father would understand, then Matt turned on his heels and went to find Pearl.

To save time, he cut down an alley that led to Jasper's shop. As soon as he rounded the corner, he heard a woman sobbing. The misery of it carried over the splash of the rain and the thud of his boots. As he picked up his pace, he heard a gasp and the crying stopped.

Peering down the alley, he spotted a stairwell that offered cover from the storm. The dusky light had the sheen of pewter, but he could still see colors. Between a wood pile and barrel of scraps, he spotted a tangle of white-gold hair, blue calico, Pearl's pink cheeks and her red lips rounded with fright.

Looking at her now, Matt surrendered to the love he was utterly powerless to stop. It consumed him. It bullied him. Instead of setting him free, the depth of his love enslaved him. He had to protect her, and that meant shielding her from storms of all kinds—the one in his heart, the one raining down on her now. He didn't know what had driven her into the rain without her cloak, but he had his suspicions. If Jasper had harmed her, justice *would* be served.

First, though, he had to get Pearl out of the rain. Her dress was clinging to her legs and her hair was a soggy mess. When he reached the stairwell, the wind gusted. To shield her, he stretched his arms to make a wall of sorts with the slicker. He put one hand on the beam supporting the stairs and the other on a riser, making himself a wall between Pearl and the wind. He felt a hint of warmth and hoped she felt it, too.

"What happened?" he said gently.

She shook her head.

He couldn't tolerate silence. "Did he touch you? Did he—"

"No." The word came out in a choked cry. "He—he—" She pressed her hands to her face. "Go away, Matt. *Please.*"

"Absolutely not."

"I'll—I'll be all right. I just need to—" As a cry escaped from her throat, she buried her face in her hands. Her shoulders shook with tears she couldn't stop.

Matt knew too much about women who'd been assaulted. Some got mad and wanted to murder their attackers. A few fled. Far too many blamed themselves for what a man did. That reaction troubled him, but he understood the logic. No one wanted to admit to being a victim. It stripped a man of his pride and a woman of her peace. He couldn't let Pearl believe that lie.

"Look at me, darlin'."

She shook her head.

He kept his voice low. "You know I won't leave you like this."

A squeak came from her throat.

"That's right," he drawled. "I'm here to keep you safe."

If he touched her, she'd balk. Except for the sound of their breath, he stayed silent. The next move had to be hers and it was…. Her index fingers twitched, then she moved her pinkies and revealed her tear-stained eyes. He'd never seen a woman so vulnerable, so in need of a man's strong arms. He ached to hold her, but he feared the consequences. The shape of her would be sealed in his memory. Even worse, the closeness might frighten her. Whatever Matt did, he wanted it to be best for Pearl. Whatever she needed, he'd give to her.

He used the tone he used with Sarah when she skinned a knee. "I'm right here. Tell me what you need."

Slowly she slid her hands down her cheeks until they cupped her jaw, then she crossed her arms over her heart and squeezed hard. After a deep breath, she lowered her hands to her sides and looked defiantly into his eyes.

Matt saw fear and something deeper, something he recognized as a man. She wanted to be kissed. The slicker made a wall of sorts, a covering. It made the space small and dark…intimate. More than anything, he wanted to kiss her fully. He wanted to hold her in his arms and keep her safe. But at what cost? He couldn't promise her more than this moment. A woman like Pearl deserved everything a man had to give.

He touched her cheek with his thumb, wiping rain and tears from her hot skin. His heart pounded with a love beyond his understanding. "Ah, Pearl," he murmured. "How did this happen?"

"I—I don't know."

"Neither do I," he said. "But it did."

The both knew what *it* was. She wanted to be kissed, and he wanted to kiss her. He swallowed hard, feeling the tightness and the longing, then he touched her cheek. Gently he tucked a strand of damp hair behind her ear.

He opened his mouth to speak, to say *We shouldn't do this.* But her lids fluttered shut and her chin lifted. When he didn't move, she opened her eyes. What he saw tied his heart in knots. She wanted to kiss him, but she feared her reaction. Would she triumph or panic?

One code of honor required him to maintain his distance. He had no business kissing a woman outside the bounds of courtship, especially not a woman as vulnerable as Pearl. Another code—a code of men at war—demanded he help her up and over this hill. Was she ready for this moment? What if kissing her destroyed the fragile progress she'd made? He saw costs to himself, as well. If they kissed, he'd never forget it. He'd remember the silk of her lips, the saltiness of tears mixed with rain. Not even whistling "Dixie" would chase away the wanting.

So be it. Pearl needed his help.

Stepping closer, he touched her cheek with the pad of his thumb. She bit her lips, then relaxed them. A tremble pulsed to his fingers, but her eyes flared with courage. When she swayed ever so slightly in his direction, he brushed her lips with his. Once, twice. When her eyes stayed closed, he lingered over the third kiss without reluctance. A cry came from her throat. Before he could draw back, she wrapped her arms around his neck and pulled him as close as she could. The kiss turned fierce, as if she were fighting memories. Just as suddenly, she relaxed in his arms and he knew she'd won the war.

He kissed her back sweetly, tenderly…long enough to feel her confidence build. He didn't want to stop, but he had to pull back. A sweet saint and a bitter sinner… They had no future. As he broke the connection of their lips, he tucked her head under his chin. "I didn't mean for that to happen."

"I did," she whispered.

With their hearts beating in perfect time, he searched for the right words. She'd crossed a battlefield today. Together they'd fought an enemy and she hadn't panicked. He hoped the kiss was enough, because he had nothing else to give.

"Now you know," he said with authority.

"I do?"

If she needed reassurance, he'd give it to her. "That kiss… You don't need to be afraid anymore. Someday you'll meet a man. He'll—"

She whispered against his jaw. "I've already met him."

He understood but wished he didn't. "Don't say that."

"Why not?"

"I'm not right for you, Pearl. I've done things. I've—"

She pushed back and looked into his eyes. He saw questions in her gaze, but he also saw a bold certainty. This woman didn't believe in cowering before anyone. She'd risk her heart for him.

"Ah, Pearl." He couldn't deny his feelings, but neither could he tell her the truth. If he admitted to loving her, where would they be? In a hole deeper than the one he'd just dug. He needed to explain himself to her, but not here. Not with the rain pelting them and Pearl soaked to the skin. Not next to a heap of garbage in a dirty alley.

He took off his hat and put it on her head, then he hunched out of the slicker and wrapped it around her shivering body. He put his arm around her waist to protect her as much as he could, then he led her away from the stairwell.

"We have to talk," he said. "My house is around the corner."

Chapter Nineteen

When Matt put his hat on her head, the warmth of the headband reached Pearl's skin. She thought of her mother calling a woman's hair her crowning glory and wondered if Virginia Oliver had ever worn her husband's hat in the rain.

She wanted to skip and dance and celebrate her victory. Franklin Dean had left her with scars, but he hadn't maimed her for life. She loved Matt Wiley with her entire being, and she'd tested herself with a kiss. She couldn't think of a more challenging circumstance than being cornered in a dark alley. Matt's slicker had blocked the light. Shiny and black, it could have reminded her of Franklin Dean's buggy, but it hadn't. She'd been aware only of Matt studying her expression, gauging her courage and giving her a choice.

Today's kiss did more than conquer her fears. It had revealed Matt's heart. He wouldn't have kissed her with such care if he didn't have feelings for her, but something—the gophers holes she'd sensed earlier—were holding him back. As much as she wanted to shout with joy, her happiness had to be contained until they sorted their differences.

The wind pushed them up the street with powerful gusts. Hunkering forward, Matt tucked her against his side. As they rounded a corner, he indicated the third bungalow on the left.

"This is it," he said.

"It's homey."

What it lacked in feminine grace, it made up for in masculine effort. Brown gingham curtains, store-bought and an inch too short, hung in the window, and a scraggly juniper grew next to a rickety porch. The needles shimmered in the fading light, a reminder her father would be worried. She hated to upset him, but she had to speak to Matt.

As he held the door, she stepped into a mix of shadows and empty walls. Another window allowed light into a corner kitchen. Near a galvanized sink she saw a shelf stacked with canned goods and another one holding tin plates, glasses and jars.

A match scraped and she turned. As the tip flared, orange light bathed Matt's face and illuminated a stone fireplace. As he touched the tiny flame to the kindling, it caught with a whoosh and lit up the room. Pearl saw a chair, a table, a hurricane lamp and a horsehair divan. Sarah had left her doll, Annie, sitting primly in the chair.

Matt added a split of wood to the fire, then faced her from across the room. Much like the day they'd met, he looked her up and down. "Are you hurt?"

"I'm fine." She took off the slicker and hung it by the door, then she walked to the fire to dry her dress. Matt had gotten wet, too. She considered telling him to change into a dry shirt, but he looked lost in thought as he stared into the blaze. Pearl stepped to his side. Soon the fire would warm them both.

Staring into the flames, he broke the silence. "We have to talk."

Would he start with the reason she'd run into the rain or with the kiss? Pearl cared far more about the kiss, so she tipped up her chin and smiled at him. Feeling bold, she stood on her toes and brushed her lips across his cheek. His whiskers tickled her lips, and she smelled the dampness of the storm on his shirt. When she stepped back, he looked completely undone.

More confident than she'd ever been, she rested her hand on his biceps. "That kiss was the nicest thing that's ever happened to me."

"Don't say that," he answered. "It was a mistake."

When he looked into her eyes, she saw turmoil in the pale green depths. Just as she'd been hurt, so had Matt. She felt certain of the reason. Sarah's mother had broken his heart. Just as Pearl had needed someone to help her bury the past, so did Matt. Full of hope, she took a chance. "I love you."

A groan rumbled in his throat. "Don't love me, Pearl. I can't love you back."

She didn't believe him. "Why not?"

"I just can't."

The fire showed every crease in his face, the dark crescents under his eyes. The log hissed and snapped. The roof echoed with the rain. Pearl had learned from her father to let troubled souls find their own way. She'd wait all night if that's what Matt needed. Still silent, he poked the fire with an iron rod. Sparks shot up the chimney and died. He set down the poker, then indicated the divan. "Sit down."

As she sat, he stayed standing with his back to her. The glow of the blaze turned his body into a black silhouette. "You don't really know me, Pearl. You don't know what I've done."

"It doesn't matter."

He gave a snide laugh. "You don't know what you're saying."

"Then explain it to me."

A gust of wind rattled the door. A draft reached the fire and made it flare. Still silent, he stood with his hands on his hips, his back straight and his feet planted wide as he spoke to the flames. "I'm a murderer, Pearl. It happened in the war, but that doesn't excuse what I did."

She'd been expecting him to say he'd been a bad husband, that he'd driven Bettina away by being cold and obsessed with his work. A murderer? She knew he'd been a Texas Ranger and a soldier, a man likely to have blood on his hands. She'd never expected some of that blood to be innocent. Her entire body recoiled, a first reaction she chose to ignore. She believed in the God who forgave everyone, including lawmen who made mistakes and men like Franklin Dean who deserved punishment more than mercy. She didn't care what Matt had done, but she cared deeply about his soul.

Her heart ached for him. "How did it happen?"

"I didn't start out bad," he said wearily. "I served proudly as a captain in Hood's Texas Brigade." His voice rang with the pride of a soldier. "We were in northern Virginia near Spotsylvania. We stopped two federal corps that day, but it came at a price. Most of my men died."

Pearl knew firsthand that violence begat violence. After being attacked, she'd beat her pillow as if it were Franklin Dean's face. "It must have been terrible."

"It was." His shoulders relaxed, but he kept his back to her. "Only eight of us lived. That night, we were ordered to patrol for spies. To this day, I don't recall approaching Amos McGuckin's farm. One minute we were in the thick of the forest. The next we'd ridden into a clearing with a big house and a barn. It was late, almost midnight. The old man came out carrying a lantern as if he'd been expecting someone."

Matt blew out a breath. "One of my men—Hardin was

his name—accused him of being a spy for the Blues. Why I believed him, I'll never know."

Pearl sprang to his side. "War makes people crazy. You were—"

"Don't make excuses for me." He clipped his words. "I was in charge. I should have stopped what happened. We had cause to question the man, but we didn't take the time. Three of my men charged up the porch and dragged McGuckin into the yard. The torches burned like the sun that night. I saw every line in the old man's face."

Pearl closed her eyes, but she smelled the kerosene and saw the faces of crazed men. She stood up from the divan. "Matt—"

"I'm poison."

She touched his arm, but he jerked away. "You're human. God forgives."

He turned to her with a look of pure hate. "Maybe *He* can forgive me, but I can't forgive *Him*. He let me murder a harmless old man. Why didn't he break my arm or shoot me in the head? Why not strike me blind? I deserve to die for what I did."

"There's still forgiveness." Her words seemed paltry compared to his guilt, but she had to try.

He shook his head. "We lynched him, Pearl. Hardin tossed a rope over a branch, and the next thing I knew McGuckin was kicking and leaking like a side of beef." His voice dropped even lower. "His daughter saw the whole thing from an upstairs window."

Pearl couldn't bear to picture her father dying such a death. She wanted to comfort Matt, but he'd gone to a place she'd never been. "I can't imagine."

"No, you can't." He stood taller. "Do you know who the old man was waiting for?"

"No," she said quietly.

"He was waiting for his son, a soldier just like me...a Confederate officer. He rode into the yard five minutes too late. Why he didn't shoot me dead, I'll never know."

"What did he do?"

"He went crazy with grief. We rode out before he came to his senses."

She had to bite her lip to keep from crying for him. He didn't need her pity. He needed to know he wasn't the first man to do something unforgivable. "I see," she said. "You're as bad as the man who raped me."

His eyes burned with righteous indignation. "I'd *never* hurt a woman."

"Sin is sin, Matt." When it came to forgiveness, Pearl knew the need to give it and the need to receive it. God's love filled the gap in between. "Everyone falls short. Some mistakes are worse than others, but they're all fish from the same barrel. If we leave them to rot, they stink."

She'd earned his attention, so she took a chance and tugged on his arm. "Sit with me."

They stepped to the divan and sat. As she angled her knees toward his, he met her gaze. "I want to ask you something."

"What is it?"

"Have you forgiven the man who raped you?"

A hard question demanded an honest answer. "Not completely, but I've tried. It helps that he's dead."

He sat back as if she'd slapped him. "I should be dead, too."

Belatedly she saw the meaning behind his question. He'd been seeking forgiveness for himself and hadn't found it. She had to explain before he lost hope. "I'm glad he's dead because he can't threaten me anymore." She thought of the harrowing days at Swan's Nest and winced. "If he'd *asked* for forgiveness, I'd have given it. He never did."

Matt held up his hand, taking hers with it in a kind of pledge. "I'd give my life to change what I did."

"Does the man's family know that?"

"I don't know."

"Why not?" Out of respect, she made her voice firm. He needed a man's reckoning, not a woman's pity.

"I wrote a letter," he admitted. "If the son received it, he never wrote back."

Pearl held his hand tighter. "You might not be able to make amends to the McGuckin family, but you don't have to carry the burden. Jesus paid the price for what you did."

As he stared at the fire, she saw their future teetering on the scale of "what if…." If Matt found forgiveness, they could be together. If he clung to his bitterness, he'd be pulling in one direction and she'd be pulling in the other. They'd always be at odds. If she pursued him, she'd be going against both God's ways and her desire for a husband who shared her faith. Even worse, she'd be standing between God and Matt. If he rejected God's grace, she'd have to let him go. Even more than he needed a wife, he needed a day of reckoning for what he'd done.

Abruptly he released her fingers and shot to his feet. He strode to a dark corner, then faced her with his hands on his hips. "That's enough about my stupidity. What happened with Jasper?"

Please, God. Touch Matt's troubled heart. She wasn't ready to give up on him. "I can see why you're mad at God. I was mad at Him after what happened to me. Sometimes I still am, but that's part of being human."

His mouth pulled into a sneer. "I hear that kind of talk from Dan all the time. When some fool gets himself shot, he tells him about Jesus and those pearly gates." Sarcasm turned his drawl to syrup. "I've had about all I can stand, Pearl. Don't pester me."

"You're being stubborn," she said quietly.

"I'm being honest."

"So am I. God's merciful. He loves us."

Matt's lips hooked into a sneer. "How do you know that? Are you going to tell me Toby's a *blessing* to you? Are you going to say God's good because you were raped but not murdered?"

"Of course not!"

He glared at her. "God's either cruel or He doesn't care. Either way, I'm not interested."

His words were meant to build a wall between them. She couldn't go through it or around it, nor could she scale the height of it. All she could do was speak to him from the other side. "I may not understand everything that happens, but I know there's more to this life than being miserable. There's love, Matt. There's family and hope and helping each other. I believe in Heaven with my whole heart. When we get there, we'll reap rewards."

With the wall at his back, he chortled. "If God *rewards* me, I'll be frying in Hell."

"That's right."

Matt eyed her thoughtfully. "I wasn't expecting that answer."

"You murdered a man." She spoke with calm certainty. "Someone has to pay for that crime, and someone has. Jesus died for all our mistakes—every lie, every murder and yes, every rape. That includes what you did to that poor old man."

Matt stayed by the window, a shadow backed into a corner. She prayed he'd find peace. *Please, Lord. Soften his heart.*

She looked for a softening of his features. Instead a hateful gleam burned in his eyes. "Forget it, Pearl. I'm asking you again. What happened with Jasper?"

Pearl gave up. If Matt didn't want to make peace with God, she couldn't force the issue. Until that day came, she had no choice but to love him from afar. With a deep breath, she hid the kiss in her heart, tucking it away just as she'd tucked away the ribbons.

Looking at Pearl, aglow with the fire in the hearth, Matt wished things could be different. A long time ago he'd had the faith of a child. But then he'd gone to war and his eyes had been opened. The past hour had opened them even wider. When he'd kissed Pearl, he'd expected to pay with his heart. Instead he'd paid with something far more costly. He'd told her his secret.

Between the fire's warmth and her sweetness, he'd lost his ability to hold the shame inside. He could have stopped the lynching, but he hadn't. Matt knew men like Jasper in his marrow because he'd been one of them. If he could stop the Golden Order now, perhaps he could forgive himself for murdering Amos McGuckin.

Until he crossed that line, he had no business kissing a preacher's daughter. When she'd kissed his cheek, he'd almost kissed her back. But then she'd told him she loved him and he'd come to his senses. He had to get her home and out of reach, but first he had to know about Jasper. Something had sent Pearl running into the rain without her cloak. "Tell me," he repeated. "Why were you in the alley?"

She stared at him for five seconds, then sighed. "I asked Jasper if I could leave early because of the rain."

She told him how Jasper had followed her into the storeroom and trapped her. With each detail, Matt clenched his jaw tighter. Whether Jasper meant to scare Pearl or harm her, he couldn't say and it didn't matter. The shopkeeper had meant to frighten her.

She raised her chin. "I didn't panic until afterward. That's when you found me. I have to thank you. That kiss—"

"Pearl, don't."

"Don't what?" She said, scolding him. "Don't thank you for finding me in the rain? For being good to me?"

"I'm not good." Hadn't she been listening? Talking about God and Amos McGuckin in the same breath had Matt all churned up. Even if he stopped the Golden Order, he'd never forgive himself for what he'd done. He'd never forgive God, either. With that hate burning in his belly, he'd never be the right man for Pearl. She deserved to hear the decision from him.

"About that kiss," he said. "Don't read too much into it. It was nice. That's all."

She looked at the fire, then spoke in a voice he could barely hear. "It was more than nice."

He tried to sound bored. "I don't mean to be harsh, but you don't know about such things."

Confusion clouded her wide eyes. "The kiss was special. I felt—"

"Forget it, Pearl. It's over."

He'd told the truth and lied in the same breath. The kiss was over but not the memory of it. He wanted to kiss her again. He'd make that one *nice,* too. Nice and long. Nice and slow. So full of *nice* she'd feel loved and cherished until death did them part. As much as he wanted to tell the truth, he couldn't. Unless he could be a husband to her in heart, soul and deed, he had no business courting her. He'd been half-hearted with Bettina. He wouldn't repeat that mistake with Pearl.

He crossed the room and added a log to the fire. Sarah's doll caught his eye and his belly lurched. His little girl still needed a mother, and they both loved Pearl. Toby needed a father, and Matt wanted to be that man. With the flames bright, he looked at Pearl. The misery on her face nearly broke him, but he had to protect her from false hope. "I enjoyed kissing you, but it *was* just a kiss."

"I see."

"You didn't panic. That's what counts." He felt like a two-faced liar. What mattered was that they loved each other.

She looked at him with a fresh glint in her eyes. "You're making excuses."

"It's the truth."

"I don't believe you."

How could he escape this mess without lying? "Forget it happened. No matter what's going on between us, I'm not the right man for you."

She jumped to her feet. "But you are. I love you."

Her hope rubbed salt in his wounds. "I can't love you, Pearl. Not like you deserve. What happened just now— It's not what you think. It's not love."

"Then what is it?"

"Just...stuff."

"Stuff?"

"Yeah." He latched on to the one thing he knew for sure. "Life isn't a fairy tale, darlin'. You're not Cinderella and I'm not Prince Charming."

"I know that!"

"Do you?"

"Yes." She looked him in the eye. "I also know a lie when I hear one."

He put grit in his voice. He had to stop this before he found himself on his knees begging for her hand in marriage. "Let me make this clear. The kiss meant nothing. If you had more experience, you'd know that."

She turned abruptly to the fire to hide her face. He imagined tears streaming down her cheeks, mimicking the rain that had coursed down them in the alley. He'd never felt lower in his life. He couldn't leave her hurt and confused, so he stepped closer. As he raised his hand to touch her hair, someone pounded on the door.

Pearl shot to her feet. "Who could that be?"

"I don't know." He went to the window and peeked through the curtain. He saw two men. One he welcomed. The other scared him to death.

Chapter Twenty

Pearl desperately needed a moment to collect her thoughts, but Matt had already opened the door. Dan strode into the room with rain dripping off his slicker and the brim of his hat. Behind him she saw her father. A heavy coat protected him from the rain, but his face had lost its color. She hurried to his side and hugged him. "Papa, I'm fine."

He squeezed her tight, then looked at her from head to toe, taking in everything from her wet hair to the muddy hem of her gown. His cheeks changed from pale to ruddy. "What happened?"

"I'm not hurt, but Jasper—"

"What did he do?"

A bluish vein bulged on his temple. She thought of his weak heart and wished they'd never come to Cheyenne. She wished she'd never set eyes on Jasper Kling or Matt Wiley. They'd both hurt her today, Jasper with the threat of violence and Matt with his bitterness. Pearl didn't want to believe the kiss had been "just stuff" to him, but his arrogance about it shook her confidence. Had he meant it? Or was he protecting her from the man he believed himself to be? Pearl didn't see a murderer when she looked at Matt. She saw the man she loved.

"What happened?" her father said again.

She told the story with complete calm, but his expression turned murderous. When she finished, Dan explained how Tobias had come to the sheriff's office and together they'd gone to Jasper's store.

"We saw him leave in the rain," Dan explained. "He went to the bank. Troy Martin, Howard Moreland and Gibson Armond walked in right after him."

"Everyone but me," Tobias said quietly. "We all know what that means."

"They no longer trust you," Matt answered.

Tobias's brow furrowed. "I was told to be at Martin's place Saturday afternoon at three o'clock."

Far from town…far from witnesses. Pearl shuddered at the implication.

Tobias looked at Matt. "I'm afraid I'm not cut out for this kind of work."

"You did fine, sir."

He looked chagrined. "I have to admit, I spoke my mind at the last G.O. meeting. The way Jasper was talking about those women from the Silver Slipper had to be stopped. He took offense."

"I didn't help," Pearl added. "I let them in his store. Today he'd treated me like one of them."

"Don't blame yourselves." Dan crossed his arms. "Wiley and I have been questioning members of the G.O. for days now. We expected trouble, just not this soon."

Matt looked at her with a fury she hadn't seen in him before now. "You're both targets." He turned to Dan. "What time does the train leave for Denver?"

"Denver!" Pearl gaped at him.

"That's right." He put his hands on his hips. "You and Toby and your father are getting on a train *tonight*."

"You can't send us away," she protested. "You don't have that right."

"Oh yes, I do."

No, he didn't. Not if he didn't love her...not if he thought the kiss was "just stuff." She opened her mouth to argue, but her father cut her off.

"Pardon me, Deputy. But I have a say—"

"Not anymore." Matt tapped his own chest so hard she heard bone hitting bone. "This is *my* fight."

"I won't go," she argued.

"Yes, you will," Tobias insisted.

"But Papa—"

"You'll do it for Toby."

If she returned to Denver, she might never see Matt again. How did a woman choose between her child and the man she loved? Even as the question formed, she knew the answer. A mother protected her child. She ran in front of freight wagons, and she got on trains for Denver even if it meant leaving her heart behind. She turned to Matt. "My father's right. When's the next train?"

Dan answered. "Tomorrow at nine."

"We'll go then," Tobias replied.

With her heart breaking, she focused on the tasks at hand. She needed to pack and say goodbye to Carrie. Sarah, too.

Matt let out a breath as if he'd been holding it. "The G.O. knows where you live. A night at a hotel would be wise."

Tobias's brow furrowed. "If we act out of the ordinary, they'll know you're on to them. *We* might be safer, but you'll be in more trouble."

Dan looked at Matt. "He's right."

"We'll stay at Carrie's," Tobias said firmly.

Matt turned to the window. "I don't like it. Things have a way of getting out of control."

"It's the best choice," Tobias argued. "We'll stick to the plan and trust God for protection."

Matt looked back at Tobias with a sneer. "Trust whoever you want, Reverend. *I'm* trusting my instincts. I'll stand guard tonight."

Tobias nodded. "Fair enough."

Pearl saw a problem. "What about Sarah?"

"She can stay with Mrs. Holcombe."

"I need to say goodbye," she said softly. "If I just disappear, she'll be hurt." Sarah would recall her mother leaving the same way. Tonight would leave another mark on her tender heart.

Matt looked as if he'd been kicked. "You can say goodbye at Carrie's. I'll take her to Mrs. Holcombe's, then come back."

Pearl dreaded saying goodbye to Sarah. She'd do it gently, but how did a woman *gently* break a child's heart? Pearl couldn't change the facts, but she'd try to soften the loss. "I'll be careful with her," she said to Matt. "I promise."

"Thank you." His eyes held gratitude and something more…something sharp and painful. She didn't want to leave him, but the Golden Order had given her no choice.

Her father watched her thoughtfully, then spoke to Dan. "Would you take Pearl to Carrie's? I'd like a word with Matt."

"Sure."

"I'll wait with you," she protested. Her father knew how she felt about Matt. She didn't want him interfering.

Matt indicated the door. "Go on now. Your father and I have business."

When the men traded a look, Pearl knew they had a secret. She didn't like it, but nothing would break her father's will and Matt had the same stubbornness. When she looked at Matt, his eyes were as bitter as ever. Tomorrow she'd be on that train to Denver. There would be no tender goodbyes, only the memory of a kiss and a drawer full of ribbons. With her heart aching, she headed for the door.

As soon as Pearl left with Dan, Matt faced Tobias. For one crazy moment, he'd wondered if the old man was going to give him another Bible lesson. Tobias sincerely believed God would be watching over them, but Matt knew otherwise. *He'd* be watching. *God* would be sleeping like he'd slept that night in Virginia. "What's on your mind?"

"They want you dead, Matt."

"Figures." He'd asked a lot of questions and pushed some high-powered people. Chester Gates and Howard Moreland had been among them. "How do you know?"

"Martin's having second thoughts." Tobias described how he'd run into the rancher and they'd had a chat. Martin didn't mind hanging a horse thief, but he'd balked at taking down a lawman for doing his job. "The man's got blood on his hands and he knows it. Under the right circumstances, I believe he'll turn on the others."

"Would he testify in court?"

"Possibly," Tobias replied. "Moreland's the one who's leading the push to see you dead."

"I talked to him last week." Matt had seen craziness in the rancher's eyes, the kind of rage that fed on violence. "The man's got a mean streak."

"So does Jasper." Tobias grimaced. "He said terrible things about those women who hassled him about the mirror. Why he turned so hard against you, I don't know."

"He's got a secret." Matt stared at the dying embers. "I know what it is, and I let him know it. What about Gates?"

"He goes along with Jasper."

"And Armond?"

"He got robbed again. He says you should've stopped it."

"I wish I could have." Matt wished a lot of things. He wished Amos McGuckin was still alive, and that Pearl hadn't been attacked. If he were God, she wouldn't be in danger. "I'm sorry for what happened to Pearl today. It's best that she leave. You, too."

"I didn't go into this blind," Tobias replied. "I knew it was dangerous, possibly for both of us. I have no regrets, but I *do* have a question."

"What is it?"

"I just walked in on you and my daughter alone in a dark house. I'm not questioning your honor. I know the need that brought you here. I'm questioning your intentions."

"Pearl and I have no future, sir."

"She loves you, Matt."

"She shouldn't."

"That's not your call."

Matt didn't want to be having this conversation, but he respected Tobias. "I'd never do anything to hurt her, and that's why I'm sending her away. Pearl and I…" He shook his head. "She's too good for me."

"We agree there," Tobias said drily. "My wife deserved better than me, but I'm the man she chose." He looked at Matt for a long time, giving him time to speak. Matt refused. If he opened his mouth, they'd be talking about psalms and night lunacy and men standing watch like he'd do tonight.

Tobias finally broke the tension. "We'll be on the morning train, but I have another request."

The old man had a lot of requirements. "What is it?"

"Be straight with her before we go."

"That's not wise, sir."

"Why not?"

"It just isn't."

"You're being stupid again. Prideful, too."

Matt took the insult. He'd hurt Pearl and had it coming. Eager to be done with the conversation, he crossed the room and lifted his hat. "Let's go."

Tobias frowned. "We shouldn't be seen together."

"There's more risk to you walking around alone," Matt countered. "We're headed to the livery. I have to get my horse."

Side by side, they walked across town. The rain had stopped, but massive puddles mirrored the clouds in a way that made the world seem huge. Matt felt that weight on his shoulders. If he blinked, it would crush him. Tonight he'd stand watch. Tomorrow he'd make sure Pearl got on the train to Denver. Once Jasper and the Golden Order were brought to justice, he'd sleep. If the dreams didn't come, he'd take Sarah and find Pearl. Until then, he'd stand guard. He'd be the watchman, sleepless and alone as he protected the people he loved.

Chapter Twenty-One

As Pearl walked up the porch steps with Dan, Carrie flung open the door. When she saw Pearl's disheveled appearance, her eyes flared and she hurried across the porch. As they met, she gripped Pearl's elbows. "Are you all right?"

"I'm fine." Pearl looked past her to the foyer. "Is everyone gone?"

"Everyone except Sarah. She's in the kitchen with Mrs. Dinwiddie." Carrie turned to Dan with a question in her eyes. The sight of them sharing a meaningful look hit Pearl hard. Tonight Matt had sent her away. He had a good reason, but she yearned for a promise. *I'll find you in Denver.* Did he love her? She'd thought so in the alley, but what did she know about men? Maybe the kiss really had been "just stuff" to him. Her heart told her otherwise, but it had been wrong before. Another first reaction…another mistake.

Damp and chilled, Pearl indicated the door. "Let's go inside."

The women turned and stepped into the foyer. Following them, Dan closed the door tight, then hung up his hat and slicker. Carrie led Pearl to the parlor where they sat on the divan. Dan stood by the window, watching the street with his arms folded across his chest.

Carrie took Pearl's cold hand in her warm one. "I was worried to death. What happened?"

"I'll tell you everything, but where's Toby?"

"Asleep in his crib."

Pearl wanted to hold him, but he needed his rest. Calm and confident, she described the trouble with Jasper and how Matt had found her in the alley. She wanted to tell her about the kiss, but not in front of Dan. She finished by telling Carrie about Tobias's involvement with the Golden Order and the fear that the vigilante group would try to harm him. "That's why we have to go back to Denver. We're leaving on the morning train."

"But you can't," Carrie cried. "I'll miss you too much."

"I'll miss you, too." Pearl loved her friends at Swan's Nest, but she and Carrie were family. "I have to think of Toby. And you, too. As long as we're under your roof, you're in danger."

The color drained from Carrie's face. Instinctively, she turned to Dan. "Do you think they'll come here?"

"Possibly." His brown eyes filled with a protective gleam. "You won't be alone, Carrie. I'll be standing guard with Matt. All night if that's what it takes."

"Thank you, Dan."

Carrie's voice rang with the richness of love. Envy washed through Pearl in a wave. Not only did Carrie have the security of her own home, Pearl sensed that she'd soon have a husband to go with it.

Slightly flushed, Carrie turned back to Pearl. "I know you have to leave, but promise me you'll come back."

"Maybe for a visit." Pearl glanced at Dan and saw him trading another look with Carrie. A second rush of envy sucked the air from Pearl's lungs. She wanted Matt to look at her that way. Instead she had to say goodbye to his daughter. She was about to excuse herself when the silence turned awkward.

Dan spoke to Carrie. "I'm going to look around outside. We want to be sure the doors and windows are locked."

When Carrie bit her lip, Pearl sensed Dan's longing to comfort her. She would have left them alone, but he'd already turned to leave the parlor. Carrie's eyes stayed on his back until he disappeared from view.

Hoping to lighten the grim mood, Pearl teased Carrie with a grin. "I may not come back to Cheyenne to live, but I'll be here for your wedding."

"Wedding!"

"I hope so." Pearl had been hurt tonight, but she wanted Carrie to be happy. "Dan's a good man."

"So is Matt." Carrie looked her square in the eye. "You didn't tell me everything that happened in the alley, did you?"

"No, I didn't."

"You're different," Carrie said quietly. "In spite of what Jasper did, you're calm."

She owed part of that new confidence to Matt. With Jasper she'd relived the attack. By kissing Matt, she'd taken back control of herself. She looked at Carrie with all the confidence she felt. "He kissed me." Such simple words. Such powerful words.

"Was it…nice?"

She knotted her hands in frustration. "*I* thought it was wonderful. *He* said it wasn't anything. I don't know what to think."

"Me neither," Carrie admitted.

Pearl knew her cousin had never been kissed, at least not more than a peck. The conversation had nowhere to go, so she stood. "I have to say goodbye to Sarah."

Carrie pushed up from the divan and they shared a hug.

Pearl went to the kitchen where she saw Mrs. Dinwiddie putting on her cloak. Sarah was seated at the table with a pencil and paper. She looked adorable in her pink dress, and her hair crowned her head in a perfect coronet complete with pink ribbons. If Pearl had done nothing else for this child, she'd taught Matt how to make a decent braid. She also realized she'd broken her promise to be at the tea party. She owed Sarah an explanation for missing the party as well as a goodbye.

A lump pushed into Pearl's throat, but she managed a smile. "Are you practicing your letters?"

The child held up the sheet of paper. Pearl saw a backward *S,* but the *A*'s were flawless and so was the final *H.* She looked pleased. "This spells 'Sarah.'"

"It sure does." Pearl glanced at Mrs. Dinwiddie. "How was the party?"

"Exhausting! I'm looking forward to putting my feet up." She smiled at Pearl. "I'll see you tomorrow."

No, she wouldn't. Pearl needed to say goodbye to the woman who'd been so kind to Toby. "I'll walk out with you."

Mrs. Dinwiddie gave her a curious look. "All right."

Pearl turned to Sarah. "I'll be right back, sweetie. Why don't you write some more letters for me?"

"How do I write your name?"

Pearl took the pencil and wrote her name in upper case letters. As Sarah went to work, Pearl walked with Mrs. Dinwiddie to the porch. In the quiet and the dark, she told the cook that she and her father were leaving on the morning train to Denver. Mrs. Dinwiddie clearly wanted to ask why, but she settled for pulling Pearl into a hug. "I'm going to miss you, especially that boy of yours."

"We'll miss you, too."

Holding Pearl by the arms, Mrs. Dinwiddie stepped

back. "Are you sure you have to leave? Denver is just a train ride away, but it's still far."

"I'm sure."

"Whatever's chasing you away, I hope it stops."

So did Pearl. As they hugged goodbye, a man cleared his throat. Expecting Dan, Pearl looked to the bottom of the steps. Instead of the deputy, she saw an adolescent boy holding her cloak and hat. Her stomach filled with nervous butterflies.

"Miss Oliver?"

"Yes?"

"Mr. Kling asked me to deliver these to you." He walked up the steps and handed the clothing to Pearl. "There's a note in the pocket. He told me to tell you."

How much had the boy heard? Did he know she and her father were leaving on the morning train? Would he tell Jasper? She couldn't ask without raising suspicion. And the note... What did it say? She wanted to read it now, but she couldn't see in the dark.

"Thank you," she managed through her tight lips. She wished she had a coin for a tip, but her pockets were empty. Sensing the need, Mrs. Dinwiddie gave him a couple of pennies. He left and the women hugged goodbye again. Pearl watched Mrs. Dinwiddie disappear into the dark, then she went back to the kitchen where Sarah had a death grip on the stubby pencil.

The poor child looked tense and fearful, as if her life depended on spelling out Pearl's name in the unfamiliar letters. Pearl sat at the table next to her, turned the paper and studied the crooked consonants and wobbly vowels.

"That's perfect," she said with a lump in her throat.

"It's for you."

"Thank you, Sarah." She touched the girl's perfect hair.

"I'm sorry I missed the party. Something happened and I couldn't come."

"That's okay."

The acceptance cut Pearl to the bone. The disappointment in Sarah's life had made her an accepting child. She took what love she could get and treasured it. Matt had given her that hope. In spite of his troubles, he was a good father.

Pearl dreaded the next words. "I have to tell you something else."

"What is it?"

"It's sad." Pearl cupped Sarah's little hand in both of hers. Her fingers were sticky with cake from the party, and she thought of the birthdays they wouldn't share. "My father and I have to go back to Denver."

"That's like Texas!" Sarah cried. "It's far!"

"I know, sweetie."

Sarah's lips quivered. "Are you taking Toby with you?"

The question stabbed Pearl in the heart. Sarah's mother had left her. Being abandoned colored the child's every thought, her every reaction. Pearl couldn't erase Sarah's scar, but she refused to make it deeper. She held her hand even more securely. "Toby's my son. I will *never* leave him. But sometimes bad things happen. People get sick or hurt, or they make mistakes like your mama did."

The child's lip quivered. "She didn't like me."

"Oh, sweetie."

"That's why she left." Tears ran down Sarah's cheeks. "She didn't like my daddy, either." She looked up hopefully. "Do *you* like my daddy?"

Pearl could hardly breathe. "I like him very much. He's a good man, Sarah. He will *always* be there for you." Except

Pearl knew too well that life was full of uncertainty. What if Matt got sick? What if he died in the line of duty?

Sarah looked at her with too much hope. "I want a mama, too."

"I know, sweetie."

"I want *you* to be my mama."

Love welled in Pearl's heart, but she didn't have the right to express it. *I love you, too, Sarah. I'd be honored to be your mother.* But Matt hadn't chosen her. He'd sent her to Denver without a word of love or even the hope of a letter. Pearl made her voice neutral. "It's up to your daddy to pick a mother for you."

"He won't." She pouted. "He works all the time."

In spite of her disappointment, Pearl ached for Matt. Until he wrestled with his need to forgive and be forgiven, he'd be bitter and Sarah would suffer. The poor child needed a mother as much as Pearl needed to be one, as much as Matt needed a wife. Pearl hurt for them all. "Finding the right mama isn't easy."

"It's not hard, either." Sarah sounded wise beyond her years. "He just has to marry you."

Just.

The word belittled everything it touched. Matt *just* had to open his heart to God. Pearl *just* had to have faith God would provide for her. She didn't want Sarah to see her upset, so she kept her voice low. "Sometimes people have to make hard choices, especially daddies. Just know that he loves you. I care about you, too."

"Then why are you leaving?"

How did she explain vigilantes to a child? "Some bad men are causing trouble. My father has to leave to be safe."

"Will you come back?"

Pearl weighed her words carefully. If Sarah was going to ever trust again, she needed the truth. "I don't know."

The child sat as still as a stone cherub. Like Pearl, she knew the futility of hoping for things she couldn't have. With tears in her eyes, Pearl took a sheet of paper and the pencil Sarah had set down. In block letters she wrote her name and the address for Swan's Nest, then she slid the paper to Sarah. "This is where I'm going to live. I'll ask Miss Carrie to help you send a letter, and I'll send one back."

"Really?"

"You bet." Pearl couldn't fix all of Sarah's problems, but she would always be her friend. Sarah looked at the paper for a long time. "I see an *S* like Sarah!"

"That's right." Pearl pointed to the *W*. "That says 'Swan's Nest.' It's where I'm going to live again."

Sarah said each letter out loud. Before she got to the *T* in 'Nest,'" Carrie tapped on the open door. "Matt's here."

Her cousin looked flushed and out of breath. Pearl wondered why. Later she'd ask, but for now the time had come to say goodbye. Pearl stood and pulled Sarah into a hug. She didn't want to see Matt, but neither would she make the moment harder than necessary for Sarah. She also had to tell Matt about the errand boy and Jasper's note.

She took the letter out of the pocket of her cloak, glanced at the writing and felt a cold certainty that it held a threat. Together she and Sarah went into the foyer, where Matt stood with his hat in hand and a grim expression.

Chapter Twenty-Two

Five minutes ago, Matt had arrived at Carrie's house with Tobias. The old man was on foot, so Matt had walked his horse. They'd exchanged a few words but not many. The danger spoke for itself. As they'd neared Carrie's house, Matt had gotten a pleasant surprise. On the far corner of the porch, he'd seen Dan and Carrie kissing in the shadows. Later he'd joke with his friend about dropping his guard while on duty, but for the moment he couldn't have been more pleased.

Tobias had seen them, too. He'd given Matt a sideways glance, but Matt had ignored him. Until he could be the man Pearl deserved, he had no business thinking about kissing her. To give Dan warning, he had cleared his throat. The couple had broken apart, then they'd all gone into the house together with Carrie looking more flustered than Matt had ever seen her. When she left to fetch Pearl and Sarah, Matt slapped Dan on the back. "Now who's the Romeo?"

Dan glared at him. "No jokes, Wiley. I'm going to marry that woman."

"Did you ask her?" Matt half whispered.

"Not yet, but I will."

Matt wished he could ask Pearl the same question. When she came into the foyer with Sarah and Carrie, he recalled seeing her with his daughter for the first time and being reminded of Bettina. He'd never been more wrong in his life. Pearl was nothing like his first wife. She had a sweetness he loved, a generosity of spirit Sarah needed as much as he did. He didn't want her to go, but he had to keep her safe from the G.O. and from his own dark heart.

She still looked disheveled from the rain, a sign she'd spoken to Sarah rather than make herself more comfortable. She also had a white envelope in her hand and a worried expression. Instead of running to him, Sarah clung to Pearl's other hand and glared at him. Tonight he'd read *Cinderella,* but he doubted the fairy tale could ease his daughter's heart.

Looking tense, Pearl offered him the letter. "It's from Jasper. I haven't read it yet."

As Matt took the envelope, their fingers touched. Hers were still cold. So were his. "Who delivered it?"

"An errand boy." She told him about the boy who'd brought her things and her conversation with Mrs. Dinwiddie. "I don't know how much he overheard, or if he'd go back and tell Jasper."

Matt's brow furrowed. "We have to figure on the worst."

Pearl bit her lip. "That means—"

"Let me read the letter." He opened the envelope, unfolded a single sheet of paper and saw Jasper's penmanship. Every letter was slanted at the same angle. The capitals matched in height, and the lower case letters made a straight and perfect line.

"Read it out loud," Tobias urged.

"Dear Pearl." Matt hated having Jasper's words on his tongue. "We seem to have had a misunderstanding. As you know, I think very highly of you and your father. I trust we'll be able to speak tomorrow when you arrive at the store as usual. With warm regards, Jasper Kling."

He folded the letter and looked at Pearl. "Whatever you do, don't go near that place."

"I won't," she murmured.

Matt turned to Tobias. "Sir, Dan and I will put you, Pearl and Toby on the train first thing in the morning. In the meantime, everyone needs to stay alert."

Carrie spoke up. "You'll need coffee. I'll put some on the stove."

"Thanks," Matt answered. He put the letter in his coat pocket. It might be needed for evidence. "The G.O. could be planning something at nine o'clock tomorrow, or they could be watching the house right now. Either way, Tobias knows too much. Once we catch them in the act, his testimony could seal a conviction."

"I'll do whatever I can," the old man said.

"Me, too," Pearl added.

Matt looked at Pearl and felt a surge of love. Instead of trembling at Jasper's threat, she looked defiant. She'd come a long way from being "Miss No Name" and running from a crowd. In some small way, he'd helped her find that strength. It made him proud, but not proud enough to stop the nightmares.

He turned to Dan. "I'll take Sarah to Mrs. Holcombe's. I'll be back with your horse."

"What about more deputies?" Dan asked.

"Dibbs and Murray are on duty tonight. I'll tell them to keep an eye out."

With their business settled, Dan gave Carrie a nod and went to stand guard on the porch. Tobias excused himself and so did Carrie, leaving Matt alone with Pearl and Sarah. Their eyes met and held, but neither of them spoke. He couldn't bear the sight of Sarah clinging to Pearl's skirt, glaring at him as if he were an ogre about to snatch her away. A man did what had to be done, so he gave her a stern look. "Come on, darlin'. It's time to go."

"No!"

"Sarah—"

"I don't want to go to Mrs. Holcombe's house! I want to stay with Miss Pearl." She stuck out her bottom lip. When Matt saw it tremble, he hated himself with the full force of all his guilt. Unwillingly, he looked to Pearl for help and wished he hadn't. Her eyes matched Sarah's too perfectly. The females belonged together. Matt belonged with them both. If he were a better man, he could have told Pearl he loved her. He could have given Sarah a mother and ended this charade of uncaring. He would never have participated in a lynching and he'd be free to sit in church without resentment coloring his every thought.

He wasn't that man, so he stepped forward and lifted Sarah to his hip. She kicked so hard he'd have a bruise. "Sarah—"

"Wait," Pearl said gently. "Let me talk to her."

Shamefully grateful for her help, he stood so that Pearl and Sarah were nose to nose. She cupped the child's head with her hand, kissed her temple and then rested her forehead against Sarah's smaller one.

"I love you, Sarah," she whispered. "I'm going to write to you, remember?"

The child sobbed.

"And we're going to be friends forever, right? I won't ever forget you, and you won't forget me."

Sarah settled a bit, but tears kept spilling down her cheeks. "I don't want you to go!"

"I know, sweetheart." Pearl pulled back, but she kept

contact by touching Sarah's chin. "How about this…I promise I'll come and visit. I don't know when, but someday I'll come and see you. Would you like that?"

Slowly, as if her head weighed a hundred pounds, Sarah nodded.

"Good," Pearl said with false enthusiasm. "We'll look forward to it. Now go with your daddy, okay? He's a good man and he loves you very, very much. He'll take good care of you, always. I know it."

If Pearl had looked into his eyes, she'd have seen tears. The feelings embarrassed him, but they didn't humble him enough to tell her he loved her. First he had to settle matters with God and the Golden Order. Turning his back, he walked out the door with Sarah in his arms.

"Bye, Miss Pearl," the child said in a shaky voice.

"Goodbye, Sarah."

With the words echoing in his ears, Matt closed the door and headed for his horse. Sarah felt as lifeless as a sack of flour. He'd have preferred a tantrum to the deadweight. He lifted her into the saddle, climbed up behind her and wrapped his coat around her for warmth. She usually chattered when she rode with him. He'd tease her about taking the reins and they'd think of funny names for horses. Tonight she curled sideways against his middle and clutched his shirt, a sign she'd said goodbye too many times. Either God didn't know, or he didn't care. Matt's blood boiled with a consuming anger. He could understand the Almighty turning His back on a man like himself, but how could He forget Sarah?

When they reached Mrs. Holcombe's house, Matt climbed off his horse and carried Sarah to the porch. Mrs. Holcombe opened the door and greeted them with a smile. "Looks like I'm going to have company tonight."

Sarah usually liked staying with Mrs. Holcombe. Tonight she muttered, "I guess."

"What's wrong?" the woman asked.

Sarah shrugged. Matt chose not to enlighten her, either.

Mrs. Holcombe respected his silence, but Matt knew her opinions. More than once she'd told him Sarah needed a mother. Tonight he had to agree. "She's tired," he said. "I'll put her down, then fetch her nightie from the house." He'd get the *Mother Goose* book, too.

As he set Sarah on the divan, Mrs. Holcombe sat close. "How about a story when your daddy gets back? We could read *Cinderella*."

"No, thank you," Sarah replied, sounding overly polite. "It isn't true anyway."

It pained him, but Matt had to agree. When it came to Pearl, he'd failed miserably as Prince Charming. He'd failed Sarah, too. He couldn't pray for himself, but he could pray for his daughter and Pearl.

Help them, Lord. They need more than I can give right now.

He didn't expect God to answer, but a small part of him hoped that someday he'd be able to trust God the way Pearl did. Until then, he'd stand guard like the watchman. It wouldn't be in vain, either. He intended to stop the Golden Order on his own. He'd fight and he'd win. If God wanted to watch, so be it. But Matt wouldn't count on Him.

When Pearl walked into her room, she saw her father in the rocking chair, pushing gently as he hummed a lullaby to his grandson. She'd had a harrowing day and still needed to pack, but she welcomed his company. She'd never have a husband, but she had the best father in the world. She sat across from him on the seat of the vanity. "How are you doing?" she asked.

"I'm fine." He kept rocking. "I just wish things had turned out better."

"You did your best," Pearl said. "I'm proud of you."

"I'm proud of *you*," Tobias replied. "Here's hoping Matt finishes the job fast. I'd like to come back here."

Pearl had the same hope. "If anyone can stop them, it's Matt."

"He's troubled, Pearl."

"I know."

He looked at her with the love she'd known her entire life. "You know I'll be praying."

"Thank you, Papa."

He indicated Toby with his chin. "This little boy's asleep. I'll put him to bed and go pack. I don't think either of us will get much sleep tonight." Her father carried Toby to his cradle, then kissed Pearl on the cheek and said goodnight. As he lumbered down the hall, she closed the door and slumped against it. The emotion she'd been holding back for Sarah's sake leaked into her eyes. A tear trickled down her cheek, then another one. She wiped them away with her knuckles, then went to the wardrobe and opened the doors. One by one, she removed the dresses from the hooks.

The blue one she'd worn the day she arrived reminded her of her first glimpse of Matt. He'd struck her as handsome and troubled, a good man with a chip on his shoulder. He hadn't changed at all, except now she loved him.

As she lifted the gray dress she'd worn to the interview, she thought of Matt taking her to the bakery. She recalled the tenderness of the moment, then the look in his eyes when he realized she'd been the victim of violence. Was that when she'd started to love him? Or had it been sooner?

Pearl didn't know and it didn't matter. Unless Matt had a change of heart, her feelings had to be put aside.

As she lifted the fancy dress she'd worn to Carrie's party, she thought of Adie's wedding and her own hopes for marriage. Those hopes had been dead when she'd arrived in Cheyenne. Matt had brought them to life, but they'd faded again when he said the kiss was "just stuff." Had he been lying? Or did he mean it? Either way, the words hurt.

Last, she removed her everyday dresses, the ones she'd worn in Jasper's store. They held no memories, good or bad. She could wear them in Denver without remembering Jasper and running into the rain.

She packed her petticoats and underthings, then opened the vanity. With her throat tight, she took out the blue ribbons one by one, recalling when she'd worn them. When she lifted the one Matt had touched, it warmed beneath her fingers and she remembered everything…the moment they'd met and Sarah's messy braid. The night in the kitchen and the kiss in the alley. Closing her eyes, she pictured Matt's face as she prayed for peace for his soul.

She whispered "Amen," then looked at herself in the mirror. Slowly she unwound the coronet she'd made with her braid, then she loosened the plaits until her hair hung unbound down her back. Over and over, she brushed the strands until they crackled.

Looking at her reflection, she felt beautiful and strong. Never again would she pull her hair so tight that her scalp hurt. The blond lengths were indeed her crowning glory.

"Be with him, Lord," she said out loud. "Remind him of Your mercy. Remind him that he needs You. Amen."

Pearl needed the Lord, too. She also wanted a husband and a father for Toby. With those prayers on her lips, she felt a rush of courage. Not once in her life had she regretted being brave, but she'd paid dearly for being timid.

Tomorrow she'd wear her hair down for the first time in a year. She'd wear Matt's ribbons, too. As he'd believed in the note that came with the ribbons, she'd become a woman of uncommon courage.

Chapter Twenty-Three

By sunrise, Matt's bones ached like an old man's gout. The coffee he'd consumed tasted bitter on his tongue, although he was certain Dan felt otherwise. Carrie had been up half the night, making sandwiches for them all and keeping coffee on the stove. Matt couldn't help but hope he'd see Pearl, but she'd stayed upstairs. He knew, because he'd watched the light in her window. Long after midnight, she'd blown out the wick.

Alone in the dark, he'd looked up at the sky. Instead of stars, he'd seen a thousand blind eyes. Bands of clouds had swept over the points of light, hiding them and then revealing them again as if God were blinking. Each time he wondered why he couldn't do the one thing that might have given him peace. He couldn't forgive God, and he couldn't ask for forgiveness for himself.

While standing guard, he'd thought a lot about what Pearl had said about that night in Virginia. She'd been wounded by a crime as heinous as the one Matt had committed, yet she'd gone on with her life. He wanted the same freedom, but how did he get it? He owed a debt for what he'd done in Virginia. Somehow it had to be paid. He'd heard what Pearl had said about Jesus dying for his sins.

He'd once believed in that gift and supposed he still did, but somehow believing God could forgive him wasn't enough. He felt dirty inside. And he still thought the Almighty had blinked on that fateful night.

Would his feelings change if he stopped the Golden Order? Matt didn't know, but he wanted to sleep without bad dreams. He couldn't bring Amos McGuckin back to life, but maybe he'd find peace if he could stop the Golden Order.

Even more important, he had to protect Pearl and her father. The Golden Order hadn't struck during the night, but Matt couldn't relax. If the G.O. wanted Matt and Tobias, Pearl was the perfect bait. Matt intended to put her on the train before Jasper opened his shop, but what about the errand boy? If he'd revealed the plan to Jasper, anything could happen.

Yawning, Matt leaned against the railing at the far end of the porch. He'd been up all night along with Dan and two other deputies. He'd sent Jake Murray home an hour ago. Charlie Dibbs was checking the horses, and Dan had gone to the livery to fetch a hack for the ride to the train depot. Until Matt saw the train pull out of the station, he wouldn't take his eyes off Pearl for an instant.

As if he'd called out her name, she stepped through the front door. "Matt?'"

"Over here."

As he pushed off the railing, the sun turned the day into a haze of gold. The light glinted off her hair, and his mouth gaped at what he saw. In place of the braid he'd come to expect, she'd swept half her hair up and let the rest fall down her back. Matching blue ribbons held the waves in place, the ribbons he'd given to her to say thank you…the ribbons that now said so much more.

When she saw him, she smiled. It didn't look the least

bit forced, though she had to be hurting. "Good morning," she said. "I thought you might want breakfast. Dan and the other deputies, too."

"Jake left and Charlie's busy."

"What about Dan?" Her eyes twinkled. "I'm sure Carrie would be glad to see him."

"No doubt." Matt was sincerely happy for his friend. "He's getting a hack from the livery."

She paused. "What about you? Are you hungry?"

"I'll pass." A single meal wouldn't satisfy him.

Dressed for the trip in a paisley skirt and a royal blue jacket, she looked both gracious and bold. Only the shadows below her eyes hinted at yesterday's trouble. Matt thought of Tobias urging him to tell Pearl how he felt. He hadn't done it last night, and he wouldn't do it now. He had to stick to the business of protecting her. "Are you packed?"

"Yes."

"And your father?"

"He's having breakfast with Carrie." She spoke as if nothing were wrong. "She leaves for school in a few minutes."

"Good." He wanted today to be like any other day, although he hoped Carrie would pay extra attention to Sarah. The child hadn't been herself when he'd left her with Mrs. Holcombe.

Pearl glanced down the street. "I guess we didn't have any visitors."

"No one. We'll leave for the station as soon as Dan gets here."

"So this is it," she said mildly.

"I guess so."

She looked at him with a kindness he didn't deserve. "I have to say something."

"Pearl, don't."

"Please," she said quietly. "Give me this moment."

How could he deny her a final request? How could he deny himself? Even dying men got a last meal. "What's on your mind?"

She raised her chin, then tried to smile. Her lips quivered, but her eyes stayed dry. "You, Matt Wiley, will live in my heart forever. You've given me gifts I'll treasure, and you've restored a part of me I thought was gone forever. Thank you."

"Pearl, I—"

"Please." She touched her index finger to his lips. "Don't say anything." Leaning forward, she closed her eyes and kissed him sweetly on the cheek.

Every instinct told Matt to pull her into his arms. She deserved to be kissed properly, by a man who loved her and would cherish her. He couldn't be that man, so he settled for taking her hand in both of his. Unable to let her go, he raised her fingers to his lips and kissed her knuckles. He yearned to tell her he loved her. Instead he spoke a painful truth. "I'm sorry, Pearl. I can't say what you deserve to hear."

Her eyes filled with unshed tears, maybe a hint of anger, but she kept her chin up. "Don't be sorry, Matt. I'm not."

"I've hurt you."

"You've helped me. I have no regrets and neither should you."

Just like that, she'd forgiven him…. He'd tied Pearl in knots, yet she stood here loving him without expectation. Saying nothing felt all wrong, but speaking from his heart would confuse them both. Vaguely he thought of Tobias asking him if he was cowardly or stupid. The question fit now, and he didn't have a good answer.

A hack rattled in the distance. Matt looked down the street and saw Dan. At the same moment, Charlie arrived with Matt's horse and his own. Feeling grim, he let go of Pearl's hand. "I'll have Charlie fetch your trunk."

"Thank you."

As she went back in the house, Matt spoke to the deputy. Five minutes later the trunks were loaded and Charlie had climbed on his horse. Everyone else gathered on the porch. With Toby in her arms, Pearl hugged Carrie goodbye. Teary-eyed, Carrie hugged Tobias, then told Matt she'd give Sarah an extra hug when Mrs. Holcombe brought her to school. Dan got a kiss on the cheek. After a last look at them all, she hurried down the steps and headed to Miss Marlowe's School.

Tobias offered his arm to Pearl. "It's time, princess."

Without looking back, she took her father's arm and walked to the carriage. Tobias handed her up, then climbed up and sat next to her. As Dan took the reins, Matt mounted his horse and the little entourage took off for the train depot, with Matt in the lead and Charlie guarding the rear. As they rode down the empty streets, Matt peered between houses and down alleys. He saw nothing out of the ordinary. In the business district—the section well away from Jasper's shop—Cheyenne began to stir and he felt hopeful the G.O. hadn't learned of Tobias's escape. If Matt had been planning a kidnapping, he'd have sprung the trap in a quiet neighborhood, not in a part of town with witnesses.

As they neared the depot, the locomotive sent puffs of steam into the morning sky. Carriages pulled up to the station, leaving passengers and their baggage on the crowded platform. Dan steered to an empty spot, hopped down and went to unload the trunks. Charlie joined him, leaving Matt to hand Pearl and Toby out of the carriage. Silent, he escorted Pearl and her father to the ticket window. He made the purchase, then handed the tickets to Tobias. "There you go, sir."

The man's brow furrowed. "I expected to pay."

"The city's paying," Matt answered. "You've earned it."

Tobias put the tickets in his coat. "I'll want to know what happens. You'll be in touch, I'm sure."

"We'll need you to testify."

"Of course."

The three of them walked through the crowd to the waiting train. When they reached the passenger car, Pearl stopped at the bottom of the steps. She turned to say a final goodbye, but Matt wasn't about to let her board without seeing who else had gotten on. Brushing by her, he climbed the steps, surveyed the other passengers and saw only strangers. Reassured, he motioned for Pearl and Tobias to come aboard.

Hugging Toby close, she slipped into a window seat. Before sitting, Tobias turned and offered Matt his hand. "Deputy, it's been a privilege to know you."

Matt grunted. "I'd hardly call it that."

"Nonetheless, that's how I feel."

Tobias broke the handshake and sat. Against his better judgment, Matt looked at Pearl. She'd turned to the window, giving him a view of the hair cascading down her back. With her face turned, he could indulge in a long last look and that was what he did, until Toby cooed and reached for him. It would have been the most natural thing in the world to lift the baby and hold him high like he used to do with Sarah, kissing her tummy while she laughed and kicked. Matt imagined holding Toby like that, until the conductor announced the train would leave in five minutes.

"Goodbye, sir," he said to Tobias. "Pearl?"

Turning from the window, she met his gaze with an arched brow. "Goodbye, Matt. Stay safe."

"I will," he murmured. "You, too."

Her chin stayed firm, even defiant. In her own quiet way, she was daring him to speak from his heart. Matt wanted to offer a dare of his own. *Marry me.* But he wouldn't do it. Until he could be the man she deserved, he had no business telling her he loved her. Deliberately stoic, he tipped his hat and left the passenger car.

He had to get off the train, but he'd be watching from the edge of the platform. He wouldn't budge until it vanished from sight. Then he'd go home and sleep…maybe.

"He's gone," Pearl said to her father.

"You'll see him again."

"I suppose." If Dan proposed to Carrie, Pearl would come back for the wedding. Aching inside, she snuggled Toby against her chest. "Today feels so final."

Disheartened, she looked out the window. Hoping for a glimpse of Matt, she scanned the crowd. Instead of the man she loved, she saw a little girl with hair that matched her own.

"Papa!" she cried. "It's Sarah!"

He leaned across her lap and peered out the window. "That poor child! She's crying."

How had Sarah gotten to the train station? Had Mrs. Holcombe brought her? Maybe Carrie? Except Carrie had a class to teach. Pearl didn't see her cousin anywhere. Neither could she see Matt. Pearl jumped to her feet. "I have to help her." She handed Toby to her father, then squeezed past his knees. "I'll be right back."

"Hurry!" he called after her. "The train's about to leave."

She had three minutes, maybe less. Hoisting her skirt, she raced down the aisle of the train car and down to the platform. Waving frantically, she called Sarah's name. The child spotted her and ran sobbing into her arms.

"What are you doing here?" Pearl crooned.

"I runned away from school."

The poor grammar showed the child's distress. Pearl's belly knotted. "We have to find your daddy."

"I don't want my daddy!"

"But Sarah—"

"I want *you!*"

Pearl felt torn in two. Sarah needed her, but the boilers were chuffing and building up steam. The excess spilled into the air, filling it with the smell of water and grit. She pulled Sarah into a hug and lifted her into her arms. Had Matt waited for the train to leave? It seemed likely, so she scanned the platform. She spotted him at the far edge, staring at the window where she'd been seated with a worried frown.

"Matt!" she cried.

At the sight of her with Sarah, his eyes filled with the worry she'd seen the day they'd met, the day Sarah had nearly been run over. Pearl hurried in his direction, but a man with a bushy beard blocked her way.

"Excuse me," she murmured.

When he didn't move, she looked up and saw the man who'd been driving the freight wagon that had nearly run over Sarah.

"Excuse me, missy." He tipped his hat—a black derby.

Pearl's blood turned to ice. She tried to step around him, but he blocked her path. As she turned, a man in a mask ripped Sarah from her arms. A blanket seemed to fall from the sky, suffocating her and blacking out the sun. When she tried to scream, a hand clapped against her mouth.

"Don't do that, Pearl. We have the little girl."

Jasper!

Shouts filled the air and a woman screamed. A man shouted, "Don't shoot! They've got a child!"

Pearl could only imagine the depth of Matt's fear. With Sarah in harm's way, he couldn't fight back. But Pearl could…. She didn't have a chance against her kidnappers, but she kicked and screamed as they manhandled her into a carriage.

Someone, possibly Jasper, tied her hands and feet with a laundry cord. Bound and still covered by the blanket, she felt a man's hand snake through her hair. Forcing her neck to bend, he tugged a black mask over her face, pulled a drawstring and tied a vicious knot. Without a word, he shoved her against the far door of the carriage, maybe the one that had dropped off her father. To both her relief and horror, their kidnappers shoved Sarah on to the seat next to her.

As the carriage lurched forward, the child pressed her face against Pearl's arm. Judging by the lack of a hug, Sarah's arms were bound and her muffled cries meant they'd masked her face. With her own arms tied behind her back, Pearl couldn't embrace the girl like she wanted. She tried to calm Sarah the only way she knew. "Do you know how to pray, sweetie?"

"A little."

"When I'm scared, I pray like this." Pearl moistened her lips. "'The Lord is my shepherd. The Lord is my shepherd.' I say it over and over."

As they spoke the verse together, the carriage lurched forward. Pearl heard shouting and gunshots, then the rhythm of hoofbeats as the driver sped away from the train station. Sarah started to cry. "Who took us?"

"I don't know exactly."

She'd recognized Jasper's voice and had hunches about the others, but Matt and her father had been careful to never mention names. Judging by Jasper's customers, she figured

Chester Gates and Troy Martin were among the captors along with the freight driver.

"Where's my daddy?" Sarah whispered.

"He'll come for us."

"How will he find us?"

"I'm not sure," Pearl answered. "But he will." They were bait. The Golden Order wanted Matt and her father to come after them, which meant they wouldn't be hard to find. Pearl heard the fading sounds of Cheyenne and shivered. Wherever they were headed, they'd be at the mercy of the Golden Order. Her captors could harm her body, but they couldn't touch her soul. No matter the cost, she'd fight to keep Sarah safe.

Chapter Twenty-Four

"Sarah!"

The cry tore from Matt's lips. Sick with fury, he watched as a black carriage whisked Sarah and Pearl away from Cheyenne. Seconds ago he'd seen his daughter snatched out of Pearl's arms by a man in a mask and a black derby. He'd drawn his pistol, but the men in masks had rendered him helpless by using Sarah as a shield. Dan and Charlie had drawn their weapons, as well, but they couldn't fire without endangering Sarah and Pearl.

The big man who'd blocked Pearl's path had sauntered away as if he were an innocent bystander, but Matt recognized Gibson Armond. Three men in masks had conducted the kidnapping. The tallest one had called out to him, summoning him to the place where the Golden Order had committed its first crime, to the valley where they'd lynched Jed Jones. *Grass Valley, Wiley. Be there. And bring the preacher.*

The Golden Order couldn't have made their intentions more clear. They'd kidnapped Pearl and Sarah to make a trade. Fathers for daughters…the guilty for the innocent.

Vaguely Matt thought of the errand boy. He'd obviously reported back to Jasper, but Matt didn't blame him for today's chaos. He blamed himself. How could he have missed Gibson Armond lurking in the crowd? Why hadn't he noticed the carriage behind the ticket office? The masked men had hidden inside it. He didn't know how Sarah had gotten to the train station, but he'd seen enough to guess that she'd run away from school, and her presence had drawn Pearl off the train.

What happened next confirmed every doubt Matt had about God. The Almighty had blinked, and the Golden Order had kidnapped the two people Matt loved most.

Dan and Charlie jogged up to him. At the same time, Tobias pushed through the crowd with Toby in his arms. If Pearl died today, the baby would be an orphan. Matt couldn't stand the thought. Neither could he bear to think of Sarah.

Tobias looked ready to kill. "I'm going with you, Wiley."

"Me, too," Dan answered.

"We need weapons and a plan." Matt had long guns in the sheriff's office. "Follow me."

Tobias grimaced. "What about Toby?"

"We'll leave him with Mrs. Holcombe."

Matt and Charlie mounted their horses. Dan took Tobias in the hack. They met at the sheriff's office and went inside. Matt considered the Colt on his hip. Six shots wouldn't be enough, so he opened the ammo box and took a handful of bullets. He put them on the desk, then opened the drawer where he kept the Colt Navy he'd carried in the war.

He didn't like the gun at all. The feel of it brought back memories of Virginia, but today it would serve another purpose. He put the weapon in his holster and his regular Peacemaker in his waistband. He took a Derringer out of the top drawer, loaded it and stuck it in his boot. Last he strode to the gun rack and lifted a coach gun. The shotgun had been cut down to eighteen inches and packed a wallop. If he had to use it, the twelve-gauge would knock Jasper Kling and the Golden Order into eternity.

As Dan and Charlie made similar preparations, Tobias stood by the window with Toby. When the baby started to fuss, the old man rocked him as if nothing were wrong. Matt figured they both needed the comfort. So did Matt, but comfort wouldn't come until Sarah and Pearl were safe.

He put on a canvas duster that would hide his weapons, then swept the extra bullets into the pocket. "Here's the plan," he said to the men. "We'll ride out to Grass Valley—"

The door burst open. The men went for their guns, but the intruder turned out to be Carrie. "Matt!" she cried. "It's Sarah. She ran away."

"I figured," he said calmly. "We're going after her now."

Carrie looked confused. "Where is she?"

"She's been kidnapped."

She gasped. "Who would do such a thing?"

Tobias glowered. "The Golden Order. They have Pearl, too."

"What can I do?" she asked.

"Take Toby." He put the baby in her arms.

Her eyes misted. "If something happens to Sarah, I'll never forgive myself. I turned my back for a minute and she ran off. And Pearl—"

"Don't blame yourself." Matt was responsible for Sarah's upset, not Carrie. He'd failed Pearl, too. He should have seen Gibson Armond on the platform. He should have admitted he loved her.

Carrie looked at Dan. "Be careful."

"I will," he answered. "Go on home."

She gave him a hopeful look, then headed for the door.

As she turned the knob, she stopped. "Bring them back, okay?"

"We will," Tobias said with confidence.

Matt thought of the watchman. Either the Almighty would be with them, or He'd be napping. Matt prayed He'd be wide awake, but God had failed him before and he had his doubts. As soon as Carrie left, he looked at Charlie. "Fetch Dan's horse from the livery. Get one for Tobias, too."

"Yes, sir."

As the deputy left, Matt explained to Dan and Tobias what he intended to do. "Tobias and I will ride ahead and we'll go alone. We'll meet up with the kidnappers. Dan, you and Charlie follow with more deputies. Don't let them see you. It'll complicate the trade."

"What trade?" Dan asked.

"Fathers for daughters." Matt's life for Sarah's. Tobias for Pearl. "That's what they're after." It was a trade Matt would gladly make. What would happen, he couldn't say. But he didn't intend to die.

Dan furrowed his brow. "Pearl could recognize these men. If she can identify them, she's as much a threat as Tobias. What's to stop the G.O. from hurting her?"

"Their own code of honor," Tobias replied. "Twisted or not, they have *some* scruples, at least that's my hope."

Matt agreed. "They put a mask on her. As long as she can't identify them, she should be safe." He turned to Tobias. "Do you want a weapon, sir?"

"I do today."

Matt took another Colt from the gun safe, checked for bullets and handed the pistol to Tobias.

The minister jammed it in his waistband. "I believe in turning the other cheek, but not when women and children are in danger."

"Same here," Dan said.

"Here's what I expect." Matt spoke more for Tobias's sake than Dan's. His partner knew what to expect. "They'll order us to throw down our weapons. I'll comply, but not completely. They won't expect the coach gun and the second Colt, and they won't know if you're armed. Handle the moment as you see fit."

The men locked eyes. Tobias deepened his voice. "I'll do whatever has to be done."

Matt had had the same thought in Virginia. That night he'd been willing to kill. Today he was willing to die for the people he loved. The difference struck him full force, and he recalled Pearl talking about God's love for him. Matt had thought a lot about dying for a good cause, but until now he hadn't thought about Someone dying for him. Somehow in his angry outbursts at the Almighty, he'd overlooked the fact that Christ had suffered far more than Matt had, more than Amos McGuckin and anyone else. Matt didn't understand why God had made that choice, but today he understood the cost.

It was hard to stay angry with a God who'd make such a sacrifice. Matt couldn't explain the mess in Virginia or why Sarah and Pearl had been taken today, but he knew God wasn't to blame. Human beings had committed those ugly acts.

His anger at God eased, but the guilt remained. He still had to stop the Golden Order. Feeling both the threat of death and a lightness of soul, he led the way out the door. Charlie had arrived with the horses, so the men climbed into the saddles and headed for Grass Valley.

For almost an hour the carriage bumped down a twisting road. Pearl worked feverishly to loosen her hands, but the rope tightened with every effort. Sarah had nestled so far into her side that Pearl's ribs hurt. The little girl had stopped crying, but only after endless assurances that her daddy would be coming for them.

The long ride had given Pearl time to piece the morning together. As she'd feared, the delivery boy had revealed their plans to leave on the morning train. She and her father would have escaped if Sarah hadn't run away from school and shown up at the train station. Pearl didn't know exactly what the G.O. had planned, but they wanted her father and they wanted Matt. She and Sarah were the bait to draw them out. She suspected they had been planning to kidnap Sarah at school but had lucked out when she showed up at the train station.

She'd didn't know how many men were riding with the carriage. She could hear the thud of hooves but no voices. The wheels rattled and spun, changing speeds as they climbed and coasted along the hills.

When the carriage lurched off the road, Sarah cried out, "Where are they taking us?"

"I don't know, sweetie."

As the jostling intensified, she heard the rush of a rain-filled stream. The wind blew against the windows, shaking the carriage as it swayed to a halt. When the driver jumped down, Pearl prepared to be dragged into the open. Instead he walked away, leaving her alone with Sarah in the middle of nowhere. Pearl hadn't tried to remove the mask during the ride. If she saw the faces of her captors, they'd kill her. Now, though, they'd left her alone. If she could see, she could escape.

"Sarah, I'm going to try to get this mask off. That means I have to wiggle around."

"I want mine off, too."

"See if you can drag your head against the seat."

As Pearl rubbed her own head against the leather to get

traction, the cotton scraped her face. The sensation brought horrible memories of Franklin Dean's buggy, but she didn't stop. She twisted until her skin felt raw, then she tried to chew through the fabric. Nothing worked. The drawstring held the mask tight.

"Mine's off!" Sarah cried.

Thank you, Lord.

"What should I do?" the child asked.

"Don't look out the window, sweetheart. We don't want them to know you can see."

"The windows have curtains," Sara said. "It's dark."

"The dark won't hurt us." Pearl had to get her own mask off. If Sarah could reach the drawstring holding it tight, maybe she could bite through it. "Do you see a string on my mask?"

"No."

Pearl turned around. "Look in the back."

"There's a big knot."

"See if you can undo it with your teeth."

Sarah scooted closer and Pearl bent low. The girl gnawed at the string, but the knot only tightened. Pearl gulped stale air. Close to suffocating, she sat back. "We'll try later."

"*Now* what do we do?"

"You stay low and out of sight." Pearl felt nauseous from the lack of air. "Whatever you do, don't open that curtain. I don't want them to see you."

"Okay."

"Let's see if I can untie your hands. We'll sit back-to-back." Pearl did her best to loosen the rope around the child's wrists, but her own fingers were numb from lack of blood.

Sarah moaned. "My fingers hurt."

"I know, sweetheart."

"And I'm scared."

"Me, too." Pearl searched her mind for encouragement. "Your father's coming for us, and so is mine." She blinked and thought of another rider who'd be coming to their rescue, a man on a white horse, a man whose Name was Faithful and True. "Jesus is coming, too. He'll be with us."

Sarah looked quizzical. "Is he like Prince Charming?"

In spite of her fear, Pearl smiled. "In a way, sweetie. But he's more...much more. Now let's work on these ropes."

Chapter Twenty-Five

Matt and Tobias said next to nothing as they rode into Grass Valley. Autumn had turned the grass to gold and the cottonwoods into yellow torches. The sky couldn't have been more blue, nor could the clouds have been any whiter. A handful of evergreens dotted the meadow, rounding out a spectrum of color. It was a beautiful day. A perfect day except for the danger to Sarah and Pearl.

When they rounded a bend, Matt saw the cottonwood where Jed Jones had died at the hands of the Golden Order. As he'd expected, the leaders of the organization had congregated beneath the tall branches. Dressed in dusters, derbies and white masks, they resembled a macabre gathering of the dead. Four of the riders stood in a row. A fifth was holding a bare-backed roan. A rope that ended in a noose hung from a thick branch. They'd come to hold court, and they'd come to sentence Matt and Tobias to death.

To the right of the proceedings and several yards away, he saw a carriage with drawn curtains. He figured it held Pearl and Sarah. He wanted to call out to them, but he couldn't. The less the G.O. thought about the females, the safer they'd be. Matt had fought a lot of battles in his life, but never had so much been at stake. The lives of his daughter and the woman he loved hung on the next five minutes. So did Tobias's next breath…and his own.

Matt would do his best to protect them all, but he couldn't guarantee the outcome of today's encounter. He no longer blamed God for the awful things that sometimes happened, but he hoped that his peace of mind wouldn't be tested with the loss of someone he loved. No matter how he felt, the time had come to trust Tobias's watchman.

"Wait here," he said to the older man.

Loose and tall in the saddle, Matt rode halfway down the hill before the riders noticed him and pointed their guns. "Good morning, gentlemen!" he shouted. "Let the females go and we'll call it a day." He had no illusion they'd agree.

"Deputy Wiley!" The voice belonged to Chester Gates. "We're principled men. We have no intention of harming your daughter *or* Miss Oliver. By the same token, we do *not* tolerate traitors. I'm proposing a trade."

Matt had suspected as much. "What do you want?"

"An eye for an eye," the man replied. "If you and the reverend surrender, we'll let your daughters go."

"Give us a minute to talk," Matt called back.

"Not a chance." Gates's horse shifted under his weight. "The reverend comes down now, or we sacrifice his daughter to the cause of justice."

"You're bluffing," Matt shouted.

"Hardly."

The man next to Gates lifted his chin. Through the eye holes in the mask, the sun reflected off a pair of spectacles. Matt recognized Jasper. Judging by the size and shape of the others, Martin and Moreland were next to him. Gibson Armond had donned a duster and mask and was holding the horse to be used in the hanging.

Matt stalled. "You're asking a man to die. Five minutes is nothing."

"Who said anything about dying?" Gates said in a smooth tone. "We'll have a trial right here. If the reverend's innocent of deception, he'll understand. If he's guilty, he'll hang."

"And me?" Matt asked sarcastically.

"You know too much." Gates smirked. "I'm quite sure you'll trade your life for your daughter's."

Matt wanted to kill this man. He wanted to kill them all, but they had him outnumbered and outgunned. The longer he kept Gates talking, the better his chance of surviving. "How do I know you won't hurt Pearl?"

"You have my word."

"That means nothing."

Gates ignored the insult, but Jasper turned to the man Matt assumed to be Howard Moreland. "Fetch Miss Oliver."

"No!" Tobias shouted.

If the old man hadn't ridden past Matt, Matt would have offered himself in Pearl's place. Wisely Tobias stopped halfway to the hanging tree. "Release our daughters."

"Just one," Gates said to Tobias. "You pick."

"Send out the child."

Matt had never known a deeper gratitude. Tobias loved Pearl beyond measure, yet he'd put Sarah first. Matt would never forget his sacrifice.

One of the riders, probably Moreland, went to the carriage. He opened the door, said something Matt couldn't hear and reached into the interior. Sarah screamed. Matt's fingers itched to pull the trigger, but then where would they be? If he acted on instinct alone, they'd all die. He had no choice but to trust the watchman, so he waited.

To his relief, Moreland pulled Sarah out of the coach

and waved her away with his gun. She saw Matt and ran in his direction. "Daddy!"

"No, darlin'! Run away."

Whimpering, she stopped in midstep.

"Go on," he said firmly. "I'll find you."

Please, Lord. Don't let that be a lie. Sarah ran up the hill. If the worst happened, Dan would find her, but then what? If Matt died today, who'd love his little girl? He had to live and so did Pearl. So did Tobias because they were meant to be a family.

Gates called out, "Throw down your weapons, Reverend."

Tobias raised his hands. "I'm armed with the sword of the Lord. It's sharp enough to separate bone from marrow, truth from lies. You men are Pharisees! You're—"

"Get off your horse!" Gates shouted.

Tobias slid out of the saddle. Still quoting Scripture, he walked toward the hanging tree with his hands high. "The Lord is my shepherd! I shall not want! The Lord—"

"Shut up!" Jasper shouted.

"I'm a dead man," Tobias replied. "I've got something to say and you're all going to listen."

He started shouting the Lord's prayer. The familiar words made one of the riders, probably Martin, back pedal his horse. Disgusted, Moreland grabbed Tobias by the collar. "Shut up, old man!"

Gates turned to Moreland. "*You* shut up! *I* give the orders!"

"Then give them!" he shouted. "We're wasting time."

"I promised this man a trial."

"He's guilty," Jasper declared.

With Tobias still shouting, Moreland dragged him to the hanging tree. The man holding the roan shoved him belly down on the horse and attempted to tie his hands. If they got the noose around Tobias's neck, he'd die.

Matt put his hands in the air. "You want me, too. Let the reverend and his daughter go, and I'll come peacefully."

If Gates accepted Matt's surrender, he'd regain the authority he'd lost to Jasper and Moreland. The banker signaled the men by raising his hand. "The deputy wants to do some negotiating."

Tobias went still, and the men stopped wrestling with him. Gates looked at Matt. "Throw down your guns, Deputy."

Matt dragged his left arm down, pinched the Colt Navy from the holster and dropped it to the ground. It landed with a thud, useless and out of reach.

"Throw down the other one," Gates ordered.

Matt slid the Derringer from his boot and dropped it next to the six-shooter. He still had the coach gun under his duster and the Peacemaker in his waistband, but weapons alone wouldn't win this fight.

"Come down here," Gates ordered.

The masked men cocked their pistols and took aim. With his arms in the air, nothing stood between Matt and death except God's grace…the grace he didn't deserve, the grace he'd scorned because of his own arrogance. Without God's mercy, he'd die at the end of a rope. Sarah would be an orphan. Pearl would escape with her life, but she'd be at the mercy of men like Jasper Kling.

In a silent breath, Matt cried out for mercy for them all. With mercy, he knew, came justice. *Forgive me, Lord, for murdering an innocent man. Forgive my pride and my arrogance.*

With his hands up and his eyes on the men in masks, he saw an ironic truth. He was just like these men. He'd taken justice into his own hands, not only in Virginia but in his own life. For the murder of Amos McGuckin, he'd sentenced himself to a life of good deeds. Where had it gotten him? Nowhere… Unless God intervened, today he'd die. Matt had done his best. Now he needed help.

It's up to You, Lord. I'm willing to die, but I'd rather not.

Peace washed him clean. His thoughts cleared and he knew what he had to do. The outcome of this day belonged to the Lord, but Matt had two guns, eight bullets and something to say. With his hands high, he called out to the men who intended to kill him. "Don't do this, gentlemen. You'll regret it. I know, because I've been in your shoes."

"Shut up!" Jasper shouted.

"You need to hear this," Matt declared. "Back in the war, I was part of a lynching. We murdered an innocent man. That's what you're doing now."

Jasper spat on the ground. "We're administering *justice!*"

"No, you're not."

Gates steadied his revolver. "Shut up, Wiley!"

"Not yet," Matt said in a steady voice. "You've hurt a lot of people, both guilty and innocent. You've destroyed property and peace of mind. And for what?" He looked at Howard Moreland, then turned to Martin. "To punish a fool for stealing horses? Jed Jones deserved to go to jail, but it wasn't your call."

Matt turned to Gates. "You love money, don't you? You have a wife and a lovely daughter, but it's not enough. You wanted to destroy Scottie Fife, because he bought land you wanted."

"Shut up, Wiley," Gates ordered.

"Not yet." He looked at Gibson Armond. "I don't know why you're here, Mr. Armond. You've been robbed, I know. But kidnapping a woman and a child? Threatening a minister? You must have lost your mind. Someone's going to know what happened, and you're going to go to jail."

The freighter looked shaken, but he didn't speak.

Last Matt turned to Jasper. "I know why *you're* here. You've got a secret and it's ugly."

"You're lying!" he shouted.

Matt laughed out loud. "Obviously not. You just denied a secret I haven't even told."

Jasper yanked off the mask. "Don't you dare—"

"Dare what?" Matt raised his voice. "Tell your good friends that you're a regular at the hog ranch? That you pay women like the ones you won't let in your store?"

"He's lying!"

Matt spoke to the others in a loud voice. "Kind of hard to imagine, isn't it? Mr. Kling got caught red-handed."

Someone snickered.

Jasper sputtered a protest, but the men knew Matt had told the truth. He'd told the truth on all of them, even himself. The truth had set him free. He was a mere man, a failed man...a man redeemed by love. Before he did what he had to do, he needed to ask one last question, the same question he'd asked himself. He looked each man in the eye. "You're proud men. You're willing to kill for what you believe in."

"That's right," Moreland shouted.

"Killing is easy. It doesn't cost you a thing." Matt looked straight at Jasper. "I want to know what you're willing to die for."

"Nothing!"

"Then you're a coward," Matt shouted.

Goaded by the taunt, Jasper raised his pistol. As he fired, his horse sidestepped and the bullet went over Matt's head. Matt grabbed the coach gun from under his duster and took aim at Jasper. With a prayer for mercy for them all, he shot the man dead.

As if he'd cut the head off a snake, the other four fell back with their hands in the air. Jasper lay dead in the grass, his chest still and his blood soaking into the earth.

With the coach gun in one hand, Matt pulled his colt with the other and aimed it at Gates. "Get that mask off your face."

When Gates did as he ordered, Matt put the coach gun away. "Now hit your knees!"

Gates hit the ground, but his eyes gleamed with the bitterness of a man who regretted his capture but not his acts.

A strange thought ran through Matt's head. He could kill these men and no one would blame him. They'd threatened his daughter and they'd kidnapped Pearl. They'd intended to hang a minister, and they'd have gladly shot a lawman to hide their crimes. They deserved to die, but Matt had no desire for vengeance. The man who'd lynched Amos McGuckin was dead and gone. No more blood would spill today, but he wouldn't let down his guard. He cocked the Colt and aimed it at Troy Martin. "Do you want to die, too?"

"No, sir."

Next he pointed the pistol at Howard Moreland. The man had put his hands in the air, but he hadn't hit his knees. "Get down," Matt ordered.

Moreland raised his chin. "What if I don't?"

Matt cocked the Colt. "I'll have to change your mind for you."

The man must have believed him, because he dropped to the ground one knee at a time.

Matt eyed Gibson Armond next. He'd followed the commands Matt had given to Moreland and hit his knees. He looked truly remorseful. Matt didn't bother to rebuke him. The man's nightmares would be his punishment. Instead he looked back at Moreland.

Tobias had pulled the Colt out of his waistband and was drilling it into the man's temple. "I'm not prone to violence, Mr. Moreland. But if my daughter's been harmed, I *will* hold you accountable."

"No one touched her." The man spat on the ground. "No one wanted to."

Fast and hard, the urge to shoot Moreland filled Matt's trigger finger. Being human, he couldn't stop the hate. Being wise, he ignored the reaction.

He had to get to Pearl. Working fast, he and Tobias tied up the men. As Matt picked up the guns he'd dropped, he heard horses approaching and saw Dan, Charlie and Jake. A fourth deputy came at a slower pace. Matt looked again and saw Sarah tucked behind him. Later he'd hug his little girl. Right now, Pearl needed him. He ordered the deputies to take in the prisoners, then he galloped his horse to the carriage.

From the moment Sarah had been snatched, Pearl had strained to hear what her captors were doing. She'd heard voices, but she couldn't make out the words over the rush of the nearby stream. Out of nowhere, she heard her father shouting the Lord's prayer. Blinded by the mask, she prayed for God to keep them safe. Matt's voice rose above the others and she prayed some more.

A shot rang out and she shrieked.

A second one echoed.

"Matt!" she cried inside the mask. Was he lying dead on the ground? Had her father been lynched? She couldn't bear the thought of losing either of them. And Sarah? What had happened to the child? Pearl struggled again to free her hands. She scraped the mask against the seat, but the drawstring tightened and cut off her air. She strained to hear voices or boot steps, anything that would give her hope, but all she heard was her own labored breath.

"Please, Lord," she murmured. "Let Sarah be safe. Let my father be alive. Dear God in Heaven, save Matt—"

The thunder of hoofbeats jarred her thoughts. As the horse pulled to a stop, a man's boots hit the ground with a thud. She couldn't see a thing. She could only feel the buggy seat, the fabric over her face and the rope binding her hands. No matter who opened the carriage door, she'd be at his mercy. If Jasper touched her, she'd kick and fight. She'd—

"Pearl!"

"Matt!" she cried. As he flung open the door, tears streamed down her cheeks. "You're alive."

"Very much so."

"My father—"

"He's safe. So is Sarah." The seat dipped with his weight. Scooting close, he tried to untie the mask. When the drawstring didn't budge, he cut it with a knife and pulled the black cotton over her head.

Air rushed into her lungs. Breathing deep, she took in the brightness of his eyes. He caressed her cheek, then as he'd done twice before, he looked her up and down for injuries. "Are you hurt?"

"I'm fine."

At the sight of her bound hands, his jaw tightened. "Turn so I can cut the rope."

She shifted to give him access. With a single slice of the knife, he cut the laundry cord digging into her wrists. Blood rushed to her fingers. It hurt and felt good all at once. Matt bent down and sliced the binding from her feet. She was free, but what about Matt? The ties binding her body could be severed with a sharp blade. His bonds were harder to break.

"What happened?" she asked.

"Jasper's dead." He told her briefly about the gunfight. "Dan's taking the others to jail."

"Thank God." She meant it.

Matt's eyes took on a shine. "I won't argue with you, Pearl. God's mercy alone explains what happened today. I'm grateful for it."

When his lips relaxed into a smile, he looked peaceful. She touched his face. "You're different."

"I feel good."

She wanted more, needed more. "Tell me."

He shrugged. "Let's just say God and I did some talking. He made some good points. I'm not stupid enough to still be angry with Him."

Pearl wanted to cheer. She also wanted to kiss him, a reaction that filled her with joy. She blushed at the thought.

He touched her cheek. "I lied, you know."

"About what?"

"Kissing you…it was a lot more than nice." His eyes burned with their old intensity. "I love you, Pearl. Will you marry me?"

Her breath left in a gasp. *Yes! Yes!* But she couldn't force the words past the lump in her throat.

With one arm around her shoulders and the other cradling her legs, Matt lifted her up and out of the carriage. When she was steady on her feet, he dropped to one knee. "I can't promise you a perfect life. I'm a hard man with a hard job, but I will live and die for you. I'll—"

"Yes!" she finally cried. "I'll marry you."

He rose to his full height and drew her into his arms. The kiss they shared was joyous and confident, full of love and so nice that her toes curled. Laughing, she stepped back. Matt grinned, then lifted her into his arms and spun her around.

When she landed, she saw her father and Sarah approaching the carriage. Her father's eyes had a knowing shine. Sarah looked hopeful but worried. Hand in hand, Matt and Pearl closed the gap between them. When they reached Sarah, Matt dropped to a crouch. "Hi, there, darlin'. Are you all right?"

She bit her lip. "I was scared."

"Me, too." He smoothed her messy hair. "The bad men are gone now. You were very brave."

"I was."

"I'm proud of you." He touched her cheek. "Do you think you can handle another surprise today?"

She looked uneasy. "Will I like it?"

"I think so." He smiled at her. "Pearl and I are getting married. She's going to be your mama."

Sarah rushed headlong into Pearl's skirts and hugged her. It was just like that first day in Cheyenne, but this time their dreams were coming true.

Tobias smiled. "Looks like I've got a new granddaughter."

"That you do," Matt replied.

The only person missing from the moment was Toby. Still hugging Sarah, Pearl looked at Matt. "My son—"

"*Our* son," he said with a twinkle in his eye.

She smiled. "Where is he?"

Tobias looked pleased. "Carrie has him."

Pearl let out a long breath. She could hardly wait to hold Toby, but mostly she wanted to see Matt cradling their son in his strong arms. "Let's get home. I can't wait to start forever."

Matt made show of rubbing his chin. "That sounds like a

good ending for a fairy tale. Do you think we can do some imagining?"

"Like what?" Pearl asked.

He indicated the carriage. "Let's pretend this ugly old coach is white with gold trim, just like Cinderella's."

Sarah giggled. "I want glass slippers."

"Me, too," Pearl echoed.

Matt laughed. "How about fancy dresses?"

"I have one," Sarah declared. "It's pink."

"I have one, too," Pearl said. "It's blue, and I have pretty ribbons that match."

Matt gave her a sly grin. "I seem to recall those ribbons. They look pretty in that blond hair of yours."

When he touched the wave falling down her back, she shivered with happiness. From this day forward, she'd wear his ribbons every day.

Her father cleared his throat. "Matt, you take the girls in the carriage. I'll follow with the horses."

"Sounds good to me, sir."

Sarah tugged on her daddy's sleeve. "I want to ride outside with you."

"Me, too," Pearl said.

Matt agreed. "Let's go, ladies."

Tobias offered Pearl his arm. "Climb up, princess. Your carriage awaits."

And so it did…. Her father led her to the front of the coach and handed her off to Matt. With a debonair smile, he helped her up to the high seat, then he lifted Sarah, so she could sit with them. After a salute to her father, he joined them and took the reins. With the sun bright and the sky a perfect blue, Pearl rode into the future with her very own Prince Charming, the man she'd love forever and ever.

Epilogue

"It's time to toss the bouquet," Adie Blue announced. "Ladies, get ready!"

From the back of the foyer, Matt watched his new wife climb to the third step of a staircase. Less than an hour ago, Tobias had presided over their wedding vows. Dan and Carrie, newly engaged, had stood with them. Sarah had been a flower girl, and Pearl had held Toby to complete their ready-made family.

Matt would have gotten married anywhere, but he'd been glad when Pearl suggested Swan's Nest. The trip had given him a chance to meet her friends. Adie Blue had spunk, and her husband, Josh, had a wry sense of humor. The sisters, Caroline and Bessie, had cooed over Toby and Sarah.

Matt had especially enjoyed meeting Mary Larue. A former actress, she reminded him of someone he used to know…a man with a chip on his shoulder and an angry past. Pearl had told him a lot about Mary. She'd taken some hard knocks in life. Judging by the way she stood apart from the women waiting for the bouquet toss, she didn't intend to take any more.

With the bouquet in hand, Pearl surveyed her friends. When she spotted Mary against the wall, she waved at her. "Mary! Get over here!"

The blonde shook her head. "Oh no, you don't! I'm *not* getting married. Not ever!"

Matt stifled a grin. He'd once thought the same way.

Adie called to the crowd. "Okay, ladies! Here it comes."

As Pearl turned to throw the bouquet, Matt caught a look in her eye and knew what she'd do.

Adie counted down. "One...two...three!"

Pearl tossed the flowers high and to the left. Sure enough, the bouquet landed smack in Mary's arms. She looked mad enough to throw it back. As she sputtered objections, Matt grinned at his wife. Knowing what he did about love, he had no doubt he and Pearl would someday return to Denver for another Swan's Nest wedding.

* * * * *

Dear Readers,

When I was a little girl, I used to sit on my bedroom floor with a big book of fairy tales. The cover showed Rapunzel with her long hair, Little Red Riding Hood in a forest, and Puss in Boots. I loved this book, especially the color plates for *Thumbelina* and *The Flying Trunk*. Every story fed my imagination.

That book of fairy tales came to mind as I described Deputy Matt Wiley reading a bedtime story to his little girl. Children's books as we know them weren't common in 1875. He would most likely have read from *The Tales of Mother Goose,* a collection of fairy tales collected by Charles Perrault in 1658. The first American edition was published in 1787 and had many of the stories we love today. Among them were *Cinderella, Sleeping Beauty in the Wood* and *Little Red Riding Hood.*

In addition to traditional stories, children's books in the nineteenth century contained short rhymes, moral lessons and simple drawings. Some of the rhymes would be familiar to us, things like "One, Two, Buckle My Shoe" or "Hey Diddle Diddle." I can't read those words without smiling. Both my sons (now grown) were fascinated with the idea of a cow jumping over the moon.

My book of fairy tales and a children's book from 1875 would have been quite different, but the feeling of discovery would be the same. Like me, Matt's daughter would have been transported to another place and time. No matter where we live or when we were born, stories have the power to open our eyes to amazing possibilities.

Looking back I see God's hand on my book of fairy tales. Who could have known? The little girl reading about Cinderella and Rapunzel grew up to write stories of her own.

Victoria Byb

QUESTIONS FOR DISCUSSION

1. After a traumatic experience in Denver, Pearl decides to start a new life in Cheyenne, Wyoming. Which of her problems is she able to leave behind? Which problems follow her? What are the pros and cons of a change in geography when a person is recovering from trauma?

2. Matt is grateful to Pearl for saving his daughter's life, but he doesn't want to be in her debt. How would you describe his attitude? Does it show integrity or pride?

3. Matt gave up a job he loved with the Texas Rangers and moved to Cheyenne. Have you ever made a big move? How did it affect your family?

4. When Pearl is interviewed for a position as a teacher, she refuses to hide the fact that her son was born out of wedlock. What were the consequences? What might have happened if she'd been less open?

5. Matt's daughter needs a mother, but he's reluctant to remarry. Why? What are his biggest fears? What factors contributed to his doubts?

6. Carrie and Pearl have a special friendship. What makes them so close? Do you have a friend like Carrie in your life?

7. The Golden Order was once an honorable civic organization. With time, the group's leaders lost their moorings. Why do you think this occurred? What makes good people go bad?

8. Matt is more than troubled by his past. He's crippled by guilt and shame. What must he do to find redemption? Describe the steps of his journey, starting with his offer to write a letter of reference for Pearl.

9. The blue ribbons are significant throughout the story. When does Pearl wear them? What do they represent to her? How does their meaning change for Matt?

10. When two prostitutes visit Jasper Kling's store, Pearl treats them with courtesy even though she knows she might lose her job. Have you ever had to make a similar choice? What were the circumstances?

11. What motivates Tobias to help stop the Golden Order? Does he compromise his morals when he goes "undercover"?

12. Matt initially criticizes the psalms as poetry. Do you have a favorite psalm? Which one is it? What do you love about it?

13. Pearl's journey from timidity to courage takes several steps. What are the most significant events in her recovery? How do fear and faith interact?

14. What is Matt's deepest motivation for stopping the Golden Order? What is he seeking? What does he need to do to find peace?

15. Sarah's favorite story is *Cinderella*. Do you have a favorite fairy tale? How would you describe the relationship between today's romances and the tales we all grew up with?

Love Inspired.

HISTORICAL

TITLES AVAILABLE NEXT MONTH

Available November 9, 2010

MAIL ORDER COWBOY
Brides of Simpson Creek
Laurie Kingery

SOARING HOME
Christine Johnson

REQUEST YOUR FREE BOOKS!

2 FREE INSPIRATIONAL NOVELS
PLUS 2
FREE
MYSTERY GIFTS

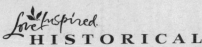

Love Inspired.
HISTORICAL
INSPIRATIONAL HISTORICAL ROMANCE

LIH10R